EPIC

BESTSELLING AUTHOR
TRUDY STILES

LIES

EPIC FAIL SERIES

ISBN: 978-0-9976190-0-3

This book is intended for mature adults only. It is not suitable for anyone under the age of 18.

Content Warning:

This book is not suitable for young readers. It is intended for mature adults only (18+). It contains strong language, adult/sexual situations and potential trigger subject matter.

Cover Design by Sarah Hansen of Okay Creations
Interior Design and Formatting by Elaine York of Allusion Graphics, LLC/
Publishing & Book Formatting (http://www.allusiongraphics.com)
Editing by Chelsea Kuhel of Madison Seidler Editing Services
Proofreading by Julie Deaton of Author Services by Julie Deaton

To contact Trudy:
Website: www.trudystiles.com
Facebook: http://www.facebook.com/authortrudystiles
Instagram: https://instagram.com/trudystiles/
Goodreads: http://www.goodreads.com/trudy_stiles
Twitter: @trudystiles
Email:authortrudystiles@gmail.com
Amazon: http://www.amazon.com/Trudy-Stiles/e/B00H3O0OJ8

DAX ANDERSON has always been the one to keep it all together.
~ His family~
~ His friends~
~ His band~

His heart is huge, but guarded. He's the best friend. The protector. The shoulder to cry on. But he's never been able to protect his own heart or himself. Lies from his not-so-distant past have destroyed his outlook on love - until he meets her.

GISELLE ANDREWS is confident and happy, but cautious. She's learned to overcome many obstacles despite her past. She's fiercely loyal and loves beyond measure. When she's reminded of her past and the pain that she lived through, will her perfect world begin to crumble?

What connects Dax and Giselle?

And will EPIC LIES destroy their future?

EPIC LIES is the second book in the EPIC FAIL series and can be read as a standalone novel.

This series is a spinoff of the FOREVER FAMILY series.

DEDICATION

To my FTN sisters — I love you!

PROLOGUE

I WANT TO DIE.

I *need* to die. And I'm ready. I realize how selfish this is, but I'm really doing this for all of you. As much as you want me around, you have no idea how bad it's going to get because I've been here before. The endless hours of watching me in pain, knowing there's no hope for me. Knowing that every breath I take is a struggle. Watching my chest rise and fall, hoping and praying it's not the last breath I'm going to take. My pain causes you grief and sadness. My pain rips me from within and shoots through my bones with purpose. Every moment hurts. Every single breath hurts. Every single touch hurts. I just want it to end. I want to be at peace. Please don't hate me for this. Eight years ago, I felt this. I lived this. I remember every single stabbing pain. I've suffered like this before. Please don't make me do it again.

Your pain is emotional. You struggle with trying to see a world without me in it. You cry over the loss of my future. You weep when you realize that I don't have one. Your tears fall for the time I no longer have. For the time you no longer have with me.

I can't stand the thoughts swirling through your heads. I can hear them all.

EPIC LIES

You feel sorry for me. You feel sorry for yourselves.

My father, strong and stoic. You have been amazing and I wish I had your strength. I can see it in your eyes every single time you look at me. Your voice booms in my head. *What am I going to do without you? My baby girl. Why is this happening? Lord, please don't steal my dreams from me. Please don't take away her future. Please don't take her away from me. My only girl. Our only child. The girl I'm supposed to die before. The girl I'm supposed to live through. Kiss away her scrapes. Take away her pain. The girl I'm supposed to give away at her wedding to her true love. Please take me. Take me in place of her. Please. I'm begging you. Take me.*

My mother, so confident, yet fragile. I want this to be over for you as much as I want it to be over for me. Every single day is a struggle. You're putting your best face forward, pretending that everything's going to be fine. Pretending like I'm miraculously going to stand up and shout, "I've been healed!" You do so much for me, hoping your optimism will be contagious. Your voice is soft and shaky in my head. *This isn't happening. I won't let it happen. I read this amazing article about your body's pH and how cancer can't live in an alkaline environment. We're going to beat this! You're going to beat this. Your father is out, buying ingredients now to make you an amazing cocktail. You're going to drink it three times a day, and it's going to heal you. You're going to live, I promise. You're going to one day know what it's like to be a mother. To love your daughter as much as I love you. You have to. I want you to know what it's like to feel this kind of love. To live for someone else. To wake up every day and wonder what amazing words are going to come out of your child's mouth. The smiles that she shares. The laughter that fills a room. I want this for you. I want you to know what it's like to have this much love for another human being. You've given that to me, and I so desperately want this for you. Please fight. Please live. I'm begging you. Your future daughter is begging you. We're all begging you.*

My boyfriend. You're so angry with me. You tell me every day that you love me. That you want me to fight for you and for us. But you're also angry I lied to you. I never told you what was wrong with me. My parents had to. They told you everything after I was admitted to the hospital this last time. I know you're mad. Upset that I didn't trust you enough to tell you that I am dying. Your voice is hoarse, like you've been crying for days. *How are we even here? Why are we here? You don't deserve this horrible disease. You should be filled with life. You should be in my arms, dancing with me like nobody else is in the room. Your eyes should be bright and clear. Your lungs should be full of oxygen and not struggling. Your hand should be in mine, forever. But we no longer have a forever. Not unless you fight. You need to fight for you and the future you're supposed to have. Don't give up. You can't give up. I need you. Fucking Christ, I love you. Isn't our love enough for you to fight with everything you have? Please. I don't know who I'll be without you. Please, don't give up. I love you.*

My best friend, my cousin. Your heart is huge, and your entire life is ahead of you. You have so much to live for and so much to fight for. I want you to siphon what strength I have left and use it to help fight your own demons. We don't talk nearly as much as we used to, and I wish we lived closer to each other. You've been through so much lately, and I rarely share my own ups and downs. You will be strong again, and I want to make that happen. You're the only one that I haven't been lying to. You know the truth and know how much I need this all to end. Your voice is chipper and animated in my head. *Seriously, get over this already. We've been here before, when you were eight. You beat it then, and you're going to beat it now. Remember when I shaved my hair when you lost yours? We called ourselves cousin twins. We looked almost identical, and we became sisters that day. You can do this. You have to. You need to keep showing me what true love is. I don't know how to love like you do. I'm learning from you. So much. Who says a teenager can't find love? You have. You're proof that true love exists. Help me find that in my heart. Help me love like you do. Drink those disgusting shakes that your parents make for you. Show them who's boss. Fuck cancer. Fuck it. Beat it to death and fight.*

Your voice starts to waver in my head, and I know what's coming next. You know me better than anyone. *I'm sorry, erase all of that. I take it back. Don't fight anymore if you don't want to. I know what this is doing to you. I know how much it hurts. It's going to hurt so much when you're gone, but I know how much you're hurting now. If I could take your pain away from you and swallow it whole, I would. I would do anything for you. I love you so much, and I give you permission to go. Take your memories and your huge heart with you. Never forget the love that we have for you. Promise me you'll be there for me when I need you because I know I'll be calling on you in the future. I'll get my cell phone charged to call you in Heaven. It's going to be epic—our own cousin twins divine hotline. Please watch over all of us and smile. I love you.*

All of your voices are swirling together. Your words jumbled and clamoring in my head.

Shouting.

Crying.

Begging.

Laughing.

Sobbing.

Please, don't give up.

I love you.

Take me.

Please, fight.

I hear you all, and I feel everything. You don't know what it's like every single day, living with the grief that I'm going to cause. I'm sorry that I can't live for all of you. I'm sorry that I can't live for myself. I hope none of you ever have to suffer with the pain that I feel every day. Please don't hate me for giving up. I just want it to go away. To be at peace.

I would tell you all what you want to hear. I would say that I have the strength to fight longer, harder.

But that would be a lie.

CHAPTER 1

Giselle
Past
Age 16

I'M SCARED. Terrified. Fear and doubt swirl in my head, and I want to run, but I can't move. My fingers are tingling as I tighten my fists against my sides. My heart pounds so hard in my chest I can feel it in my throat. I swallow and nearly choke. I attempt to pull my arm up to cover my cough, but it's pinned to the ground.

"Are you okay?" he asks and loosens his grip on my arms. My coughing fit subsides, but it's still hard to breathe. The weight of him on top of me is making it worse. I quickly nod and gasp for air, embarrassed. "Are you having some kind of panic attack?"

I try to relax and I'm able to slightly loosen my clenched fists. My eyes search his face for a reason not to run. He looks concerned, but different. His eyes look cold and uncaring. When he told me he loved me just ten minutes ago, his eyes were much softer, kinder. I'm suddenly confused by his expression. Is this Troy McIntosh, my boyfriend? Or is this someone else entirely? *What am I even doing here?* I was supposed to be at my cousin's house this weekend, celebrating her fifteenth birthday. I told her that Troy invited me to a party, and she told me I could celebrate with her another weekend. I haven't missed her birthday ever, and I chose to miss it this year for *Troy*.

"No, I don't think so," I whisper and take another deep breath. *Can he feel my heart pounding? Am I supposed to be this scared?*

He shakes his head and pushes my hands back down into the blanket. A warm gust of air reminds me that we're outside on the golf course behind his house. His cool lips brush against my neck, and his hips press into mine. I inhale deeply, turn my head, and see my clothes that he expertly removed. His grasp tightens around my wrists as he poises himself above me. *What am I doing?*

"Stop, Troy," I say. "I can't do this." None of this feels right.

He tenses above me, and his eyes become even colder. "You wanted this, Giselle. You've been practically begging me for it." He ignores my plea and presses himself between my thighs. I feel how ready he is, and I attempt to close my legs. "No," I gasp, but it's too late. He plunges into me in one movement, and I cry out in pain. Blinding, shooting pain. He pushes his forehead into my chest as he thrusts and grunts and thrusts and grunts. "No," I attempt to say again, but my words don't come out as I intend. I choke on my tears and cry as his pace quickens, the friction tearing me up inside. I try to push him off of me, but the weight of his body is too heavy, his grasp on my hands too tight. I'm trapped beneath him as he continues to plunge in and out of me, burning me. Destroying me. *I just want this to be over.*

"Ah!" he yells into my chest, ramming me one last time, his sweaty forehead leaving a damp residue behind. "That wasn't so bad, was it?" He pulls out of me quickly and removes his condom, tossing it into the bushes. He jumps up, pulls up his boxer briefs and zips his jeans. I'm lying cold and naked. *Ashamed.*

I can't look at him. He kicks my pile of clothes closer to me. My hand shakes as I reach for my underwear, but I can't sit up. Everything hurts and aches. My head is pounding from my unheard tears. He turns his back to me and looks out into the darkness. "I bet you'll remember your first time forever, Giselle." His words are cold and unfeeling and I shiver.

My first time wasn't supposed to be like this. I imagined us in a four-poster bed, candlelight dancing off of the sheer fabric drapes that surround our bodies. Soft music playing and him gazing at me through loving eyes, caressing me, loving me. I imagined warmth and heat and *love*. His body wrapped around mine, protecting me. Holding onto me until the sun comes up and loving me all over again.

Lies.

As I pull up my panties, I see drops of blood on the blanket. I'm hyper aware of the tenderness and burning between my legs. Warm tears continue to stream down my cheeks. I sniffle. No, there are no soft pillows and glowing candles here. There's only rough grass and dirt. And music coming from somewhere. It's loud with electric guitars and banging drums drowning out the voices. "We should get back to the party." He turns back to me. "Are you ready yet?" he asks, his voice tense and annoyed. The warm August air is heavy, weighing me down. Sweat drips down the back of my neck, and the stickiness between my legs makes me shudder.

I pull my tank top over my head and attempt to stand up. My knees are weak, and I fall back down onto the blanket. "Are you drunk?" He knows better than to ask me this. I've never had a drink in my life. *Maybe if I did, this would have been easier.*

"Of course not," I say and look up at him. He shakes his

head and huffs. "Hurry up then. The party sounds like it's raging!"

Can't he see my tears?

"Do you love me?" I blurt out, needing reassurance for what just happened.

"What kind of question is that?" he scoffs. "I told you that I did, didn't I?"

I nod and look into his eyes. I see everything I need to know in his dark, cold gaze. He doesn't love me—he never loved me.

"I'll catch up. I need a minute to get myself ready." I reach for my purse, hands shaking. I fumble for the zipper and can't open it. The strength in my hands is gone. I place my hand on my lap and cover it with my free one, but the shaking doesn't stop.

"You should freshen up a bit," he sneers. He points back at me and grins. "Let's keep making memories." His words make me shiver as I watch him jog across the fairway toward the music and laughter. The darkness swallows him, and I'm alone.

Alone in my tears.

Alone with his lies.

CHAPTER 2

Dax
Past
Age 16

"WHAT ARE THE CHANCES he actually comes back?" Alex asks as he places his guitar into his gig bag.

"He seemed interested and sincere," I say. I slide my sticks into my back pocket and walk toward the driveway. We'd been practicing for the past few hours when some dude around our age tried to find the guy who lives next door to Tristan. He seemed nervous and curious about where he may be. He noticed us in the garage and came over to find out if we knew anything. We don't know much about the guy at all, and that's exactly what we told the kid. *Garrett.*

But, more importantly, he can shred on guitar! He picked up one of Alex's Strats and played with us like he's always been part of Epic Fail. Mighty impressive.

"Later, guys," Tristan says as he opens the door from the garage into his house. "See you tomorrow in school."

"See ya," I say. Alex and I grab our things and close the garage door on our way out. We walk across the street to our house. Alex moved in with me and my family about two years ago after his father tried to kill him and then killed himself. It was a totally fucked up situation, but now Alex is like a brother to me. Now he's safe.

"Hi, boys," my mother says as we walk into the kitchen. The smell of garlic fills the air, and my stomach immediately growls. Dinner is almost ready. "Dad will be home soon, but I didn't want this to get cold, so help yourselves." She places covered dishes onto the hot plates in the center of the table and removes the lids to reveal my favorite meal, spaghetti and meatballs. "Garlic bread is in the oven and will be ready in a few minutes," she adds.

Alex and I fill our plates and start devouring our food. *I ate lunch today, right?* I can't believe how hungry I am.

My mother starts cutting the garlic bread and says, "Oh, Dax. Lara called about an hour ago. She says you can call her after dinner."

Alex snorts, and I shuffle my feet under the table.

"Shut up," I say to him and lightly kick his shin.

"Ow, you ass!" he says with a mouthful of food.

"Boys," my mother says, semi-sternly. She slides into the seat at the end of the table and fills up her own plate. "I like Lara. I wish she would come by more." She smiles at me, and my ears get hot. How embarrassing. *Why did she have to call the house phone?* She knows she can call me on my cell.

"Yeah, I wish your *girlfriend* would come by more often, too," Alex chimes in, and I just want to crawl under the table. Ever since last week, when kids in school declared us the new 'it' couple, Alex has been relentless. He thinks it's funny that I have a 'girlfriend.' She's a sophomore and I'm a junior and somehow this is also a huge topic discussed in the halls of our school. I really don't see the big deal, but her friends are obsessed with the fact that she'll attend the Junior Formal with me at the end of the school year.

"Her mother works in the hospital, and I see her now and then when I have to be there. Such a lovely woman." My mother is a social worker and is at the hospital several times a week.

I nod and shovel more spaghetti into my mouth. I don't want to talk about Lara, especially with my mother.

The garage door opens, and my father comes in. "Looks like I made it just in time," he says, dropping his briefcase in the hallway and kissing my mother on her forehead before sitting across from her. Alex keeps his eyes lowered while he finishes the food on his plate. My parents have always been affectionate, and I can't help but notice Alex's discomfort every time he witnesses it. He still hasn't grown used to seeing how a 'normal' family treats each other after what he went through with his own father. His life totally sucked for too long.

"I think we found a new lead guitarist," I blurt out, trying to make Alex feel more comfortable.

"Oh?" my father asks, and my mother smiles.

"Yeah, some dude came looking for the guy across the street. He's about our age. He played a few songs with us, and man, he's amazing." Alex looks up and nods in agreement.

"Why would he be looking for John Horton?" my father asks, concerned.

"Who knows," I shrug. "He probably had the wrong house anyway."

My parents exchange looks with each other, and I wonder what they know about that crazy dude from across the street. "I know I've told you boys in the past, but please stay away from Mr. Horton's house. I've seen all sorts of people in and out of there, and I just don't like it." My mother's lips tighten, and she tenses up.

I nod, "Yeah, we never see him. Don't worry about us."

"I think he's gone. I haven't seen him or any sign of his visitors in months," my father chimes in.

"Maybe he's gone for good," my mother says, with finality in her voice.

"I hope so," my father responds.

Without missing a beat, my mother says in her sing-song voice again, "Lara called for Dax today."

"Oh? That's nice. I like her." My father grins, and I avoid eye contact. *Why does everyone have to talk about this?*

I push my plate away from me and swipe my napkin to clean my mouth. "I'm finished. Can I be excused?" I'm annoyed that they keep bringing her up. Alex does the same and stands up. "Dinner was really good, Mrs. Anderson."

"Alex, you know you can call me Lila," my mother reminds him as she does every time he calls her Mrs. Anderson.

He nods, and I follow him upstairs. He goes straight to his room and says, "Later," as he shuts the door.

After I close the door to my own room, I pick up the phone and immediately dial Lara's number. "Daxton," she answers, calling me by my full name. She's literally the only person on the planet that calls me Daxton, not even my parents refer to me by the name on my birth certificate. *I kind of like it.*

Her voice is a little hoarse, and she sounds tired.

"Hey, Lara. You called?" I say, trying to sound as cool as possible, ignoring the wildly pounding heart in my chest.

"I did. I talked to your mom, she's so nice. How was band practice?" She's our biggest fan. Really, our only fan. She's not allowed to come over to any of our houses by herself, but I give her every recording we make so she can listen.

"It was okay," I say, twirling my drumsticks in the air with my free hand. I've been practicing this a lot. She thinks it's totally cool.

"My mom is taking me to the mall tomorrow after school so I can get a new pair of shoes. You should meet us there for dinner. She says it would be okay." Her voice is shaking slightly, and I think she's nervous. I smile as I realize she just asked me out on a date.

"What time?" I ask.

"Around six?"

"I should be able to." I need to make sure my mother can drop me off. I feel bad leaving Alex behind, but it would be awkward if I brought him along. "I'll get a ride there."

She exhales deeply, almost with relief. "Oh, good," she says. "I'll see you tomorrow, then." She seems reluctant to hang up, but says, "Goodbye?"

"See ya," I say and hang up the phone, dropping my drumsticks at the same time. Lara and I have known each other since grade school. She was in fifth grade when I was in sixth. She's always been quiet and reserved. She still wears her hair in long, blonde braids, like she did the first time I saw her. I remember some of the idiot boys pulling her braids every once in a while, just to tease her. Nothing fazed her though; she just shook it off and laughed along with them, never accepting being the butt of any joke. They quickly stopped pulling her hair and started treating her with more respect. Now that we're in high school, she blends in and doesn't draw attention to herself. But she's always stood out to me. She's just *different*. Special. I think about her all of the time, especially when I–

My door flies open, and Alex comes running in. "Dude, check this out." He's hyper. Excited. He shoves his sketchpad under my nose. It's filled with all of his drawings that he rarely shows anyone, including me. "This is going to be my first tattoo." The vision of Lara in my head is quickly replaced by Alex's sketch. He's been obsessed with getting ink for as long as I can remember. He's too young, but that doesn't stop him from designing the art that will someday be on his arms and God knows where else. He's drawn two closed fists with the words EPIC FAIL spanning across all of his knuckles. I have to admit–it does look cool. "We should all get this. All of us in the band," he says. It's good to see him so excited and animated.

"That's rad," I say, nodding in agreement. I know for a fact that my parents will never go for this.

"My sister will take me to get this, so don't worry about your parents." His older sister, Reagan, was initially named legal guardian of Alex after his father died, but she was barely out of high school, and there was no way she could take care of the both of them. Thank God for my mom. She knew a few people in family court and worked it out so Alex could stay with us. She and my dad have legal guardianship now. "I think my parents will have something to say about this, Alex. I don't want to bring you down, but they're responsible for you. I don't think they'll let you get a tattoo."

"Whatever, I'll figure it out. We all need this one."

"Cool," I say, picking up my drumsticks and twirling them again.

"So, *Daxton,* what's up with Lara?" Alex chuckles.

"What do you mean?"

"Is she really your girlfriend? Everyone in school thinks she is."

"I guess," I say and suddenly feel very possessive of her. I grab the sticks and sit up straight. "I'm going out to dinner with her tomorrow night," I state, proud of my official first date. With Lara and *her mom. Fuck.*

"Right on," Alex says and leaves the room.

After he shuts the door, I lie back on my bed and smile, and my heart jumps.

I have a girlfriend.

24

CHAPTER 3

Dax
Present

"DUDE, NICE BIKE!" Heath says as I cut the ignition to my new motorcycle. "Are you sure you know how to ride that thing?"

I shove the keys into my pocket and walk toward Garrett's house. "Yes, *asshole.*"

"Not like you needed another ride, but hey, whatever floats your boat." He smirks and opens the door. Since I moved out to the suburbs, I've bought a few vehicles. The SUV and cars were a necessity, but the bike was an impulse purchase. I went with Tristan to the Harley Davidson dealership this morning so he could bring his in for routine maintenance and wound up driving this beauty home. I'll admit that I'm a bit nervous riding it, but I'll get used to it. It's fucking fast. *I'll definitely get used to it.*

I follow Heath into Garrett's foyer, and Kai runs toward us laughing and screeching. "Hey, buddy!" I say as I bend down to give him a high five. He instinctively reaches into my jacket to find my drumsticks in the inside pocket and swipes them out, giggling.

Sam, Garrett's wife, walks into the foyer smiling. "Ever since you gave him that drum set, it's all he wants to do." She gives me a quick hug and chases after her son. "Make yourselves at home. You know where Garrett is." As active as Kai is, Sam never seems flustered. I follow Heath toward the basement stairs and down to Garrett's studio. Kai's giggles are coming from the family room as he begins to bang on his drums with my sticks. That kid is too much.

"Gentlemen! So good of you both to be on time," Garrett says sarcastically. Tristan is already here, lounging on the leather sectional couch.

"Dax rode here on a new motorcycle, so he was probably crawling along like an old fart in traffic!" Heath laughs and slaps my back.

"What's your excuse?" Tristan asks.

"None of your business," Heath responds and sits on the opposite side of the couch from Tristan.

"We have some work to do, boys." Garrett shakes his head as he walks toward the studio. We have to finish mixing our album and get it to the label in three days. I see our producer, Chuck, already at the boards with headphones on. He's adjusting levels on the board while chewing the end of a pen cap. He nods a silent greeting and goes back to doing his thing.

"Alex isn't here?" I ask.

"He was here all day, like the rest of you turds were supposed to be." Garrett slides into his seat next to Chuck and unfolds a sheet of paper. I see the list of ten tracks for our album with notes scribbled all over with Alex's handwriting.

Alex wrote most of the lyrics for our latest album and plays rhythm guitar on three of the studio tracks. Although he stepped away from touring with the band, he's still a huge part of our music.

"We're here now," I huff and walk to my chair in the corner.

Hours pass. I don't know how many, but when I see Peggy,

Garrett's housekeeper, place a stack of pizza boxes on the table in the outer room, I realize that I'm starving.

"Pizza Thursday!" Heath exclaims, and tosses his headphones onto the console.

We all grab a few slices and sit around the sectional. "I'm not sure how much more I can do tonight, guys," Tristan says with a mouth full of pizza. "I have to be somewhere early tomorrow morning."

Garrett looks up from his food. "Seriously? We need to get this finished. Can you make time for us tomorrow afternoon?" he asks, annoyed.

"Anytime after eleven," he responds. Tristan has been pretty elusive lately. I know it's not any of our business, but I hope everything's okay.

"I'm good anytime," I say, trying to make up for my tardiness today.

"Let's meet here at three so Tristan can get his beauty rest. But, plan to be here all night until we're done," Garrett adds, and we finish inhaling the pizzas that are in front of us.

Heath jumps up and tosses his paper plate into the garbage. "If we're done here, I'm out." He takes the steps two at a time and disappears. Garrett shakes his head.

"Lighten up, man. We'll get it done," I say, trying to diffuse the anger that's about to spew from him. Lately, he's been putting so much pressure on himself to finish this album, and I hate it when he gets like this. "We always make it happen, right?" I add, and he nods.

Tristan is next to stand up. He stretches and sighs. "I'm not trying to make things difficult, G. But things have been challenging lately, and I'm trying to make it right." He's vague, once again, but I don't pry.

Garrett looks down and shakes his head, "Sorry, man. I

know what you're going through and let me know if there's anything you need."

Wait. Now I feel out of the loop. "Everything okay?" I ask.

Tristan walks to the stairs. "It will be. Don't worry, I'm fine." And with that, he's gone.

Garrett and I stare at the demolished pile of pizza boxes in front of us, and I laugh. "I hope Sam and Kai had something to eat upstairs because there's nothing left for them here."

"Peggy always makes sure they get fed before we do." He chuckles as he tosses the boxes into a large garbage bin in the corner.

"Kai is getting so big, dude. And he looks just like you." Garrett has done some really shitty things in his life, but raising Kai is not one of them. Kai and Sam are the best things that have ever happened to Garrett, and it really shows, despite his pissy mood earlier.

"Yeah, he's my little man," Garrett muses. "I don't know what I'd be doing if he weren't here."

"Let's not think about that."

"Anyway, yeah, Sam had to buy him all new shoes and socks the other day because his feet grew like two sizes in the past month. His doctor can't believe how fast he's growing. I guess he's had some catching up to do." Kai's first few months were miserable, and he barely ate. Sam helped nurse him back to health, got Garrett on track, and now they're a happy family. It's funny how things work out.

"I'm really happy for you, seriously. You've changed for the better since that little dude and Sam walked into your life."

"Stop talking to me like a chick!" He punches my shoulder, and I follow him up the stairs. "But, thank you." We leave Chuck downstairs so he can finish working.

"Daddy!" Kai screams from his seat at the kitchen table.

His face is covered in sauce, and the slice of pizza he's holding looks demolished. "Pool?" he asks his father with a mouth full of food. He points to the pool house nestled at the back of Garrett's property and smiles.

"Finish eating, and then you need to digest your food," Garrett responds. "Then, *maybe*, we'll go swimming tonight."

Sam looks at him disapprovingly. "It's already late. Why don't we plan on it tomorrow?" Kai's face drops, and Garrett jumps in.

"Ten minutes of swimming tonight and as soon as the album is finished tomorrow, we can swim as long as you want. Deal?"

Sam nods, and Kai smiles. "Yay!"

He turns to me. "You fuckers better have your shit together tomorrow, or Kai is going to make your lives miserable."

"*Language*," Sam chides, and Kai is back to eating his pizza.

Garrett smiles. "He doesn't know that fuck is a bad word. It's said enough around this house by both of us to be considered normal."

Sam wraps her arm around his waist and he kisses her forehead.

"Alex and Tabby are coming with the kids. We can spend the day out at the pool while you guys finish up things downstairs. He'll be plenty water logged by the time you're done, so you won't have to worry about disappointing anyone." She kisses him back and swipes a bag of wipes from the counter. Soon, Kai's hands and face are clean, and he runs toward us, arms outstretched. "Pool?" he asks again.

"Okay, little dude, let's go." Kai high-fives me, and his smile warms my heart.

As Garrett and his son head toward the back door, he turns to me one last time. "Seriously, don't be late. Come with your ideas, and let's get it done."

I nod and smile, "Of course. I've got no other place I'd rather be."

I have no intention of letting him or the guys down tomorrow.

"I'll be here, I promise."

CHAPTER 4

Giselle
Present

"DON'T WORRY, DAD, I'm being careful." I grip the steering wheel tightly with both hands and tap the brakes. The highway lines blur. The rain is coming down so hard it pelts against my windshield, rendering the wipers useless. Cars in front of me aren't moving, and I slow down to a complete stop. Red taillights are stacked ahead of me for miles, and I let out a huff.

"It's not supposed to let up any time soon. They're calling for hail and dangerous cloud-to-ground lightning." My father is the source of all things weather and traffic related, which is why I'm talking to him right now. He called to tell me that the interstate is closed about three miles ahead of me, and I may be stuck on the highway for a while. "Do you have enough gas?" he asks.

"Yes, Dad." I roll my eyes. Who needs OnStar when I have my very own *BobStar.*

"The traffic reporter said that the overturned tractor trailer contained hazardous materials. I wonder if they're going to divert you elsewhere. Where are you?"

"I'm between mile eight and nine," I say, straining to see the mile markers.

"Darn, there isn't another exit for at least five miles," he says to me, and I shift uncomfortably in my seat.

"Thanks for reminding me," I groan. I just finished the last sip from my oversized Starbucks' Trenta black iced-tea lemonade. *Shit.*

"Be careful and call me when you get home, okay?" I hear my mother's voice in the background. "Love you, Giselle!"

"Love you too, Mom. And I'll call you when I get home, *Dad.*" I grin and hang up.

I shift my car into park and switch my windshield wipers onto high. Rain slams onto my roof, and large hail bounces off the hood of my car. The sound is deafening and terrifying at the same time. It's so loud that I barely hear the motorcycle pass me on the right hand side in the shoulder. *Wow, that sucks.*

I watch as the driver stops under the bridge just ahead of me and jumps off his bike. He's attempting to shield himself from the splattering hail, but it's useless. The bridge provides little protection from the rain as it's coming down sideways at this point. He removes his helmet, and his dark hair becomes instantly soaked. He's looking up into the rain as it pummels his face, trying to find a clearing in the sky. According to my father, this storm isn't going anywhere anytime soon.

A loud crack causes my ears to pop, and the biker jumps straight up into the air as thunder booms, enveloping my car. *Holy shit. Did lightning just strike nearby?*

I watch as the biker climbs the embankment underneath the bridge, but water is pouring down toward him. He's really struggling, and it's so dangerous out there. *Why isn't anyone letting him take shelter?* Maybe he's a serial killer, and they can sense danger. Water blurs my vision as my windshield wipers are rendered useless from the teeming rain.

Another loud clap of thunder rumbles, and this time it

seems to be rolling over us. The biker looks around, desperate. He doesn't want to be outside any more than I want to be sitting here stuck in traffic about to die from another lightning strike. He pulls the collar of his leather jacket high up to his ears.

Without thinking, I beep my horn, and he quickly looks over at my car. I wave my hands, telling him to come my way. *My father would kill me if he knew what I was doing. Hell, what am I doing?* He looks at me curiously. Another boom of thunder rocks my car, and he makes a mad dash toward me. I unlock the doors, and he's suddenly in my passenger seat, soaking wet.

"Holy shit," he says, panting. "Thanks for letting me in." He drops his helmet to the floor between his legs and turns to face me. His dark eyes pierce into me, and I shudder. Tall, dark, and handsome doesn't even come close. His hair is saturated, water dripping over his thick, black eyebrows, down his cheeks, and to his chiseled jaw. His lips are parted, and he's still breathing heavily. This man is pure perfection. And he could be a serial killer. Yet, there's something familiar about him. *Do I know him?*

I fumble for my phone and turn off the Bluetooth. I hit speed dial for my best friend, Mia, and place the phone against my ear. As it's ringing I say, "Can I have your driver's license, please?" He furrows his brow, looking extremely confused, but reaches into his back pocket, pulling out a wallet attached to a chain.

"Hey! You were supposed to be here like an hour ago," Mia says, without saying hello. We're not only best friends, but we're also neighbors. Our townhouses are next to each other and we share a patio in the back.

"I'm stuck in traffic… and a bad storm." The stranger holds out his license, and as I reach out to grab it, our fingers touch, sending a jolt straight through me. Thunder crashes around us, and he shudders, dropping his hand to his thigh.

"I also just picked up a hitchhiker or something like that. His name is..." I bring the license in front of my face, and I'm grabbed by how incredibly hot he looks in the picture. My own license looks like I slept in the garage on a steamy, humid night. My hair is frizzy, and I have a stunned looked on my face. Not attractive at all.

"Dax Anderson." I read her his address and say, "Now if anything bad happens to me, you know where to send the cops." He runs his hands through his soaking wet hair and shakes his head, laughing.

"Dax Anderson?" she screeches into the phone, interrupting my thought. "Where the hell are you?"

"On the interstate, and I'm stuck in at least a three-mile backup. Mr. Anderson was stranded on his motorcycle in the pouring rain, and I let him hop into my car. I probably saved his life." His grin grows wider, and his face softens.

The cell phone starts to crackle, and I hear what seems like every other word from Mia, "Dax...do...he...fail...Oh. My. God."

"Mia? You're breaking up," I say loudly into the phone. "I'll see you when I see you." Before I can hang up, the call is dropped. Another bolt of lightning streaks in front of my car, and I gasp, dropping my phone onto the floor. Thunder claps and booms all around us.

"So you think I'm a serial killer?" he asks amused as the rumbles shake my car.

"Just covering all bases," I reply and wonder what my father would say if he knew I picked up a stranger. A *hot* stranger who could do really bad things to me if he wanted to.

He reaches across the seat, and I flinch a little. "Can I have that back?" he asks, gesturing toward the license I'm still holding in my hand.

"Oh, yeah." Once again, our fingertips brush against each other, and I blush. Without looking away, I reach down and pat the floor, attempting to find my phone. His hand is suddenly next to mine and brushes against me.

"Do you always act this strange?" He smirks. "Here's your phone."

I am acting strange. This is so out of character for me. I swipe the phone from his hand and tuck it between my legs. He raises his thick eyebrows.

"I don't normally pick up strange men from the side of the road," I respond and feel like curling up into a ball.

"You're a life-saver," he says. Another crash of thunder rocks the car, and the rain falls harder, if that's even possible. He attempts to look through the windshield, but it's now completely fogged up. He reaches out and presses the de-fogger button in the console and lowers the temperature in the car. "I hope you don't mind," he says.

"Of course not."

"Seriously, I don't think I would have survived out there." He peers out the passenger side window. "It's raining so hard I can't even see my bike."

"Why would you ride your bike in this kind of weather?" I ask, dumbfounded.

"An hour ago, there wasn't a cloud in the sky," he states.

Doesn't he have weather alerts on his phone? Maybe I'm the only dork that gets alerts for every type of weather event. God.

I shake my head in silent judgment.

"What happened up there, anyway?" he asks, craning his neck to see the miles of cars parked in front of us.

"My dad said that a tanker overturned about three miles up the road, spilling hazardous materials all over the place."

"Perfect," he says and clenches his fists. I immediately tense up as his demeanor changes.

"Is there somewhere you need to be?" I ask.

"It's nothing. They can wait." He takes out his phone and swipes on the screen. His thumbs move quickly over the letters, and he hits send. We sit quietly for a few minutes, and he says, "You know my name. Now I think I should know yours. You know, in case you're a serial killer." He winks, and his grin widens.

"Giselle," I answer.

"Just Giselle?" he asks curiously.

"Giselle Andrews," I say hesitantly.

"Nice to meet you, *Giselle*." He reaches out and offers me his hand. I tentatively place mine into his, and he squeezes. His hand is damp and cold.

"You're freezing," I say, but don't let go.

"I'm also soaking wet," he responds and continues to hold on to me.

"Yes, you are."

"So where are you heading today in this fabulous weather?" he asks, looking out at the window toward his bike.

"I'm on my way home."

"And your home is?"

I hesitate before answering. "Radnor."

He nods. "I'm not too far from there, but you already know that."

His driver's license. "Yeah," I say.

Rain continues to pummel my car, and I hear emergency sirens coming from behind us.

"So," he says and turns to look at me again.

My nerves are setting in, and this awkward conversation isn't making things any better.

"What do you do for a living?" I ask him. *Not getting any easier.*

"Oh, yeah. I'm—"

The emergency sirens are much closer now, and louder. Fire engine horns are blaring, and I see by glancing into the rearview mirror they are barreling up the shoulder. And they aren't going slowly.

We both turn to the see the first fire truck plow into Dax's motorcycle, and the one behind it didn't slow down to assess the damage. Groans escape his mouth as several state troopers speed along the shoulder. His bike is now up on the slope underneath the bridge in a mangled heap.

"What the fuck?" he shouts. "What in the actual FUCK?" He slams his fist into his thigh.

My hand covers my mouth as we both peer out the window at his former motorcycle. "Oh God," I say.

"They didn't even stop! I mean, I could have been on that bike. Fuck!" He gestures wildly, and his breathing hitches.

"I'm sure they would have stopped if they saw a person, right?" I try to assure him, realizing that I totally did save his life.

His fists are tight, and he leans his head against the window, his warm breath causing it to fog up. "It's brand new. I picked it up yesterday."

"I'm sure your insurance will cover it?"

"I shouldn't have bought the damn thing in the first place. Whatever. Fuck it." He pulls his phone out again and begins typing a message and laughs out loud as he hits send. His laughter fills the car as it turns into hysterics. It's contagious, and I begin to laugh, too. Tears stream out of the corners of my eyes, and I gasp for air. *Why are we laughing so hard? His bike just got destroyed. He could have died.*

His phone rings, and he answers it immediately. "Dude, you wouldn't believe me if I told you." He chuckles as he explains to whomever is on the phone what just happened. "Exactly! Well, that's the last time I'm buying a motorcycle. Chalk that up to life lessons. Oh, I'm going to be really late. This traffic jam hasn't budged at all. Can you tell the rest of the guys? Tell Garrett that I tried, but shit happens. You can send anything you want me to listen to right to my phone. Thanks, man. Tell Tabby I'm sorry I missed seeing her and the kids. Later."

He disconnects the call and drops the phone on his leg. "Sorry about that." He turns to me, and his smile once again warms me.

"You don't smile much, do you?" I blurt out as I stare at the soft creases on either side of his mouth. His teeth brush against his lower lip, and the smile fades.

His gaze falls to my lips and quickly back to my eyes. "What would make you think that?"

I blush and shake my head. "Your laugh lines are soft. Smooth. Like they're brand new."

He touches his cheek where my eyes are fixated, and then lowers his hand. "No. I don't laugh a lot." His admission makes me sad, and I'm thankful that I was able to witness his hysterical laughter just a few minutes ago. "But somehow that was the funniest thing I've seen in a long time." He points to the disfigured bike. "I mean after I got over the initial shock of it all."

I suddenly want to know everything about him. Why doesn't he smile? Did someone hurt him? Are his lips as soft as his cheeks? *I need to stop. I don't even know him.*

"I'm sorry, I didn't mean to—"

He brings his hand up, and his rare smile is back. "It's okay. You seem very perceptive, Giselle." My name floats from his mouth, and I'm hypnotized. I don't think I've ever heard my name spoken with such masculine softness, if that is even a thing?

He reaches down between his legs and pulls the lever to slide his seat back. As it clicks into place, I jump a little. He places his right foot on the dash and leans back, obviously getting comfortable. "Is this okay?" he asks and looks at his wet boot, resting on my clean dashboard.

"Sure."

The rain continues to batter my car, and I lean back, as well, to try and get more comfortable.

"Tell me about yourself," he says. "Like what on Earth would make a girl like you let a complete stranger into her car? Do you do this all of the time?" He looks worried, as if I'm naive and innocent.

"Never!" I exclaim too quickly. I've learned to not trust many people, and that's how I've lived my life for a long time.

"Good. You shouldn't make a habit of this. The next guy might not be as nice as I am."

"So, you're a nice guy?" I ask.

He shrugs, "I guess, compared to some."

"Good to know." I smile.

"So, you were about to tell me all about yourself," he reminds me.

"There's not much to tell. I'm a simple person, with a simple life." I lie.

"That's very hard for me to believe," he says. "So tell me what you're doing tonight?"

"I have a date planned with my best friend. We're going to watch a few movies, pajama style."

"Sounds like fun," he says and raises his thick eyebrows. Those eyebrows…

"What movie?" he asks.

"You're going to think I'm a nut," I say, shying away from revealing the movies to a total stranger.

"Try me," he says and gets more comfortable in his seat.

"*Bowfinger*," I say and blush.

He laughs out loud and sits up straight. "That is legitimately one of my favorite movies. Fucking hilarious! That scene where Steve Martin makes Eddie Murphy's character cross a busy street to buy Starbucks is just priceless." I start laughing, and before I can control myself, I snort. I cover my mouth, embarrassed, but I can't stop laughing.

"Oh my God. My favorite scene!" I can't believe someone else likes this movie as much as I do. I also can't believe how much I'm getting pulled into his perfect smile. His lips. Eyes. Everything about his face is perfect. Captivating.

"Then we're going to watch Labyrinth," I say, proud of our movie rotation tonight.

"Labyrinth? Really? Isn't that a Muppet movie or something like that?" He sits back into the seat and turns so he's leaning on his shoulder.

"It *is* a Jim Henson movie, but it has nothing to do with the Muppets. Although, come to think of it, *The Muppet Movie* is amazing." I pause. "David Bowie's in it and plays a goblin king. It's amazing. Magical." I look out of the window and can practically hear him singing "Magic Dance."

"Well, if David Bowie is in it, it must be good," he says sarcastically.

"You have no idea what you're missing," I retort.

"I'll have to check it out. I mean, if you like *Bowfinger*, you must know what you're talking about." He pauses, "I'm sorry you're going to be late."

"It's okay, Mia will understand. She won't start without me."

I notice cars begin to inch forward ahead of us. I wipe my windshield to see through the fog and see that cars are being diverted through the median up ahead and being forced to make a U-turn. We slowly approach the median, and I'm able to turn around and head in the opposite direction.

"I need to get you home, since your bike is totaled."

He exhales deeply. "I'm in Villanova, but you can drop me anywhere along the Blue Route, and I'll be able to get a train or a cab back home."

"No, I'll drive you. I insist." I grip the steering wheel tightly as the wind tries to blow me off of the highway.

"Can I have your phone?" He stretches his hand across the center console and looks down between my legs where I shoved it earlier.

I blush and reach down, my thumb getting caught in the hole in my jeans just above the knee. He raises his eyebrow.

He glances at my legs and back up to my eyes, extending his hand.

"Why?" I ask, giving him my phone.

"I want to enter my address into your phone so we can navigate back to my house. What's your passcode?"

"I can enter it," I say and reach back for the phone.

"You're driving, that would be unsafe." I can see his wide smile out of the corner of my eye. I've never given anyone the passcode to my phone before, so I hesitate.

"Zero, eight, two, four," I say and tighten my grip on the steering wheel. *August twenty-fourth. A date I'll never forget.* I see him type it into my phone, and he quickly finds the navigation app. I hear C-3PO's voice come through Bluetooth, telling me to stay on the highway for *"Another two miles, Master."* Dax chuckles, "Star Wars fan, too?"

I nod.

I'm suddenly uneasy sharing my passcode with him. "You like even numbers?" he says.

"What?"

"Zero, eight, two, four. All even numbers." He sounds a little odd, his voice tight.

"Yeah, something like that," I reply, and C-3P0 interrupts. *"Exit to the right, now, Master."*

We drive in an uncomfortable silence as I'm guided through the directions by my favorite Star Wars android. I notice we're weaving through a gorgeous residential area with immense homes and perfect tree-lined streets.

"Nice neighborhood," I say. *Really nice. Like, Rockefeller nice.*

"I just moved here."

I picture his wife and bazillion kids waiting in the driveway for him as C-3P0 tells me, *"We have reached our destination, Master."*

I pull into the long driveway and stop in front of a four-car garage. "Wow," I gape.

The rain has stopped, and he opens the door to leave. "Thank you, Giselle. You really did save my life back there." He swings his legs out and turns back to me. "I owe you. Let me do something nice for you. Maybe buy you dinner or something?"

What?

"No, I don't think that would be appropriate." I gesture toward his house, expecting the front door to fly open and a beautiful model of a wife to be running toward him.

"It's the least I can do," he says.

"Just pay it forward," I respond. "I'm sure your *wife* wouldn't approve."

He chuckles and shakes his head. "You shouldn't assume things, Giselle." He gets out of the car and pats my roof. "Take care of yourself, and stop picking up strangers on the side of the road." He closes the door and strolls to the garage. I watch him punch a code into the keypad, and one of the doors opens up. I can see a line of black cars, the closest a large SUV. He doesn't turn around as the door closes.

"What the hell?" I ask and turn my car around. I watch in my rearview mirror as his mansion becomes smaller behind me. I stop at the end of the driveway and enter my own address into the navigation app. C-3P0 quickly chirps the directions to me as I begin driving home.

"Did that just happen?" I say out loud. C-3P0 doesn't answer.

I'm tense as I drive home. I'm also sick to my stomach.

I've never told anyone about the significance of 'zero, eight, two, four.'

So many things swirl around that date.

Loss

Love

Lies

It's a date I'll never forget.

CHAPTER 5

Dax
Past
Age 17

I GRIP THE SIDES OF THE VANITY as I stare at myself in the mirror. Dark eyes peer back at me, eyes I barely recognize. My heart is pounding in my chest, and I try to regulate my breathing. I take a deep breath and exhale slowly, closing my eyes.

Her smile is vivid and fresh in my memory. She's all around me, I can feel her body against mine, trembling slightly. I can see her eyes, wide with excitement and maybe a little bit of fear and uncertainty. The scent of her strawberry Chapstick suddenly hits my nose, and I lick my lower lip, tasting her again. *I need to feel her again.* I quickly turn and rush from my bathroom. I need to confirm that what just happened was real and not a dream or hallucination.

She's still here. Lara is in my bed, propped up on the striped flannel covered pillows, her wavy blonde hair cascading over her shoulders. *She's still here.*

Her eyes widen as I stride across the room, still naked. I stop next to the bed, and her gaze slowly travels down over my chest and toward my…

"Lara," I blurt out, interrupting her visual assault of my no longer impressive junk. She blinks quickly, and her eyes find mine again. I pull back the comforter and jump into the bed next to her, covering our nakedness. She shivers and slides lower under the blankets, blushing and embarrassed that she was caught staring at me.

"I'm freezing," she whispers, eyes softening. I turn onto my side, clumsily twisting the sheets and covers around us. My bare ass is now completely exposed, and I quickly kick my legs, trying to fix the blankets so we're both covered again. Her cool hand touches my arm, and I settle against her, pulling her closer to me. I take care not to press my once again growing erection into her.

"Is this okay?" I ask as I wrap my arms around her waist. Our hips are touching as our lower extremities are facing up. As awkward as we are lying next to each other, it feels incredible knowing that we just had sex–made love–for the first time. And then I remember how she tensed underneath me, wincing in pain. The look of surprise on her face as I pushed into her is fresh in my mind. "Oh my God, Lara, are you okay?" I turn completely on my side, placing my chin on her shoulder. "Please tell me that I didn't hurt you."

"I'm fine," she says softly. "It's about what I expected." My heart drops as her tone tells me everything that I need to know. It was awful. It sucked.

"I'm sorry," I whisper against her skin. "I'm really sorry."

"Don't be sorry," she says, and she giggles a little bit. "I knew it would hurt. The first time is *always* painful. That's how it's supposed to be. You did nothing to cause that - it's just how I'm made." She places her hand over mine and squeezes. "It's really okay, *Daxton*. I'm fine." Her smile relaxes me, and she stretches forward to kiss my cheek, the scent of strawberry Chapstick once again filling my nose.

"Are you sure?" I ask hesitantly, wanting to find her lips again.

"Yes, totally sure," she assures me.

"Well, I hope so, because I would hate to hurt you like that again." I close my eyes and try to erase her look of panic from earlier. "Are you bleeding?" I ask, embarrassed.

She blinks rapidly, looking surprised. "I...I don't know," she says, shifting uncomfortably next to me. "I probably am, and I'm sure I've ruined your sheets." Her eyes glisten and begin to fill with tears.

"Hey, stop that. I don't care what you did - what *we* did - to my sheets. They can be washed." I make a quick mental note to wash them myself so my mother can't see the evidence of what we did here today.

Lara relaxes against me, and I nuzzle into her neck. "Are you sure you're okay?" I ask her.

"I'm wonderful," she says, and I feel her smile against my forehead.

"Wonderful," I repeat her words and tighten my hold around her tiny frame. She feels fragile in my arms, and all I want to do is protect her, never cause her pain or discomfort again.

"I love you, Daxton." Her words grab my heart and squeeze.

"I love you," I quickly respond so there isn't a doubt in her mind. "I'll always love you."

"Always?" she asks and curls into my side.

"Forever," I say without hesitating. She briefly tenses in my arms, and I can't help but wonder how much pain she's really in.

THE FRONT DOOR FLIES OPEN, and Alex strides in followed by my mother. Lara and I exchange worried glances as they enter the kitchen. Our school books are scattered on the table, and we only just began the project we were supposed to have been working on for the past four hours. "Looks like you two got a lot done," Alex says, barely audible. His mouth is packed with bloody gauze because he just had four wisdom teeth pulled. His eyes glaze over as he sinks into the couch in the adjacent den. "I need Advil," he moans.

My mother rushes into the kitchen and grabs the painkillers from the cabinet while swiping a bottle of water from the refrigerator. "Here, Alex. Take these and get some rest." Her stress is obvious. She hates seeing any of us in pain, ever.

"I'll just get some rest, right here," Alex slurs. He makes eye contact with me and attempts to wink, but both eyes close awkwardly, and he looks cross-eyed. He knows what Lara and I were planning to do today. It was his idea since he knew he'd be at the oral surgeon for several hours, and my mom had to stay with him. My dad is out of town so I had the house all to myself. It was the perfect time for Lara and I to do what we've been talking about doing for months. She shifts uncomfortably in her seat, and a pang of guilt once again grabs me. "Are you okay?" I whisper, and she quickly nods and smiles.

My mother joins us at the kitchen table, and she sinks into the chair next to Lara. "What a day," she says and stretches her legs. "How's your position paper coming along? Have you two decided on a topic to debate?" Lara's eyes widen, and she slowly nods. The project we're working on is for our debate club.

"Yes, Mrs. Anderson. We've decided to debate the right to die with dignity." I shake my head and look away. I did not want to write an opposing position paper on this topic, and Lara is fully aware of that. She knows my opinion on this already, and she also knows the topic that I wanted to debate.

"Oh? That's interesting," my mother says. She turns to me, "I thought you were planning on debating the space program and what the benefits were in investing more into space exploration."

"Apparently, that's not what we're debating," I snap as Lara looks guilty, smiling apologetically.

"Well, I'm sure whatever the two of you decide to do, it's going to be fantastic," my mother says, reassuringly.

Lara scribbles some notes onto a piece of paper. "I can't wait to discuss this paper in Debate Club. I think it's an important topic and something the majority of our country is far behind on. Oregon, Washington, and Vermont are much more progressive when it comes to this."

"It's killing yourself. Suicide, Lara. There's nothing good about that." I tense up as Alex groans from the couch.

"Some people should be able to kill themselves," he mumbles. "It's a better world without them, trust me." Gauze hangs from his mouth, and his eyes roll back into his head. The anesthesia must still be in his system.

My fingers click louder on the keyboard as I continue to write about my position. I hate that we're even having this discussion in front of Alex. His father killed himself, but I wish he didn't. I hate that fucker for what he did to my best friend, but he deserves a lifetime of punishment, not the escape of death.

"Alex, that's different and you know it," Lara chimes in. "When someone is so sick, with no hope, they deserve the right to choose to end their life. They shouldn't be subjected to the endless suffering that's ahead of them. They should be able to die in peace and with dignity. I'm not talking about psychopaths or criminals." She takes a deep breath, and her hands begin to shake. She quickly swipes a tear from her cheek and looks around.

"It sounds like you two are going to have a very healthy debate," my mother says. "This is certainly one topic that can polarize close friends *and* an entire country."

Alex mumbles something incoherent from the couch, and then starts snoring loudly. My mother quickly rushes to remove his Chuck Taylors and arrange a blanket over him. She pauses to smooth his hair and places a soft kiss on his forehead. She loves him as if he was her own.

Lara sniffles and begins to gather her books and papers. "I think I'll email you my paper tonight," she says as she shoves her things into her backpack.

"What?" I ask, surprised.

"I have to go. I'm not feeling so good."

I tense up. What if she's still bleeding? Is that even possible? What if she's in so much pain that she can't sit still?

"Are you *okay*?" I whisper, trying not to let my mother hear me.

She furrows her brow and nods quickly. "I'm okay, I'm just feeling a little lightheaded and nauseous. It has nothing to do with *that*." She wobbles when she stands up. I rush over to her. Her hand is cold and clammy.

"You're not okay, Lara."

My mother is suddenly next to us. "Honey, you look pale. Sit down and let me get you some water."

Lara nods and sinks back into the chair. Her eyes are glassy, and she has a dazed look about her. "What's going on?" I ask. "You were fine just five minutes ago." I'm terrified that I really hurt her. Fuck.

"I'll be okay," she says and looks up. "Thanks, Mrs. Anderson, water will do the trick." Her shaky hands reach for the glass, and she raises it to her lips, closing her eyes.

"Take as long as you need to relax," my mother says. "I'll drive you home when you're ready."

Lara shakes her head and says weakly, "I can walk, really."

"Nonsense, it's over a mile, and no offense, but you don't look like you could walk a block."

I slide my chair closer to hers, so our knees are touching. "Please tell me you're okay," I whisper as I place my hands on her knees and rest my forehead against hers.

"I'm fine," she says.

"You're lying," I say immediately.

She doesn't respond, but her eyes tell me that I'm right.

CHAPTER 6

Giselle
Past
Age 17

MY PHONE BUZZES on the night stand, indicating there's an incoming text message. I drop my highlighter and close my English book. There are only two people who text me often, and I cringe at the thought of one of them. I slowly walk over to pick up my phone and see the message on my locked screen. Bile rises in my throat, and I vow to get my number changed. I unlock my phone and read his message.

Troy: Why on earth did you wear those sneakers to school today?

What the hell?

Me: Because they're comfortable.

Troy: You shouldn't wear them anymore. They're ugly. You don't want to be ugly, do you? ;)

Why am I even engaging with him? He's been badgering me ever since he stole my virginity last summer on the golf course. After he lied to me. He told the entire school that I was a frigid lay, and he only took me to that party because he felt sorry for me. I can't believe what I let him take from me. *What he stole.*

Me: I'm changing my number this weekend. So, do me a favor and delete me from your contacts.

Troy: I won't ever delete you. We're tied together. You know you can't forget about me.

I roll my eyes and shake my head. If he thinks he's intimidating, he's insane. There's nothing tying us together. I'm not his property.

Me: It's over. It's been over for months. Leave me alone.

Troy: Never.

"Giselle? Are you here?" My mother knocks lightly on my door. I tuck my phone under my pillow, hiding the text conversation I'm having with Troy. She has no idea the hell he put me through and the constant badgering I'm subjected to every single day.

"Yes, Mom. Come in."

The door opens, and she comes in carrying a basket of my folded laundry. "You left this in the dryer. I had some time, so I folded it all for you." She slides the basket on the floor next to my closet.

"Thanks," I say. My mom's pretty amazing.

"Are you tired?" she asks, looking concerned. I realize that I'm still on my bed, so it must look like I may have been napping.

"A little," I lie and feel the bed vibrate with more text messages.

"Your father is coming home early today and thought we'd take a ride out to the shore and have dinner and maybe stay in that bed and breakfast we love in Spring Lake." We may live in Pennsylvania, but we spend a lot of time at the New Jersey shore, and I love it. "We're planning to meet with a realtor tomorrow to look at several rentals for this summer." That's the best part of our excursions, especially when we're looking for our summer rental. My mother and I love walking through quaint beach houses, imagining ourselves spending warm summer evenings on the porch. That's a must, any house we consider must have a porch.

I almost forget about the douche under my pillow until it vibrates again.

"Sounds good to me," I say. "I need to finish a few things for school before we leave. Should I pack for one day or two?"

"Just tonight. We'll be coming home after dinner tomorrow."

"Okay," I say, shifting uncomfortably on my bed. My phone keeps vibrating, and I'm worried about what nonsense Troy is spewing now.

My mom backs out of my room and closes the door. I quickly grab the phone from underneath my pillow and see that I have twelve missed messages.

Troy: We need to talk.

Troy: I'm calling you in five minutes.

Troy: You can't avoid me.

Troy: Are you there?

Troy: Dammit, Giselle. Stop playing games with me.

I can't read any more of this crap. I stop reading and swipe left to delete the entire thread. As soon as I hit delete, the phone rings, and his name appears. My hands are sweaty, and my heart is racing. I need to end this insanity.

"This needs to stop, Troy." I shout as I answer the phone.

Silence. But I can hear him breathing.

"Troy. Please stop this."

"I'm sorry," he says in a tone I haven't heard in a long time. He sounds sincere. Sweet, almost. But I'm not buying it.

"This ends now. I'm tired of this. We're over. We've been over for months. Do you understand?"

"No," he says simply and takes a deep breath.

I'm ready to unleash on him. It's been a long time coming. My confidence builds, and I let go.

"Accept it. I mean, how could you possibly think that everything you've done to me is acceptable? You've tortured me for months. You treat me like a piece of shit. Jesus, you raped me, Troy. You fucking *raped* me. What do you think I'm going to do? Forgive you? Date you? You're a sociopath. Take a minute, and Google the word. You're a fucking sociopath."

He remains silent, and I continue to pounce. "What is it that makes you think that you have some sort of power over me? Huh? I certainly didn't give you permission to take anything from me. And I don't give you permission to keep bothering me. It ends today. Forever. Do you understand? Because so fucking help me God, I will destroy you if you continue to do this. I will wipe your squeaky clean name all over this town. So don't push me."

"I'm sorry," he says again, his voice straining. "I didn't realize... I mean... I didn't rape you." He chokes on those words, and his breathing becomes erratic.

"Yes, you did. I told you "No." I said the word. I told you to stop, and you didn't. That's rape."

"But, you are, I mean, you were my girlfriend. That's not rape, Giselle."

"It's rape when the other person says no, and I fucking said "NO!"" My heart is still racing, and I feel my cheeks begin to burn with rage. *Why did I wait so long to do this? Why did I allow him to abuse me for so long? Why did I let him rape me?*

"No, Giselle. Oh my God," he says, his voice trailing off.

I don't relent. "Let it sink in. Think about it. You're a fucking criminal."

He gasps and begins to stammer. "I–I'm so sorry... I didn't– wouldn't... God..."

Is he sobbing? Crying? I can't tell, but he doesn't sound so good, and this makes me happy. I want him to shed tears. Lots of them. I want him to feel the pain of what he did to me physically, emotionally, and socially. His buddies mock me. Other girls call me a slut. Even some of my close friends questioned the truth. *What really happened on the golf course that night?* I've never told anyone my side of the story, and now Troy is afraid of what may come. He should be.

"But I love–I loved you."

I laugh, "You lied to me, Troy. You used those words as a weapon to steal my heart and get in my pants. You didn't love me. How on Earth could someone in love do what you did to me? The sad thing is I believed your lie. I believed you and let you steal from me. No more, Troy. No more."

"I wish I could take it back," he says softly, but I don't believe him.

"You got what you wanted and made me feel like shit every single day since. You knew exactly what you were doing."

"I don't know what to say…"

"Really? You've said so much already. You've belittled me. You've called me ugly, skank, whore…shall I go on? For once, I'm glad you're speechless because from this moment on, I will never let your words affect me ever again. You've taught me so much, Troy. I'll never trust you or anyone like you ever again."

"But…"

"Just stop. Please. And seriously, lose my number. Now." I end the call and immediately drop to my floor. The sobs don't come right away, but when they do, I let loose.

Months of embarrassment, shame, and anguish pour from my soul. I'm back on that blanket, in the warm August air, naked and ashamed. My youth was lost that night, stolen from me. My innocence gone. My tears flow with relief that this may finally be over. Troy has no control over me. No power over me. I can't let that moment dictate my future. I'm in control now. I've won in a convoluted way. *Why did I wait so long to do this?*

My phone vibrates, and his name pops up again. This time I block him. Forever.

I silently vow to never let this happen again.

One lie started this, but the truth ends it now.

CHAPTER 7

Dax
Present

I PUMP MY ARMS as I widen my stride. My feet hit the pavement harder than I want. I'm going to seriously pay for this workout later, my aching joints already throbbing. My breathing becomes labored as I enter my neighborhood and see the hill that leads to my private driveway. FitBit tells me I've already run four miles. I tap my iPhone, and the music becomes louder in my ears, engulfing my senses. AWOLNATION's 'Jump on My Shoulders' reverberates in my head as it drowns out my labored breathing. *I'm going to make this hill my bitch.*

The loud music motivates me through the pain. A vision of Giselle's nervous smile replays in my brain, reminding me that a complete stranger literally saved my life the other day. A stranger that I've been unable to get out of every waking thought. *A beautiful, yet familiar stranger.* I can't shake that feeling I know her from somewhere.

I reach the top of the hill as a tow truck backs out of my driveway and speeds off past me, the driver smirking. As soon as I reach the base of the driveway, I realize exactly why.

My brand new motorcycle is lying in the middle of it in a mangled heap. *What the fuck?*

When I called the state police and the department of transportation yesterday, informing them of the accident, they assured me they would remove the bike, and I'd never see it again. I never wanted to see it again. But here it is now, right smack in the middle of my fucking driveway.

I bend over and place my hands on my knees, trying to catch my breath. Sweat is dripping over my brows and down my face.

What the hell am I going to do with this mess?

My legs are burning, and I need to cool down and stretch, but all I feel is rage. FitBit buzzes on my wrist, indicating that I just surpassed twenty thousand steps today. My heart is pounding in my chest, and I just want to pick up the bike and chuck it into the street.

I kick the tire as I walk past it, and immediately regret my act of frustration as my toes go numb. *Fuck!*

After stretching and cooling down as best as I can, I walk through my house, into the kitchen, and grab a bottle of water. I drink half of it in one gulp when the doorbell rings.

"Coming!" I yell, but the bell rings again. *Seriously?*

I jog toward the front of the house and quickly pull the door open. I'm about to unleash on the visitor when I see Alex's smiling face.

"Collecting weird sculptures?" he asks sarcastically as he pushes past me. My mouth hangs open, unable to form a coherent response, anger still coursing through my veins.

He makes himself comfortable at the bar in my kitchen, the smile never leaving his face.

"What do you think?" I retort. He knows what happened to me the other day and why I couldn't make it to Garrett's.

"Lighten up, dude. You know I'm just kidding, right?"

"Whatever," I say and grab another bottle of water. "I wasn't expecting you."

"Obviously."

I shake my head and chug the rest of the water. He better have a good reason to be here, because I'm not in the mood for entertaining.

"Are you hungry?" I ask him as I open the door to my empty refrigerator.

"I can always eat," he replies.

"Well, I've got nothing here." I slam the door shut, just for effect.

I sit down at the other end of the bar and stare at him. Maybe uncomfortable silence will make him want to leave. And I've got a fucking mess in my driveway I need to do something about.

"I'm really fucking happy you're alive," he says, his smirk replaced by genuine concern. "I don't know what I'd do if something happened to you."

I've been trying not to think about what would have happened if I was crushed to death by the speeding fire trucks. I've had a couple of mini panic attacks over the past two days. I truly have to believe that they would have stopped just in time. They would have seen me. *Right?*

"Thanks," I respond.

"I'm serious, Dax. I know I don't say it enough, but you're my brother, and I love you, man. I'm sick over this, wondering what would have happened to all of us if you weren't around."

"Stop over-reacting. I'm totally over it. I wasn't on the bike and was sitting safely in a car."

"You should pay off that person's mortgage or something. Do something really special for him for saving your life the way he did," Alex says excitedly. He's full of ideas suddenly.

I smile. "It wasn't a 'he' it was a 'she' and I think she may feel weird if I started snooping around, trying to find out everything about her so I can pay off her debts."

"A *she?*" He's grinning now. "You spent hours trapped in a car during a crazy storm with 'a she' and you don't tell me about it?"

"Are you being serious right now?" My cheeks heat up. "One minute, you want me to pay off this woman's debt, and then you want to know if I hit on her?"

"I didn't say that," he says defensively. "You just conveniently left out the part about your savior being a woman."

"You didn't ask. Besides, I'm not out there trolling for another relationship right now, if you haven't noticed." *And I have no intention of it.*

"Are you still not over what happened with Natalia?"

"Don't fucking bring her name up again, Alex." I clench my fists and try to push her out of my mind. "In fact, don't bring up me and any other woman for the foreseeable future. I'm done with chicks. I'm done with relationships. I'm done with constantly being lied to." I know I sound like a brooding baby, but fuck, I can't deal with this anymore.

"Whoa. Easy. Sorry I brought it up." He looks at me apologetically and lowers his head. "I just want you to be happy. You deserve it."

"I am happy. Look around you. I have the house I've always wanted, hidden away in the suburbs. I'm the drummer for the number one rock band in the country. I'm even planning a vacation for next month." *Two truths and a lie.*

Alex raises his brow. "A vacation? Really?" he asks in disbelief.

"Yes, a vacation."

"Where are you going?" he quickly asks, trying to force me to admit that I'm lying.

"Mexico." *Take that.*

Shit.

"Really? Where in Mexico?" Alex presses.

"That place where you and Tabby went over the winter."

"Playa del Carmen?" he asks.

"Yes. There."

"I would think a single guy like you would go someplace more happening, like Cozumel or Cancun. Where we stayed was mostly couples."

Shit.

"Well, that's where I'm going." Now I'm determined to make this happen. I don't give a shit if he stayed in a place that was for couples. I'll book somewhere better. More exclusive. *I'll show him.*

"Good for you. You could use a vacation." He pauses and laughs. "Did Garrett approve your time off?"

Shit.

Garrett's going to lose his mind when I tell him that I'm taking an impromptu vacation after we just finished laying all of our tracks for our new album. He's going to want to play some local places to test our songs and get our playlist ready for our tour in a few months.

"I haven't told Garrett yet." *Or my travel agent.*

"Good luck with that!" Alex laughs, slapping his hand on the counter.

"He'll be fine. I'll break it to him gently."

"I'm serious when I say you should do something for that girl who saved your life. Think about it."

"What the hell can I do?"

"Find out what you can about her. Pay off her car. Her house. Something."

"Why does it have to be about money?" I ask.

"What would you suggest? Send her flowers? Candy? A card? Dude, she saved your life. It's got to be big, and you can afford big."

It's a bit presumptuous to think she needs money. I don't know a thing about her, other than her name and where she lives.

"I'll think about it," I say reluctantly.

"Good, man," Alex says.

He stands up, walks over to where I'm sitting, and suddenly pulls me into a bro hug. "I'm really glad you're alive. We all are." He quickly releases me and begins to brush off the front of his shirt. "Holy shit, you're a sweaty mess."

"I didn't ask for a hug, bro. And that's what you get for rubbing your body against someone who just got back from running."

"I gotta take off. Glad we had this little chat," he says and swipes his keys from the counter.

He's out the door before I know it.

"Yeah, me too, bro," I say into the empty foyer.

Alex is my brother, regardless of whose blood he has coursing through his veins. We've been through a lot together, and his life wouldn't be what it is today if my family didn't give him a second chance at life. We're connected. Bonded.

And I just lied to my best friend. *My brother.*

I shake my head and laugh.

I guess I need to book a trip to Mexico and figure out something nice to do for Giselle.

Priorities.

CHAPTER 8

Giselle
Present

STEAMING HOT WATER pounds into my skull, cascading down my aching body. I just finished the longest run of my life–six miles. It was painful and exhilarating at the same time. Everything hurts, so I let the heat from the water loosen my muscles. The pain feels good, though. It makes me realize how hard I'm working, how far I'm pushing my body. I'm training for a half-marathon in a few months, and I'm finally seeing positive results in my endurance and stamina.

I'm not sure how I'm going to hold up tonight, though. Mia's made plans for us to go bar hopping, and I haven't done this in a while. I actually can't remember the last time we went out. Our nights usually consist of movies, snacks, and drinks at home. The thought of finding something to wear, other than pajamas, is daunting. I dry off, and slip into a loose t-shirt, and walk over to the chair in the corner of my room. I pick up a pair of jeans and immediately sniff them. They seem fresh enough, I think I've only worn them three times since I washed them last week, so they should be good and comfy to wear out tonight. I poke my finger through the hole near the knee and smile.

EPIC LIES

These are the same pair I wore last Friday, when I picked up a complete stranger on my way home. I smell them again, almost expecting the scent of a fresh rain storm. *Or Dax.*

After I finish dressing, I dry my long hair and let it fall into a wavy, but controlled mess. I brush a light coating of mascara onto my eyelashes and a little bit of strawberry Chapstick on my lips. *Ready to go.*

Mia is already downstairs waiting for me. "It's about time," she huffs. I glance at the clock; it's only seven-fifteen.

"What's the rush?" I ask.

"I'm starving!" she yells and grabs her clutch from my counter. "And Uber has been outside for the past ten minutes." She walks past me and opens the door. "Do you have your keys?" she asks.

I rarely carry a purse or a bag, so I toss my house key to her to keep for me. My driver's license and ATM card are both tucked into my back pocket, and I have a few twenty-dollar bills in my front. "I'm ready," I say, patting my pockets and smile at my best friend, who's trying to remain calm at my tardiness.

Dottie, our favorite driver, is waving at us as we walk out of my house. She's an Uber driver, moonlighting on the side of her regular job at a diner in Philly. She prefers the flexibility of driving people around since she has a few kids at home and a very busy husband. Yes, we know her well. We request her every single time we know we'll be out drinking. We also love her stories from the city and the diner she's worked at for the last decade.

"Girls! So great seeing you again. What have you all been up to?" she asks enthusiastically. Her smile is genuine and always warms my heart.

"Giselle's been so boring lately. All she wants to do is stay home and watch movies," Mia jokes. I huff.

"Well, it's a gorgeous night to be out on the town. Where's our first stop?" she asks as she shifts the car into drive, slowly pulling away from my townhouse.

"Villanova, The Lounge on North Spring," Mia says.

"We're going near campus? On a Friday night? How old are we?" I ask. We tend to avoid any bars near the university, so I'm surprised by her choice.

"Oh, hush. We're going to have a blast."

"Mia, we have both been out of school too long to be going to a college bar. Seriously."

Dottie giggles from the front seat. "Didn't I take you two there a few months ago?"

"No," I say and turn to Mia. We haven't been there in a long time.

"Not recently, but I may know someone who works there," Mia says slyly. I smack her leg.

"What? Who?"

"Remember that guy in Starbucks last week? Well, he's a bartender at The Lounge, and I told him I may stop by this weekend to say 'Hi.'" She smiles and looks nervous.

No wonder she's been acting so funny all week. I didn't think she really spoke to him, but then again, I was in my own world that day.

"Oh," I say.

"Sounds like someone has a crush." Dottie giggles again and turns toward Villanova.

"Hey, I barely know the guy. But I have to see where this might go, right? And besides, did you see him? Holy. Hotness."

"I wasn't really looking," I admit. "Do you even know his name?"

"No," she answers quickly. "But I plan to find out tonight."

"Does that mean I'll be coming home alone?" I smirk.

"No! God, I'm not like that!"

"Right, you *never* leave a bar for a one-time fling," I say sarcastically. If I had a dollar for each time…

"Stop judging me. He's cute. I mean hot. And he seems super nice."

"Whatever. Dottie, you're going to be busy tonight with the two of us apparently. I hope you have a sitter for your kids."

"My husband is home all weekend for the first time in months, so I'm at your complete disposal. Oooh, this is going to be fun!" she chirps. "What about you, Giselle? Anyone special?"

Our Uber driver is way too invested in our love lives. Or in my case, lack thereof.

"Nope," I say.

Before we know it, Dottie's pulling up in front of The Lounge. There's a huge, shiny, black SUV with a trailer attached to the back, taking up at least three parking spaces. Two guys in black t-shirts and jeans are unloading equipment from the back. "There's a band here tonight?" I ask, annoyed. So much for a quiet dinner and drinks with my best friend.

Mia's surprised. "I had no idea."

"Sure you didn't." I turn to Dottie, "I'll text you when we're ready to leave. I have a feeling it will be soon."

"C'mon, Giselle. Stop being such a party pooper. We haven't seen a band play live in so long, this is going to be fun. I promise."

"Have a great time, girls! I'm going to spend some time in Barnes & Noble. I have a list of books my girls want to read, so I think I'll use this time to do a little shopping and browse a little for myself." Mia and I slide out of the car just in time for one of the roadies to practically run us over with a hand truck that has several amplifiers piled on it.

"Bye!" we say in unison, and Dottie drives off.

"I have a feeling you're going to owe me after tonight," I say and grab her hand. We walk into the bar, and besides the crew setting up in front, it's practically empty.

"Looks like we have the place to ourselves," she says and walks toward the hostess.

We're seated in a booth in the far corner of the room, and she immediately looks toward the bar. "He doesn't seem to be here yet."

"Relax. If he told you he was working tonight, he'll be here."

Our waitress arrives and places coasters in front of us. "Hello, ladies. What can I get you to drink?"

Mia strains her neck and looks toward the bar again. "What's on tap?" she asks. *She never drinks beer.*

The waitress rattles off a dozen micro-brews that neither of us have ever heard of while Mia keeps watch for Starbucks Guy.

"I'll have a lemon drop, please," I interrupt her. "Make it two."

Mia looks at me, "How did you know that I wanted a lemon drop?"

"Because that's what you *always* have."

She smiles and shrugs.

"I'll be right back with your drinks. Take a look at our specials while I'm gone, and let me know if you want any appetizers. I personally recommend the Bavarian pretzels with spicy mustard." She walks away, and my mouth is watering thinking of her suggestion.

"I'm not eating carbs tonight. At. All," Mia declares and shifts again in her seat.

"Really? Since when?"

"Since I put these jeans on and had to lie on my bed to pull up the zipper."

I laugh. "Stop it. You're being ridiculous."

"Says the girl who wears her jeans for weeks before washing them to ensure you never have this problem."

Zing!

"I don't wait two weeks," I lie. "And stop stalking my laundry piles."

I open the menu, feeling a little self-conscious. *Maybe I should order a salad. Nah.*

The buffalo chicken sandwich is screaming at me from the menu. That's definitely what I'm getting.

The sound of drums suddenly fills the room, causing Mia and I to turn to look at the stage. One of the roadies is banging on them like he's the only person in the room. "Isn't it a little early for the band to be starting?"

"Who knows," Mia says and looks toward the bar again.

The hostess appears again and pulls two tables together directly across from us, setting it for a larger group.

Then our waitress places two large lemon drop martinis in front of us, along with the Bavarian pretzels. "These are on me. They're seriously my favorite, so please enjoy them."

Mia scoffs at the heaping pile of carbs on the table between us, so I pull it closer to me. "Thank you. I'm sure they're great," I say to the waitress as I pull apart one of the pretzels and dip it into the spicy mustard.

"Are you ready to order?" she asks.

"I'll have the avocado and chicken salad. Please hold the cheese and croutons. Instead of the creamy dressing, I'll just take some lime, vinegar, and a little bit of olive oil." Mia's order is extremely high-maintenance and won't absorb an ounce of the alcohol that I know she's about to consume.

The waitress nods politely and turns to me. "And for you?"

"The buffalo chicken sandwich," I say with a mouthful of salty, amazing pretzel. The spicy mustard burns the inside of my nose, making my eyes water. But it's so good.

"Fries?" she asks me, and I nod vigorously. *I mean, duh.*

Mia shifts in her seat. "Who's the bartender tonight?" she asks, trying to be nonchalant.

"Oh. I'm not sure who's on tonight. The shift change happens at eight. Maybe it's Trent. But it could be Ashley. Not sure." She walks away with our order.

I take another bite of the heavenly pretzel and chase it with a sip from the martini. *Delightful.*

"What if he's not working?" she asks, almost frantic.

I swallow harshly. "Simmer down. Aren't we here to have fun?" I ask.

She huffs and reaches for a pretzel, tearing it into small pieces on the plate in front of her. "I'm just going to have a small bite."

A group of guys begins to fill the large table next to us, and the roadies are the first to sit down. Mia's eyes widen, and she practically chokes on the mouthful of pretzel.

"He should be here in about five minutes, so don't lose your shit, G." One of the guys says, attempting to keep the brooding guy calm.

"He better fucking get here. We have to go through our set list and make sure he has his shit together. And based on his track record this past week, I don't have confidence he'll get here on time."

"Stop being so hard on him. What happened last Friday wasn't his fault, and you know it."

More grumbling from the brooding dude called 'G.'

Mia's eyes widen, "It's the band," she whispers too loudly, and their heads turn toward us. Mia begins to choke.

"Are you okay?" the guy next to 'G' asks.

Another person shows up, but I'm focused on my best friend, whose face is turning shades of pink, then red, then purple. She coughs and launches a partially chewed piece of pretzel across the table, bouncing off my chest. Color returns to her face.

"I'm fine," she answers, eyes wide. "Oh. My. God."

"Are you okay?" I ask her, and she nods vigorously.

She stammers. "You're–you're–Epic Fail!" She looks crazy right now. Epic Fail? Not a chance...

I turn to the group at the table next to us as I take a sip from my martini. Their smiles are huge, and recognition sets in as one of them slides next to Mia across from me.

"Hey, lifesaver." Words float from his lips like magic, his voice imprinted in my brain. My heart begins to race, and I can't believe who is sitting across from me. Everything suddenly comes together, and I realize who he is and why he seemed so familiar to me last week.

Holy.

Fucking.

Shit.

"Hey," I say, barely audible.

His eyes lock on mine and stay there. I'm afraid to look away. My left foot starts tapping wildly on the floor, starting a chain reaction up my leg, and I have to press my hand into my thigh to calm myself down. *It's Dax.*

"Did you make it home okay after dropping me off last week?" he asks, his eyes bright and his smile still soft and welcoming.

"I had to take back roads, you know, because of the accident." *Why am I so nervous?*

Mia looks from me to Dax and back to me again. "I told you!" she yells. "I knew it!" She's so proud of herself, yet completely star struck that Dax Anderson from Epic Fail is sitting next to her. "I'm Mia, her phone-a-friend. So nice to meet you. Now, please excuse me, I have to pee," she exclaims, and Dax slides out of the seat. We watch Mia as she runs through the bar toward the restrooms.

He sits back down, and we both reach for the last pretzel on the plate in front of me. Our fingers brush against each other, and we pull the pretzel apart while our eyes remain locked together. "Do you mind?" he asks, his voice strong and deep. "I haven't had a thing to eat all day." I drop the half of the pretzel that I pulled and nod.

"It's all yours. Please take it." *And take me, too.*

"Thanks," he says and chews the pretzel.

I look around to see if Mia is finished in the bathroom and notice her leaning on the bar, talking to whom I can only assume is Starbucks Guy.

Dax clears his throat, and I turn my head to look at him again. He's staring at me. Through me. Into me.

"What are you doing here?" he asks in disbelief.

"What do you mean?" I ask, mildly defensive, but excited he wants to know more.

"How did you know I was here?"

"I didn't."

"Oh." His eyes drop but quickly find mine again.

"Mia. She knows the–I mean–she kind of knows the bartender. So that's why we're here." I tense up and feel a little dizzy. "You didn't think–you don't think I'm stalking you. Do you?"

Oh. My. God.

"I didn't know who you were until now." I would swear on my first-born child if I could. I really didn't know.

My conversation with Mia last week replays in my head, and I realize she knew who was in my car. *Why didn't she say anything?*

EPIC LIES

I twist toward the bar and see her flirting, hard. I believe her intentions were mixed for tonight. She was definitely coming to see Starbucks Guy, but did she know about Epic Fail? She couldn't have—she was just as surprised as I was. *Right?*

Dax chuckles and shakes his head. "No, I don't think you're stalking me." His smile captures me.

"How are you?" I ask. I've been thinking about him non-stop since last week. The accident that could have killed him keeps replaying in my mind. I've cringed every single time I've heard emergency sirens this past week, trying not to picture his demise underneath that bridge.

He inhales deeply and looks around the room. His bandmates seem to be preoccupied with the vast menu, everyone gesturing and pointing.

"I'm—okay," he says, furrowing his beautiful eyebrows. "But something has been bothering me all week," he says, capturing my gaze.

"What?" I say, breathless.

"How do I know you?"

CHAPTER 9

Dax
Past
Age 17

SILENCE FILLS THE ROOM, engulfing me. Strangling me. *Suffocating me.*

"Dax, honey, are you okay?" Lara's mother, Mrs. Tierney, asks quietly from behind me. We're the only people in here now.

"No," I choke. "I'm sorry, Mrs. Tierney, but I'm not okay. How could I be okay?" I'm fighting back tears, and I'm losing.

She walks over to me and places her hand softly on my shoulder. Her touch is cold, yet burns at the same time. "Do you want to talk?"

I swallow the ball of spit lodged in the back of my throat. "What's there to talk about?" *She can't be serious.*

"You must have questions."

You have got to fucking be kidding me.

I hold back the rage pulsing through my veins, and I turn to look into the eyes of my girlfriend's mother.

"Why didn't you tell me?" I need to know. "Why did you hide this from me for months?"

She sinks onto the bed next to her daughter. *My girlfriend.*

Mrs. Tierney grabs my hand at the same time she holds Lara's. The difference is mine is warm and pulsing with life. Lara's is limp, cold, and dying.

"It wasn't easy, Dax. The past few months have been so incredibly difficult for us. For our family. For *Lara.*"

I rip my hand from her grasp and move away from her, closer to Lara's shoulders. I'm hoping she can hear everything that her mother and I are talking about. She has to know how much her decision has affected us. *Affected me.*

"Why did you let her do this?" I scream. "Why? You're her parents. You're supposed to protect her and keep her safe. Help give her strength so she can thrive. So she can fucking live!" I'm pacing now, and Mrs. Tierney has tears streaming down her face. She knows I'm right. She *must* know.

She inhales deeply and lets go of Lara's hand, placing it gingerly on her chest, as if she's already in her coffin.

"You don't understand how bad it is. How bad it was going to get for her."

"No, I don't understand. Because NOBODY FUCKING TOLD ME!"

She flinches, and I watch Lara for a response, but there isn't one. She's been comatose since yesterday.

The day that I found out that her body was riddled with cancer, and she was going to die. Everything happened so suddenly. Too suddenly.

"None of this has been easy. We've been struggling with her decision every single day. But you must know, this was her decision, and we honored it. We love her and wanted to give her the right to choose how far she took her treatments."

"She's sixteen years old. How can you let her decide for herself?" I ask in disbelief. They should have been forcing chemotherapy into her veins. Prolonging her life. *Saving her life.*

"Someday, you'll understand. I promise. But for now, you'll have to trust that Lara's father and I have done everything we can to keep our daughter alive. Our only child. We've fought alongside her through some of the toughest battles she's ever had to fight. We've seen how bad it gets. We fought her tooth and nail to allow the doctors to pump her full of poison to keep her alive for a few more months. But that's all we would have had. We wouldn't have had the lifetime that we hoped for…dreamed of. Our baby girl wasn't going to last another six months with chemotherapy. So, we let her decide to stop treatment. To say she's had enough."

Her voice is strangely calm now. At peace.

Lara's chest moves up and down mechanically. She's on a ventilator that's keeping her alive. Allowing air to flow through her lungs, preventing her organs from completely shutting down.

"She barely fought!"

"That's not true, Daxton. She's been fighting since she was eight years old. She's gone through this before and had to endure over two years of chemotherapy and bone marrow transplants. Her situation was dire back then, and we've been lucky to have her with us for the past eight years. In those eight years, she's lived a full life. Those eight years were a gift. She's almost at peace."

Rage is about to spill out, and I do everything to restrain myself. How could Lara be at peace? She's fighting to breathe, requiring artificial support to keep her alive. This isn't peace; this is hell on Earth.

"She's suffering," I sputter. I'm about to lose it.

"She's not suffering at all." She nods toward the various bags of fluid hanging above my girlfriend, intravenously pumping into her body. "She's comfortable. I promise you, she's not in pain at all."

Mr. Tierney walks into the room. He looks angry and protective. "Is everything alright?"

"Yes, Dear." Mrs. Tierney nods and dismisses her husband. His gaze lingers on his daughter, and he lowers his eyes, exiting the room.

"Why didn't you tell me?" I beg her, needing answers.

"It wasn't my place to," she states simply.

Lara's frail, pale body looks so still. I want to shake her awake. Scream in her face and ask why. *Why did she lie to me?*

"Nobody thought it was their place to tell me Lara was dying? Seriously? I've been asking her for months what's wrong. And nobody could tell me?" I'm sobbing now, and I'm not ashamed. This family needs to know how much I'm hurting. How much I'm losing. None of this is fair.

"Someday, you'll understand."

"Stop saying that! How can you possibly think that I could ever understand this?" I stand up and pace next to Lara's bed.

"You need to see things from her perspective. It's the only way." Her mother's voice begins to break, and I know she's struggling with this as much as I am.

I kneel next to Lara and remove her cold hand from her chest. "Lara, you need to wake up and tell me what you want. I need to hear it from you." I glance up at her mother, and her face is buried in her hands, sobs pouring out. "Lara, please. I need you to tell me that you don't want to fight. That you can't fight. I won't believe anyone but you."

Lara's chest moves up and down in unison with the sounds coming from the ventilator. No other movement. *Can she even hear me?*

"She can hear you. Tell her what you need her to hear before she leaves us," her mother cries as if reading my mind. "Please don't ask her for anything she can't give you. This isn't about you, Daxton. Please let her go, on her terms."

I exhale and shake my head. "This all happened so fast."

"She's been protecting you from the truth, Daxton. This has been going on for months."

I've been noticing how frail Lara has been the past few months, but I shrugged it off. I couldn't imagine it would be something serious. School has been intense, especially for her. She's been studying for SATs and AP classes, trying to get ready for the next school year. She always excelled in school and fought hard to stay at the top of her class. I had no idea that she had been fighting something else entirely.

I squeeze Lara's hands, hoping for a response. Praying for a response from her. *Open your eyes.*

"She loved you," Mrs. Tierney says softly.

"I know," I say.

"Please let her go. Please tell her it's okay."

"But she's been lying to me. You've all been lying to me," I retort. "None of this is okay."

Mrs. Tierney's shoulders begin to shake, and her face is once again in her hands. "This isn't easy for any of us. Please know that we've done everything we can."

She turns and walks into the hallway, leaving me alone with my girlfriend.

I can't keep watching her chest move up and down without words coming from her lips. Without her eyes open and happy to see me. None of this feels real, yet it's tearing me from the inside out. I want to absorb her pain and suffering. I want to burn away her cancer. I want her to sit up, hop out of her hospital bed, and jump into my arms.

"Lara, can you hear me?" My face is inches from hers. My breath hovers over her cold, dry lips. My voice shakes. "Please tell me you can hear me."

I place my lips close to her ears.

"I'm not supposed to love someone this much. I'm young. We're young. We both have our lives ahead of us. But I can't help but want to take all of your pain and suffering away from you so we have a chance to find out what it's like to be in love and grow old together. You shouldn't have to suffer like this." I'm rambling, desperate to fill her brain with trigger words that might jolt her from this near-death sleep. Aside from grabbing her by the shoulders and shaking her, I don't know what other options I have.

She remains comatose. Unable to move. I'm unsure if she can really even hear me.

But I can't let it end like this.

"Listen to me, dammit." I pause to try to restrain my anger. I have to keep telling myself that this isn't her fault. Her cancer has control, and she's letting it take her, forever.

I place my hand over her coarse, dry hair. It feels brittle, about to break apart under my soft touch. "I love you, Lara. I love you so much."

I close my eyes and see her healthy smile. I see us playing Uno at my kitchen table, laughing and flirting. I see her riding her bike through the park, racing me back to my house. I see her lying in my bed, her skin glowing after making love. I see months fly by, months when I had no idea she was dying. Time I should have cherished her more. Loved her more.

"Please don't leave me," I whisper into her ear. My heart sinks with each second that she doesn't respond to my touch. My voice.

And I know she's already gone.

CHAPTER 10

Giselle
Past
Age 17

"IT'S UNIMAGINABLE what we have to do today." The priest's voice booms throughout the church, jarring me from my trance. My mother's sobs begin again, and my father places his hand over hers and grabs mine with his free one. His warm grip soothes me but causes my mother to cry even louder. "Shhh," he whispers.

For the past few weeks, we've been on a death watch since my aunt and uncle told us that they agreed to allow all treatments to stop. My mother argued with them. *How could they allow their daughter to just give up? Why would they support this?* My aunt Joyce is my mother's older sister by fifteen months. They've always been close, and I've honestly never seen them argue about anything, until recently. Until Lara decided she couldn't fight any longer.

I look up and see Father Ken bow his head. Intermittent sniffles fill the room. My cheeks are soaked from my own tears.

Lara's casket sits alone in front of the altar, adorned with flowers and a giant cross made from woven light yellow roses.

Her favorite flower and color. Light blonde, like her beautiful hair.

"Lara Grace Tierney was a young girl full of life, her soul filled with love. She gave so much of herself in her short time here on Earth." He pauses and looks up toward the pews, his eyes scanning the crowd. He nods and makes eye contact with a group of teenagers in the congregation. They look to be about my age, so I assume they were in Lara's class. A mix of boys and girls, all sniffling and wiping tears from their eyes. "She was active in our parish, her voice filling this very room every Sunday morning during our services." I remember coming here for Lara's confirmation, and she sang several hymns during the service. Her voice was haunting, yet beautiful. My mother said that she had the voice of an angel. I think it was something more beautiful than what I would imagine an angel's voice to be, light and airy. Hers was more wistful and brooding. Her soul spoke to me through her melody and tone. I can practically hear it again.

I see her bright eyes, always smiling. Although we lived over an hour from each other, we spent a lot of time together. Our families shared a beach house every summer until I was fourteen, except when Lara was eight and spent most of that summer at Children's Hospital, fighting leukemia for the first time. It was a long, two-year battle. I used to hear my parents talking about this dreadful disease back then. I also remember them swabbing my mouth and drawing my blood, taking samples to see if I was a compatible donor to help save her life. I wasn't. They were never able to find a matching donor, and they eventually transplanted her own bone marrow, heavily radiated, back into her body. She was eventually declared to be in remission, but cautioned that they had to follow her closely for many more years. She remained cancer free for a while, but then it came back with a vengeance. Five months ago, she was feeling unusually tired, and her legs began to ache, her arms were covered in bruises she didn't know how she received. She confided in me that she thought something was wrong, but she didn't tell her parents right away. They found tumors throughout her body, all inoperable. Aggressive chemotherapy would only prolong her life, not cure her.

She had more important things to do, she said. She was in love and planned to show her boyfriend, Daxton, just how much she loved him. I quickly look around. *I wonder if he's here?* I wouldn't even know what he looked like, since we never met.

She didn't want to be sick, and she ignored many of the signs early on. Somehow, she knew what was happening. She swore to me when she finished chemotherapy when she was ten, that she never wanted to go through that again. Ever. It took its toll on her, physically and emotionally. It nearly destroyed her, and it broke my heart.

Her parents got her involved in church. This church. They helped her find strength in religion, hoping it would give her a purpose for her future. Something to always fight for. She really tried, but she just knew. Somehow, she knew she wasn't going to make it this time, and she wanted to go out on her own terms. She argued with her parents constantly, threatening to kill herself if they didn't allow her to just die peacefully. After two months of fighting, she won the battle. Aunt Joyce and Uncle Jimmy prayed with her one night and promised her that they would respect her wishes to stop all treatment. We couldn't believe it. Everyone was angry and devastated. We all tried to convince her to change her mind. She couldn't be swayed, and she begged me to help her make everyone understand. I couldn't. My parents, especially my mother, wouldn't listen to me. She said that Lara was too young to give up. She needed to fight for herself and her family. As much as I wanted to agree with my mother, I know that Lara would have fought if she could. *She just knew it was the end.*

I close my eyes, warm, fresh tears streaming down my face and listen to Father Ken continue his eulogy.

"Lara will be missed, the void already felt within our church, among all of you, her family, and friends. But her soul is now eternal, her voice filling heaven with its luster and beauty. Her birthday was this week and now we celebrate the birth of her soul in Heaven. August twenty-fourth, a day when she blessed her parents with life sixteen years ago. And now she's blessed with eternal life. Please bow your heads and pray with me." Father Ken pauses, and I lower my head. Through my tears, I see my hand in my father's and realize my Uncle Jimmy will never hold Lara's again. I squeeze my dad's hand tightly, and he returns the gesture, as if he knows exactly what I'm thinking. Maybe he's thinking the same, holding onto me for dear life, never wanting to let me go.

Father Ken's prayer concludes, and he asks us all to stand. He walks over to her casket and places his hands on it, saying a final prayer. Music fills the church as he makes his way down the aisle with the altar servers behind him. He stops briefly in front of my aunt and uncle and bows his head, closing his eyes in silent prayer. Aunt Joyce sobs loudly while Uncle Jimmy holds onto her tightly.

She's at peace. This is what she wanted.

As much as I repeat this mantra in my head, it doesn't sink in. I still can't believe it. My best friend, my cousin twin, is gone. She's gone forever. The weight of her decision rests heavily on my chest, in my own conscience. I helped her. I gave her validation in her conviction to give up. Jesus, I practically told her to give up if that's what she really wanted. *What the fuck was I thinking?*

Panic fills my chest, and I rip my hand from my father's, running from the pew. I cut off the priest, who's only halfway down the aisle, and run through the vestibule out into the hot summer air. I'm gasping for breath and unable to fill my lungs as quickly as they need. My sobs turn into heaving, and I gag, suddenly puking all over the beautiful rose bushes under a stained glass window. *Shit.* I wipe my mouth with the back of my hand as I look up to see the Virgin Mother Mary, looking down on me from the stained glass, arms spread wide, eyes sad. I just puked on her flowers, her shrine. *Shit.*

The doors open, and several boys walk out. I shrink against the wall, hiding, and hold my breath, thorns from the rose bushes digging into my shins and calves. Warm blood trickles down my bare legs.

"Dude, are you okay?" one of the boys asks another, placing his hand on his shoulder while two others run toward a waiting car at the curb.

"No, I'm not fucking okay," he says and shrugs off his friend. "Give me a minute, will you?" His friend reluctantly walks down the steps toward the car without saying another word.

Pain grabs me in my gut again, and I bend over, giving in to the nausea. I lose control and puke the entire contents of my breakfast and last night's dinner on top of what I did before. Tears and vomit spew from me, and I can't stop any of it. My head is pounding, and I attempt to drop to my knees but get caught in more thorns that tear at my skin.

Once this round of vomiting subsides, I hear a voice next to me. "Whoa."

I look up and see the boy who was standing on the stairs a few seconds before. All I want to be is invisible, and I close my eyes. My mouth is dry and pasty, so I wipe it again, hoping there aren't any visible chunks. He looks around quickly and then takes off his t-shirt. *What the hell is he doing?* He's dressed in layers, so a long sleeved henley shirt remains behind. *Man, he must be sweating wearing all of those clothes.*

He reaches out toward me and begins to wipe puke, spit, and tears from my face with his clean t-shirt. I'm beyond embarrassed at this point, but thankful. He's intent on cleaning my face and arms as his eyes move lower. "Holy shit, you're bleeding." Concern sweeps over his face, and I look down. My skirt is torn in multiple places, and blood is streaming down my legs from the vicious scratches I have from the beautiful yellow and red roses beneath the Virgin Mary window. *What the hell is happening?*

"I–I'm o-okay," I stammer.

"I don't think you are," he says and drops his dirty shirt. Before I know it, he scoops me from the thorny prison and places me gingerly on the patch of grass next to the church stairs. "Can I get you anything?" His concern is evident, and my chest warms with embarrassment.

"No, you've done enough." *That came out all wrong.*

His face drops, and he turns toward the pavement. "You can keep the shirt," he says as he walks toward the waiting car.

"Thank you," I say, nearly inaudibly.

I pull my knees up to my chest and place my head on them, not caring that I'm wearing a skirt. I'm nauseous again and inhale deeply, trying to stop the next wave of vomit from spewing all over these holy grounds. Guilt continues to rip through me as I think of Lara and that I told her that all of this was okay. *What was I thinking?*

"Giselle?" My mother's voice is above me. "Oh my God, honey, what happened?" My father is on his knees in front of me with the puke-covered t-shirt, wiping the blood from my legs.

I look up, and my mother gasps. "There's blood everywhere!" she screams at my father as he begins to wipe my face. Blood stains the shirt, and I realize I put my forehead on my torn-up knees. *I must look like death.*

"I'm okay." I attempt to swipe my father's hand from my face because I can smell my vomit on the shirt he's trying to use to clean me.

"The hell you are!" my mother yells and falls to the ground next to me, opening her purse. Fresh tissues fly out that she uses to clean my face and dab my knees and shins. "Giselle, what in God's name happened to you?" Worry is evident, and I quickly try to explain.

"I felt sick. I ran out here to get some fresh air and got caught in the rose bushes while I puked," I state simply, calmly.

My father laughs and shakes his head.

"It's not funny, Bob," my mother chastises him, and soon she's fighting back laughter and tears. I have tissues stuck to my legs where all of the blood was pooling. The warm sunlight engulfs me as I lean back and lie down on the grass as my parents' awkward laughing subsides. Soon, their shoulders are on either side of mine, and they each grab a hand as they lie next to me.

My mother squeezes my left hand tightly and says into the warm breeze, "I love you more than life, Giselle. Always remember that. Even if I don't tell you every day. Please always remember." She chokes on a sob.

"I love you too, Mom," I say and fresh tears coat my blood and puke-stained cheeks. I turn and look at my dad, grass tickling my cheek. "And you too, Dad."

He purses his lips and continues to look toward the sky. "Giselle, you're our life. You're everything to us." His voice breaks, and I know he's said it all. And I feel it.

EPIC LIES

We lie here on the sloped hill in front of the church where my cousin's life is being celebrated. The thorny stems mock me from behind us, pieces of my skin still attached to the beautiful rose bushes. The Virgin Mary watches over us with her sad and forgiving eyes.

I take a deep breath, allowing calmness to sweep over my body. My parents' hands loosen in my grip. The last time I was lying in grass, I was on a golf course after Troy took away my trust. My virtue. *After he lied to me.* Today, my parents are on either side of me, protecting me, telling me only truths. And I believe them.

In this very moment, I've never felt so loved.

Thank you, Lara.

CHAPTER 11

Dax
Present

GISELLE SITS ACROSS from me, blinking rapidly. When I got here a few minutes ago, the hostess pointed to the table the guys took over–right next to her. *My life saver.* I can't believe she's here. The coincidence floors me, I'm completely shocked.

My question still hangs in the air between us, so I ask it again, "How do I know you?"

I can see in her eyes that she knows what I'm talking about. There's something so familiar about her, she must feel the same way. She's studying my face and shaking her head slowly.

"I don't know," she says softly.

I sit back in the booth and stare, making her visibly uncomfortable. She's shifting in her seat and tapping her fingers on the table. "I'm sorry, but ever since last week, I haven't been able to shake the feeling that I know you. That we've met before." *Maybe she's been to one of our shows?* "Have you ever seen us play live?" I ask.

"Nice pick up line," her friend says, returning to the table.

"Giselle saved my life, and for the life of me, I can't figure out how I know her," I say to Mia but hold Giselle's gaze.

Mia grabs her purse from next to me. "I'll be over there," she says, pointing to the bar. The bartender she was speaking to earlier waves back at her, and she giggles.

Giselle shakes her head and takes a long sip from her martini. "So," she says, uncomfortably.

"Want to join us? Since your friend left you all alone?" I gesture toward our table that's only a few feet from hers. The guys are all settling in, and drinks are being delivered. Her eyes widen. "Or maybe I can just stay here, with you?" *What am I doing?*

She takes another sip and swallows hard, her throat moving up and down. "Sure."

"Dax!" Garrett calls for me. He's already annoyed.

"Can't you see I'm enjoying an appetizer with my friend?" The pretzels are gone, an empty plate between us. Giselle turns and flashes a tentative smile toward the band.

He shakes his head, and Tristan pats him on the shoulder. "Don't worry, G. Dax has the set list memorized. *We got this.*" He smiles, and I chuckle.

"If you need to go, I totally understand," she says to me.

"Nah, it's okay. We've been rehearsing all week. Besides, nobody even knows we're here."

"What do you mean?" she asks.

"We're kind of doing a surprise show. Our manager booked us under a different name because we didn't want this place to turn into a zoo. This will be the first time we're playing any songs from our upcoming album, you know, rehearsing for our tour." She nods and takes another sip from her now almost empty martini. The waitress arrives at the exact moment she places her glass gingerly back on the table.

"Another lemon drop?" she asks Giselle.

"Sure."

"Your dinner should be out shortly." She looks over at Mia who's made herself completely comfortable at the bar. "I'll bring her salad to her over there."

"Would you like anything?" she asks me.

"I'll have whatever she's having," I say and nod toward Giselle.

"So, a lemon drop martini and a buffalo chicken sandwich for you, as well?" she asks, scribbling on the pad in front of her.

"Exactly," I say. I don't drink martinis, but I guess there's a first time for everything.

Garrett approaches us, dragging a chair with him. He turns it around, straddling it, and leans on the table. "Hey, I'm Garrett," he says, extending a hand to Giselle. *What's he up to?*

She shakes his hand tentatively.

"Sorry about that before. We're just a little unprepared for tonight, I think. We aren't the jerks that we seem." I raise my eyebrow and cough.

"Nobody thinks we're jerks, G. You on the other hand…" I laugh.

"So, Tristan tells me you saved our boy last week?"

"I don't think I saved his life. I mean, I just let him sit in my car during the storm."

"And then his bike got plowed over by a speeding fire truck. So, that's saving his life, in my book." He smiles, and it seems like his nerves are finally under control.

Giselle looks embarrassed.

"So, what brings you here tonight? How did you know we were going to be here?" he asks.

She glances toward the bar, "We didn't know. At least, I don't think we did."

Garrett looks at her curiously.

"It's nice to meet you. Anyone who saves a buddy of mine is all right by me. Are you staying for the show?" he asks.

"I'm not sure what our plans are. I think Mia had a few places in mind for tonight, but it looks like she isn't going anywhere anytime soon." Mia's giggles drift through the bar.

"Well, you should stay. But fair warning, we might be a little messy and disorganized." Garrett slaps the table and pushes himself away, dragging the chair back to sit with the guys.

Our new drinks are placed in front of us, and I realize how much I don't want a martini. "Can you bring me a pint of the Stone IPA?"

"Sure," the waitress says, leaving both drinks in front of Giselle.

"Lemon drops aren't your thing?" She laughs.

"Not exactly."

She brings the glass to her mouth, her tongue darting out, licking the sugar from the rim. *God. I could watch her do that all day.*

The waitress is back with my beer, and I gulp half of it down in one sip.

"Nervous?" Giselle asks.

"No, thirsty," I lie.

Yes, I'm nervous. Sitting across from her, mesmerized by her, I'm way out of my comfort zone.

Our sandwiches are placed under our noses, and my stomach growls loudly. "And apparently, I'm hungry, too."

She laughs and quickly bites a French fry in half. "Oh, this is so good," she says and squeezes a heap of ketchup onto her plate.

We eat in silence, and I'm amazed by the speed and efficiency with which she eats. Half of her sandwich is gone as are most of the French fries. I look down at my own empty plate and realize I've eaten just as quickly.

The guys are finishing up. Jake and Eddy, our roadies, are finishing the stage set-up.

I down the rest of my beer and wipe my mouth with the back of my hand. "So, are you going to stay?" I ask, hopeful.

"I think so. I mean, yeah, I can't wait to see you guys play." She's enthusiastic, and I'm pleased.

"Can I see you after?" *What am I doing?*

She looks toward the bar and sees Mia continuing her flirtatious assault on the bartender.

"As long as she wants to stay, I'll be here."

I take a deep breath. "Good, I still owe you."

"What?" She's suddenly embarrassed. "You don't owe me anything. Seriously."

"That's not an option." I'm determined to make sure she knows how thankful I am for what she did for me.

"Just buy me a drink, and we'll call it even," she blurts out.

The waitress comes back. "Can I get either of you anything else?"

Giselle replies, "A large ice water, please." The lemon drops line the table in front of her.

The waitress nods and turns to me, "And for you?"

"Nothing, thanks. But can you switch their bill onto our tab?"

"Of course." She smiles and walks away.

"Thank you. That was completely unnecessary."

"It's just the beginning," I say, and she flushes, a rose hue spreading across her cheeks.

"Dax!" Tristan yells from across the room.

"I gotta run." I look around the still-empty bar. "It's probably going to be a very quick set, considering there's barely anyone here. So, stay put," I order her as I stand up.

"Thanks again for the food and drinks," she says and smiles. *Her smile.*

I jog toward the stage, and Eddy tosses me my sticks.

EPIC LIES

Heath taps the microphone and says, "Hey, everyone. We're Epic Fail, and we're here to play some new stuff for all eight of you here," he chuckles. Recognition quickly sets in throughout the bar, and cell phones light up as the patrons begin texting their friends. This place will be completely full by the second song. He should have stuck with our fake name, Sinus Cavity.

I watch Giselle look around the room, her friend still throwing herself all over the bartender. Her gaze finds its way back to me, and I smile. Disbelief and awe fills her eyes, and she grins back, shaking her head. Her long hair falls and covers half of her face.

She's completely stunning, and she has absolutely no idea how amazingly beautiful she is.

I intend to make sure she knows how much. *She better not leave.*

I tap my sticks in the air above my head and start the show.

CHAPTER 12

Giselle
Present

TWO SONGS IN, and my heart is pumping. I've wanted to get up and dance since Dax started tapping his drumsticks together. The band is electrifying. The bar is packed with wall-to-wall co-eds and Epic Fail fans. This place filled up in less than ten minutes. I watched as people filed in, immediately swarming the small stage, pushing tables and chairs against the walls. *Unreal.*

At least one hundred people stand between me and the bar, and I can't see Mia anymore. Starbucks Guy is feverishly shelling out drinks. The show is incredible so far. Heath seems to stumble over a couple lyrics, but he doesn't even care. Every time he smiles, girls scream, so his mistakes are forgiven or go completely unnoticed. Dax seems to be in the zone, feverishly banging on his drums. The music is melodic, and my heart pounds in time with the rhythm from his hands. He's concentrating so hard with every single beat as sweat drips from his brow, his hair equally wild.

Several photographers are escorted from the bar, causing commotion near the entrance. Their cameras are still flashing as they hold them above their heads. I've never seen real-life paparazzi before. It suddenly hits me that I *know* Dax Anderson. THE Dax Anderson. Drummer for one of the biggest rock bands of our generation. People are screaming his name, trying to get as close to him as possible. And he asked *me* to stay so he could see *me* after the show. I smile, and my pulse quickens. *What could possibly come of this?*

Mia falls into the booth, and her forehead hits the table with a 'thud.' "Mia?" I ask and watch her hands fall to her sides. She's out cold. "Mia? Mia!" I yell, and she twitches and giggles at the same time. She's completely hammered.

"He showed me his tattoo. He likes me," she mumbles, and she's back to heavy breathing and snoring.

"What the hell, Mia?" I ask, but she can't hear me. She literally went from zero to fucked up in less than an hour. I quickly text Dottie from my phone, letting her know we're ready. I slide out of my side of the booth and next to Mia, making sure to grab her clutch. I look up, and I can't even see the stage. Fans are jumping up and down, screaming. The music reverberating from within and causing the crowd to surge. I only see Heath and Garrett as they are both in the front of the stage, bending over their fans, Heath singing into the microphone. His eyes are closed, and I can tell he's feeling every single word he's belting out. The only part of Dax I see are his hands holding his drumsticks, and they seem to be flying in the air uncontrollably.

I grab Mia's hand and yank her from the booth. As soon as she's in a standing position, I wrap my arm around her waist, her arms limp at her sides. *You have got to be fucking kidding me.*

Somehow, I'm able to make it to the door, and the bouncer looks alarmed. "Is she okay?" he asks, arms and chest pumped out like he's a superhero or something.

"I could use some help, please," I respond, and he swoops

in and takes her from my arms. If only Mia could see the fuss being made over her right now, she'd be giggling.

The warm air hits my face as soon as we exit the bar. There's a line of people that goes on for as far as I can see. Girls screaming and guys playing air guitar. Dottie's car is double-parked, and she jumps out of the driver's side and runs to open the back door closest to us. "Oh boy, is she okay?" she asks, concerned.

The bouncer slides her into the back and looks at me with pity. "Take care of your friend." He rushes back inside and has to block at least a dozen people from rushing into the bar. It's complete mayhem out here.

I get into the car next to Mia, and she falls into my lap. Dottie looks over her shoulder as she shifts into drive. "Are you girls buckled up?"

I pull the seatbelt over my shoulder, and as soon as I fasten it, I make sure Mia is secured. She's snoring so loudly that it makes me laugh.

"I don't think I've ever seen her like this. What happened tonight?" Dottie glances at the clock, and then says, "It's only nine-fifteen!"

I shrug, but then remember the salad she ordered for dinner. I have no idea how many drinks she had at the bar, but I can only imagine that it was too many in too short of time.

"I think she drank a lot. Way more than me," I say as I hold Mia's head firmly on my lap. I know I left at least one and a half lemon drops at the table. I smooth her hair out and pray to God that she doesn't puke all over Dottie's car.

"Hang on tight, I'll get you home as fast as I can." I can tell she's thinking the same exact thing. Neither of us wants to clean up vomit.

Dottie keeps her promise and pulls up in front of our townhouses. "Hold on, let me get the door for you." She jumps out and runs around to my side of the car. I lift Mia's head and try to keep her stable while I attempt to find her keys in her clutch.

As soon as I find them, I hand them to Dottie. "Can you open the door for us?"

"Which one do I unlock?" Dottie asks as she grabs the keys from my hand.

"Six," I say. My house is number eight, and Mia's is six.

Dottie rushes to open Mia's front door, and then comes back to help me walk her into the house. Mia is mumbling something, and the only coherent word I hear is 'Starbucks.'

Once inside, we place her on the couch, and her breathing begins to even out. She's snoring.

"Thank you so much, Dottie." I reach into my front pocket and find one of the twenty dollar bills that I shoved in there before we left. I try to place it into her palm, but she jerks her hand away.

"I will not take that, young lady," she says sternly.

"Why?" I ask.

"You're my best customers, and a tip like that isn't necessary. Just keep calling me when you need a ride around town, okay?" she says as she walks out of Mia's house. "Do you think she's going to be alright?" she asks, concerned.

I look at Mia, slumbering soundly on the couch.

"Yes, she'll be fine." *I hope.*

"Can you text me tomorrow morning to let me know that she's okay?"

God, I love this woman.

"Of course. And thank you so much, Dottie. You're a life-saver." Dax's words ring in my head, and I realize I left without saying goodbye. He called me his 'life-saver' more than once tonight, and I can't help but think that I deserted him at the bar.

Dottie leaves, and I hear her car drive off. I sink on the couch next to Mia and rub her hair. "What am I going to do with you, Drunky McDrunkerson?" She snores louder. Not a chance she's waking up anytime soon.

I slide off her shoes and look around the room for a blanket and spot one draped over the chair in the corner. Once I fetch it, I tuck it around her on the couch. There's not a chance I'll be able to get her upstairs by myself. But she doesn't seem to care–she breathes deeply and tucks her hands under the pillow she's resting on.

"Mia?" I say her name softly, but loud enough that she should hear me.

She snores.

"Mia, I'm leaving. Are you okay?" I ask.

"Mhm," she mumbles and her eyes flutter.

"Are you sure?"

"Mhm," she mumbles again.

She's fine.

But I'm seriously going to give her hell tomorrow. I honestly can't remember the last time I saw her this drunk. I'm thankful that I didn't drink the three lemon drops placed in front of me tonight. If I was as drunk as Mia right now, I'm certain the two of us would have wound up in an alley somewhere near the university. *Or worse.*

I bend down and kiss her forehead. "Goodnight. I love you," I whisper and walk toward the front door.

As I'm about to leave, I remember that my house key is somewhere in her clutch. I dig through it and see a napkin folded in half. My curiosity gets the better of me, and I unfold it. It says Trent and has a phone number scrawled on it. I smooth it out and place it neatly on the counter so she can see it when she wakes up tomorrow morning.

EPIC LIES

I grab my key and lock her door from the inside before pulling it closed. I walk down her steps and turn left toward my house, letting myself in and locking the door behind me.

What the hell happened tonight?

My completely wasted best friend is passed out face first, and I hung out with a rock star. A really, really hot rock star.

Whose life am I living right now?

I'M STARTLED AWAKE by ringing and slap my alarm clock, but it doesn't silence the sound. *Where's my phone?*

I pat around on the bed next to me and find it, unlocking the screen–it's midnight. Wait, that's my doorbell. *Mia?*

I run down the stairs as fast as I can and unbolt the door locks, pulling it open. My hallway is flooded with bright lights from a large SUV parked in front of my townhouse, a large figure standing in my doorway. *Holy shit, it's not Mia.*

I gasp and back away from the stranger, my heart is racing and I reach into the open hall closet for the aluminum bat my father gave me when I moved out on my own. I grip it, and bring it up to my ear, and get into a swinging–fight stance.

"Whoa, Giselle, it's me," his voice strong, but gentle. *Dax?*

I drop the bat in the hallway and back up further into my house. He switches the light on in the foyer, and that's when I realize I'm not wearing any pants, just a long t-shirt and panties. *Fuck.*

"What the hell are you doing here?" I ask, embarrassed, my eyes darting around the room for something to cover myself with.

"Oh God, I'm sorry, I didn't mean–they told me you left unconscious." The look of worry leaves his face, and now he just looks confused.

"What are you talking about?"

He looks around nervously. "Can I come in?"

Seriously?

"I guess?" I respond tentatively.

"Wait, I'll be right back." He turns and jogs down my stairs, reaching into his car to turn off the lights. I take this opportunity to swipe a pair of yoga pants that were in a ball on the couch. That's when I notice that my house is a disaster, clothes everywhere. The jeans I had on earlier tonight are on the floor near the kitchen with my shoes at the bottom of the stairs. After leaving Mia in her house, I came back here and undressed, dropping clothes and accessories along the path upstairs to my bedroom. I was exhausted, even though it was early.

He walks back in as I'm pulling the yoga pants up. My hair is a disaster, covering most of my face. I must look like that creepy girl from the horror movie *The Ring*.

After he closes the door behind him, he stops. "I'm glad you're okay, but I shouldn't be here," he says, apologetically.

He turns to leave, and before he opens the door, I say, "Wait!" His hand drops from the doorknob, and he looks at me.

"I'm sorry for scaring the shit out of you," he says.

"It's okay, but why are you here?" *And how the hell do you know where I live?*

He walks toward me, and I gesture toward the couch and watch him sit hesitantly.

"When you weren't in the bar after the show, I asked the bouncers if they saw you leave. They told me you had to be carried out by your friend because you had passed out." His brooding eyes grab mine, and my heart melts. "I was worried." *Holy Swoon. Holy shit.*

"It wasn't me," I say.

"What?" He looks confused. "No offense, but you had at least three martinis."

I feel my face flush. *Does he think I'm a lush?*

"Excuse me, Mr. McJudgey, but I didn't drink them all. I only had one and a sip of another before *Mia* passed out, and I had to carry *her* from the bar."

He drops his head into his hands and shakes his head. "Jesus, I'm sorry. I should go."

He begins to stand up, and I say sternly, "Sit. Down."

He complies and falls back onto the couch, looking slightly amused.

"How did you know where I live?" I ask.

A smile plays across his lips as my heart begins to pound out of my chest.

"I looked on your phone."

"What? When?"

"When we were navigating back to my house. The day you saved my life."

"Oh."

Wait.

"But why?" I ask, and I suddenly realize I'm standing toe to toe with him, hovering over him as he reclines comfortably on my couch.

"Like I told you tonight, I wanted to do something nice for you."

"Showing up here at midnight, scaring the living shit out of me, isn't '*something nice*,'" I say, using air quotes.

"You're standing on my feet," he smirks, and I look down.

"Oh. Sorry." I back away, folding my arms over my chest. *Crap, I'm not wearing a bra.*

I'm not sure he's noticed, but his eyes drift lower and then back up to my face.

"Are you done scolding me now?" he asks, grinning again.

I huff. "I suppose, but like I told *you* tonight, you don't have to do anything for me. In fact, we're even since you paid for our food and drinks."

He shakes his head and stands up. "I'm really glad you're okay, I was seriously worried about you." He looks around, "How's your friend Mia?"

"She's sound asleep, probably dreaming about Starbucks Guy. She lives next door, and I tucked her in hours ago," I respond.

"Good. You're a good friend," he says as he's walking toward my front door. "Lock the door behind me, please, you never know who could show up this late at night." He's chuckling as he starts to let himself out.

I reach for the doorknob, and our hands brush against each other. He pauses, then reaches for my face and brushes the wild mess of hair away from my eyes. I tense up. He's staring at me, searching my face for *something,* his eyes settling on my lips for too long. His hand grips my face, caressing my cheek. *Oh my God, is he going to kiss me?*

My pulse quickens, and I can feel my heart beating in my throat.

But then, his hand suddenly drops to his side.

"Take care of yourself, Giselle." He walks out and pulls the door shut.

I exhale loudly, heart still pounding, my hands shaking.

"Lock the door," he says from outside.

I slowly turn the locks and slide the chain into place. He waits on the other side of my door until he hears confirmation of his request, then I hear him walk toward his SUV and start the engine, pulling away.

My phone buzzes, and I grab it off the counter.

Dax: Thank you for saving my life.

What the–

EPIC LIES

I search through my contacts. He must have added his name when I drove him home. Then I search through the outbound texts. There's one from last Friday from me to him with my contact information attached.

He sent my personal information to himself.

I walk down the hallway, almost tripping on the aluminum bat that I nearly decapitated him with.

My heart drops when I realize that I probably just saw Dax Anderson for the last time.

CHAPTER 13

Dax
Past
Age 17

THE STARS AND CONSTELLATIONS in the dark sky above me begin to blend together, becoming blurry. Tears stream down my cheeks as I think of my last few days with Lara. She was comatose while I cried and complained about being kept in the dark about her condition. My anger was directed at her and her family. I shouldn't have been like that, and I feel sick to my stomach. My guilt takes control and squeezes the life out of my heart.

I've been so fucking selfish.

Death is what she wanted. She didn't want anyone taking any extreme measures to prolong her doomed existence. When they found her body riddled with tumors, her death sentence became firm, so her parents honored her wishes. She wanted to die with dignity, something we debated a few months ago in front of our school. We were on the Debate Team together, and our position paper was the culminating moment of the assembly. She received the most applause while making her points, and now I fully understand why. She not only researched her position thoroughly, she had a personal interest in it. Her emotions took over that day, and she even convinced me that my opposing position was wrong. I became a supporter of dying with dignity that day, not realizing her personal and private struggles.

And then I let it all fall apart. When I found out how sick she really was, it was too late for me to convince her otherwise. I needed more time with her.

Saying goodbye to her today was awful. None of this seems real, and I just want to wake up to Lara, smiling and healthy.

Someone kicks the hammock that I'm lying on, and I turn to see Alex, his head hung low, hands shoved into his pockets. "Hey," he says.

I swipe at my cheeks, trying to hide the evidence of my emotions.

"Are you okay?" he asks and sinks into an Adirondack chair near the fire pit.

"No," I say, stating the obvious. *And I doubt I ever will be.*

"Do you want to talk about it?"

I squint at the stars, trying to focus on something, anything to take my mind away from the past few weeks.

"Nothing to talk about," I snap.

"Bullshit," he responds.

"What do you want me to say?" My grief is morphing into anger, and I'm about to take it out on Alex.

"Anything. Everything."

"I wish she would have told me sooner," I choke.

"What would that have done? Would you have been angrier with her sooner? Broken up with her? You wouldn't have enjoyed the time that you actually did have together. Cancer would have been hanging over you every single second you spent together. She wouldn't have been able to see your true feelings, experience them the way that she did. Because you would have looked at her funny, acted differently, treated her with kid gloves. You would have started mourning long before she was ready for you to."

Holy shit. Where did that come from?

"How do you even know any of this? You don't know what I would have done if she told me months ago that she was going to die."

"The fuck I don't. That's exactly what you would have done. And you would have made it unbearable for her. You can't be mad at her for giving you the short time that you had together. She gave you a gift by hiding her cancer from you."

"She lied to me, Alex. She fucking lied."

"Cut the shit. You act like she did it to spite you. She lied to you because she loved you. The sooner you realize that, the sooner you'll forgive yourself for being so mad at her. And the sooner you'll forgive *her*."

He's so fucking right. I'm a selfish asshole.

"It's hard," I say, snot building up in my nose. Alex has never seen me cry, and now the waterworks have started again.

"I never said it wasn't. Shit, it's going to be hard for a long time. But you need to start thinking about this in a different way, or you're going to destroy yourself."

I find his words and advice completely ironic, considering his situation. I don't call him on his own past and issues with his father, because I know for a fact that he's not over his personal hell. He lives his own nightmare every single day. I keep my mouth shut, because his advice for me is true.

The hammock sways in the warm summer breeze, and I exhale deeply. I have to figure out a way to get past this anger.

"Who was that girl puking at the church?" Alex asks, changing the subject.

"I have no idea," I say. "I didn't get a good look at her, she was throwing up so much. She was a fucking mess."

"It was hard to see from the car. Was she bleeding?"

I remember the blood on her forehead and the cuts and blood on her knees. She looked like she was in a street fight. "Yeah, I think she cut herself on the thorns from the rose bushes I pulled her out of." I can't imagine why she was even in them in the first place. *Was she trying to hide?*

"I think that was the same girl who ran out of the church before the final procession was over," Alex says, remembering something I didn't even witness. I was too busy staring at Lara's casket, wishing for a miraculous resurrection. I was practically willing the casket to open and Lara to walk out of it like nothing had happened to her at all. I didn't notice anything until Alex pulled me out of the pew and out the doors of the church.

That's when I saw her, *The Puker.*

"Whatever," I say.

"It was nice of you to help her. Tristan and Garrett ran to the car when they heard her retching. They couldn't get away fast enough."

"It's alright. I couldn't *not* help her, you know?"

Alex nods.

"Now you need to start helping yourself," he says and stands up. "You hear me?" he asks, and I close my eyes.

I want to hear him. I want to believe what he told me tonight. I know that I need to accept Lara's choice to end her treatments and end her suffering.

"I'll try," I lie.

Alex walks into the house, and I open my eyes, once again staring into the vast night sky. Now the stars are fully out and shining their brightest. I find the Big Dipper and trace the outline of Orion's Belt with my hand in the air. I make an 'L' with the stars I can see and drop my hand to my side.

My guilt takes hold of me again, and I want to scream into the darkness. I want to tell Lara everything in my heart and soul. I want to spill it all for her to hear. But I know I'll get no response. I shouldn't have made her feel like she *had* to lie to me. I should have been the type of person she could confide in without fear. She should have been able to rely on me for strength, not worry. She protected me from her illness because she didn't want me to be sad while she was still alive. How could she have known how I would react when she didn't give me the choice?

I take a deep breath, my gut still twisting from my nerves. Alex's words ring in my brain, and I need to get control of all of this.

I have to let it go. I have to let her go.

"I'm so sorry, Lara. I love you, and I'm sorry."

CHAPTER 14

Giselle
Past
Age 18

"WAKE UP. WAKE UP. WAKE UP," my roommate, Mia, is chanting incessantly over me. I'm trying to ignore her. I fell asleep after dinner and was enjoying my nap, hoping to be able to sleep all night.

I pop my eyes open and pull my blanket up to my neck. "I want to sleep," I whine. She's been relentless all week and has insisted we attend every single freshmen week activity as if our lives depend on it. I haven't had a moment to rest.

"But tonight's the bonfire," she whines as she rips my blankets off of my body. "And you need to get dressed," she says, looking at me all super-judgy.

"I'm comfortable in this," I say. "Especially since I'm staying here. In. Bed." I attempt to yank my covers back from her but she pulls them out of reach.

"This is the last night of fun activities before the upperclassmen show up tomorrow. We need to take advantage of having dibs on the hot freshmen boys before the more experienced co-eds have their pick." She's constantly thinking about hooking up. Just this week alone, I swear she's kissed—or done more—with at least six guys. One per night.

"Mia, tone it down already," I say as I sit up. There's no winning an argument with her, and the sooner I relent and get dressed, the sooner she'll stop badgering me. "I need to shower," I say and grab my robe and shower bucket that's filled with my toiletries.

"Quickly!" she calls after me as I let the door slam behind me.

As I'm showering, my mind wanders to all of the fun we've truly had this week. Meeting Mia was certainly the highlight, although we've been communicating with each other for most of the summer. We decided that we couldn't have been matched with anyone more perfect. We complement each other nicely. However, if she continues to be this much of a party animal and hook up monster, I'm going to have to draw the line. I can't keep up with all of her wild energy.

I'm also not as experienced as she is. After Troy raped me, I haven't had a relationship or been with anyone else. I don't trust freely, like Mia does. And I won't ever trust another person with me or my body for as long as I live. Troy stole a lot from me, something that I'll never get back. Mia is fully aware of my chastity vow, but I haven't told her about Troy. She thinks I'm a virgin, and that's the way I'm going to keep it. She doesn't need to know about the ugliness of what Troy did to me. Besides, I like the thought of being a virgin again, even if it's only in my mind.

After my shower, I wrap a towel around my head, dry my body off quickly, and apply my favorite lotion to my body. It's the same pink lotion my parents used on me when I was a baby. The fragrance makes me think of soft and fluffy things and keeps my mind at peace. It also makes my skin amazingly soft.

I pull my robe on and grab my bucket. I'm sure Mia is pacing in our room, waiting for me to return so she can supervise me getting ready.

When I open the door, I'm shocked to see our room full of people. The two girls who live next door, Cassidy and Tammy, and two guys I've never seen before. "Giselle!" Mia screeches. "We have company." Her eyes are wide, and she's sitting between the two unknown boys, her leg practically draped over the one to her right. Everyone's eyes are on me, taking in my near naked state. *What the hell?*

"Umm…" I stammer and can't find my voice to say anything else. This is completely embarrassing and humiliating. She knew I was going to come back here as soon as I finished in the shower, and she knew I had no clothes with me. Anger rises in my chest, and my cheeks begin to burn.

"We should go," boy number two says. Boy number one can't move because Mia has him pinned in the corner, and she's still draped all over him.

Tammy and Cassidy both stand up, and Tammy says, "We'll get out of your way, see you at the bonfire."

Boy number two also stands up and looks at his buddy, "We need to leave so she can get dressed." He smiles apologetically at me as he passes while Mia lets his friend follow him out.

As the door closes, I say, "What the hell, Mia? Don't you have any regard for my privacy?"

She's grinning ear to ear, ignoring my complaint. "That was HIM!" she says.

"Who?" I ask as I towel dry my hair. "And how can you even keep track?" I'm so annoyed with her now, and she seems to have no idea.

"Rob," she says as if I should know.

"Like I said, who?"

"Rob, from Tuesday."

Her hookups this week have been so out of control that he's associated with a day of the week. Lovely. Her family should be so proud.

"Am I supposed to have a flash of memory, Mia, because I have no idea who 'Rob from Tuesday' is."

She walks past me to the sink in the corner of the room and begins inspecting her makeup. She applies lip gloss and fluffs up her already gigantic hair. "He's the one from the soccer team."

Now I remember. On our way back from the freshmen social the other night, she broke away from me and wound up hanging out with a bunch of players from the soccer team. I never met any of them, just waved at her as she went off in another direction, and I went back to the dorm to go to bed.

"Oh," I say.

"He must have remembered where my room was since he walked me back here the other night. I think I'm in love!" she exclaims, and I want to throat punch her. She's seriously out of control, and I'm sure my advice wouldn't be welcome at this early stage of our friendship. If she doesn't tone down her promiscuity, she's going to find herself in a heap of trouble. I make a mental note to chat with her about it during the week, when she's distracted by other things, like actual school work.

"Isn't he so cute?" she asks.

"I guess," I respond and pull on my favorite pair of jeans.

"You're going to sweat in those," she says. "You should wear a dress, or shorts, or something."

I love my jeans, and now they're super-soft and stretched out since I haven't washed them yet this week. I do have a maxi-length tank dress in the closet that I've been dying to wear, but I think I think it's too dressy for a bonfire.

"I'll be fine," I say as I pull my pink tank top over my head and fasten my hair in a ponytail.

"Suit yourself," she says, and her judgmental tone is back.

"I'm perfectly comfortable and happy with what I'm wearing. So stop bugging me," I say and point my finger at her nose. She pretends like she's going to bite the tip of my finger off but smiles instead.

"Yes, ma'am!" she cackles and swipes her student ID card from her desk. "I'm sorry for letting everyone hang out in our room while you were in the shower. That was insensitive of me." She hugs me, and then smiles, "Let's go already."

I grab a hoodie and tie it around my waist, then slide into my flip-flops. "I'm ready."

WE HAVE TO WALK all the way to the far end of campus where there's a huge open field. Mia talks incessantly the entire way, mostly about Rob and what a great kisser he is. She babbles on about wanting to do more with him, but since she totally hooked up with someone else on Monday night, she didn't want to overdo it. I drown most of her chatter out until she addresses me. "What do you think about Derek?" she asks.

"Who?" I have no idea who she's talking about.

"Derek? His friend?"

"You mean the guy in the room with him tonight?" I barely remember him because I was completely and utterly embarrassed.

"Yes!"

"I don't know, Mia, I was trying to figure out a way to keep my robe from opening up and hide my naked body from the room full of people who so conveniently showed up when I was in the shower for five minutes!"

"God, stop being so dramatic," she says.

She's lucky that I like her, for now.

"Look, the fire is already going strong." I change the subject and point to the huge bonfire that's right in the middle of the field. At least fifty students are here already, and I can only imagine how crowded it's going to be before long.

"Rob!" Mia ignores me and rushes toward boys number one and two. Derek sees me lagging behind and leaves his friend to walk toward me. Mia jumps into Rob's arms and kisses him all over his face.

Derek reaches me and looks just as embarrassed as I did back in my room. "I'm really sorry about earlier. Mia didn't tell us you were in the shower."

"Figures," I say, still embarrassed. "It was harmless. It's a good thing I didn't strut into the room naked, like I usually do."

His eyes widen, and his jaw drops. "Really?" he chokes out.

I snort, "No! Not really. Oh my God, that would be insane and completely uncalled for." I cover my mouth, embarrassed by my snorting.

His face relaxes, and he smiles. "You're funny, you know that?"

"I try, sometimes, but most times I fail horribly. I'm usually the only one who laughs at my jokes." This is a sad truth.

We both look to find Rob and Mia, but they've disappeared.

"Seriously?" I mutter.

"Rob's been talking about her all week. He finally got up the courage to come see her tonight."

If only Rob knew that Mia's hooked up with at least three or four guys since, but I'll keep that little tidbit to myself.

"Yeah, Mia's been going on and on about him," I lie. "What a nice surprise that he came to see her."

She's going to break his heart.

"So, what is your major going to be?" Derek asks nervously. *How original.*

"Business or Marketing. Something like that," I say. "What about you?"

"Chemistry or Biology. I'm hoping for Pre-Med. Something like that." He smiles shyly.

The crowds are really forming now, and we settle onto the grass in the field. Now I'm glad I'm not wearing that dress because I'm sure tons of bugs would be crawling up my legs at this point. I get itchy just thinking about it.

"Where are you from?" he asks me.

"My family lives in Radnor, Pennsylvania. That's probably where I'll live after I graduate." I can't see moving far away from them.

"That's cool. I live in Yardley." Someone else from Pennsylvania.

"You're the first person I've met from PA," I say. Our school is in Virginia, and so many kids in our class are widely dispersed. Mia's from Vermont, Tammy's from South Carolina, and Cassidy's from Ohio. "We're practically neighbors."

"I'm hoping to continue the Pre-Med program at either Penn or NYU." Apparently, he's really smart, too.

"Wow, impressive," I say.

"My father's an orthopedic surgeon, and my mother's a gastroenterologist. It kind of runs in the family."

"What made you apply for undergrad in Virginia?" I ask, curiously.

"This is where my father went to school. So, I guess it's our legacy or something like that." He shrugs, and I can tell he's getting uncomfortable.

"Oh, nice."

I scan the crowds to see if I can spot Mia and Rob, but I don't have any luck. I want to go back to my room, but I feel bad leaving Derek here, stranded.

"I'm not really into this bonfire," I admit and hope he isn't bummed.

"Me either," he quickly replies. "Do you want to do something together?"

I look at him, and he looks terrified of what my answer may be. "I guess? What do you have in mind?" I ask, putting him on the spot.

"There are some movies playing in the Student Center. We can check that out."

"That sounds great," I say, and he's already on his feet. He reaches out to grab my hands and pulls me up, so our noses are practically touching.

He drops my hands abruptly and smiles nervously. "Sorry," he says and backs away from me.

I'm comforted by the fact that he doesn't seem like a jerk, and he's nervous about being close to me. That tells me he's not a man-whore just looking to get in my pants. *At least, that's what I hope.*

We make small talk on the way to the Student Center. I find out that he's an only child, and he inherited two Siamese cats, when his grandmother died two years ago, named Milo and Agnes. He loves to play Yahtzee and is the reigning Jenga champion in his house. He's very proud of this fact, considering his father is a surgeon and has the steadiest hands he knows. He plays guitar and loves alternative music.

"And holy shit, this is my absolute favorite movie," he says as we walk into the Student Center, and *Spaceballs* is being projected onto the wall.

"No. Way." I say, practically squealing. "I freaking love this movie!"

He grabs my hand and pulls me to a double lounge chair that looks to be the only one vacant in the whole place. I relax in his grip as we weave through other students. We fall onto the lounge, and I try to stifle a laugh. "Eagle eyes," I say as I recline.

He does the same, and our shoulders are slightly touching. We've only missed the opening credits, so we made it just in time. As I sink further into the lounge, I realize he's still holding my hand. I wiggle my fingers a little bit, and he jerks his hand away. "I'm sorry," he whispers into my ear, causing me to shiver slightly.

"It's okay. I didn't want you to have to feel my hands get warm and sweaty." *Oh my God, what am I saying?*

He chuckles, causing his shoulder to move against mine. I'm comfortable with him. *This is good.*

By the end of the movie, we're both wailing, tears of laughter streaming down our faces. "May the shwartz be with you…" I burst out laughing, and Derek does the same. We can't catch our breath, remembering the wackiness that ensues in *Spaceballs.*

The lights come on briefly as one of the students stands in front of the room with a small microphone. "In five minutes, our double feature will continue. The next movie is *The Princess Bride.* We hope you can all stay with us. Refreshments are along the wall. Help yourselves!"

Derek turns to me, "Are you up for a double feature?"

"I could never say no to *The Princess Bride,*" I say.

His smile is huge. "I'll go get us a couple of drinks and some popcorn. Any special requests?"

"Light salt, no butter, a water, and lots of napkins."

"Coming right up," he says, jogging over to the refreshment stands.

He comes back to our lounge just before the lights are turned off again. "Just in time," I whisper, accidentally brushing my lips against his ear. A smile spreads across his cheeks, and his ears turn red. "Sorry," I say, facing forward.

He holds the popcorn out nervously, and I dig in.

For the first hour of the movie, I'm fully aware of his proximity to me. Our shoulders still touching, hips barely an inch apart, and our breathing in sync. We've bumped fingers and knuckles together at least a dozen times when reaching into the bucket of popcorn. Every single movement sends nervous shivers throughout my body, causing me to blush on more than one occasion. I realize that I'm not nervous around him at all. I'm surprisingly comfortable. *I like it.*

The moment arrives when Princess Buttercup realizes exactly who the Dread Pirate Roberts really is, after he launches himself down a hill yelling, "As you wish!" This gets me every single time, and I sniffle, knowing tears are going to spill. Derek shifts slightly in the lounge and slowly drops his hand next to mine. Before I know it, his fingers are entwined with mine, his thumb making small circles on my hand. I sink lower into the lounge and rest my head on his shoulder, causing him to squeeze my hand harder. My heart is beating out of my chest with nerves and excitement. I haven't been this close to a boy in a very long time.

"Is this okay?" he whispers. I squeeze his hand back and nod against his shoulder.

"Good," he says.

I don't pay attention to the rest of the movie because I'm concentrating on his every move, his every breath. I focus on his strong hand fused with mine for nearly two hours, the swipe of his thumb on my hand, the intermittent squeeze to let me know he's still connected to me. His head has been resting on top of mine for the past ten minutes or so, and I can feel him swallow and breathe. I can feel his heart beating against my cheek, and it's beating in time with my own. I'm so at ease, and that makes me nervous.

The movie ends, and neither of us react. I don't think either of us wants to move. He stretches his legs and says, "Can I walk you home?"

I laugh nervously, "Yes, but it's where you live, too, so it's not like you need to go out of your way, right?"

"I'm on the fourth floor, and you're on the second, so technically, it *is* out of my way." He stands, still holding onto my hand, and once again pulls me to my feet. This time, I don't flinch when our noses practically touch. This time, I welcome the feel of his warm breath on my lips. I blink and inhale softly.

"Ready?"

I nod.

We walk as slowly as possible, hand-in-hand, back to our dorm. When we walk through the doors to the lobby, he pulls me toward the elevator and presses the up arrow. As soon as we're in the elevator, he presses 2 and leans back against the wall with me. I realize he hasn't pressed the button for his floor, and my heart begins to beat harder in my chest. The doors open, and he leads me from the elevator, down the hall to my room. Now I feel like I'm going to puke. My hand is sweating, and I'm certain it's going to slide out of his grip, but his fingers remain intertwined with mine.

"Thanks for hanging out with me tonight," he says as we stop in front of my door.

"Anytime," I say, and he raises his eyebrows.

"Yeah? We can do this again?" he asks, smiling.

I nod slowly as I watch his gaze fall to my lips.

For the first time in hours, he releases my hand from his. He reaches for my face, softly cradling my cheeks, searching my eyes for permission to do what I've been afraid of for too long.

I nod again, and he places his lips on mine, kissing me softly, stealing my breath away. His thumb swirls on my cheek like it did on my hand all night, and I melt against him. I don't know what to do with my hands, so I drop them over his shoulders, pulling him a little closer to me. His kiss continues, and I begin kissing back, nipping lightly at his lips and pulling them into my own.

"Giselle," he mutters against my mouth. "I have to go."

Yes, you do.

"Okay," I say, but not before I pull his lips to mine and slide my tongue into his mouth, teasing his.

He groans and pulls me tight against his body, his lips leaving my mouth, traveling across my cheek to my neck. He breathes deeply, softly nipping and kissing his way back to my lips. I can feel the bulge in his pants growing, and I stiffen in his arms.

"I'm sorry. I really have to go," he says, and this time he releases me, backing away so he can look into my eyes.

"Okay," I say.

"I don't want this to be just a hook-up," he says, and I quickly nod.

"Neither do I." I feel myself flush, and my heart begins to race. My cheeks are burning. I don't know what I want this to be, but I'm fighting the urge to pull him into my room and see where it might lead.

He kisses me again and pulls away for the last time. "I'll see you tomorrow?" he asks.

"Definitely," I smile.

He backs away down the hall and ducks into the stairwell instead of taking the elevator. I hear him climbing the stairs for two more flights until I hear nothing more.

My room is dark and empty; Mia is still gone. I throw myself on the bed and sigh deeply.

What just happened?

My heart tells me to stay guarded. My body's not ready for what Derek wants.

Tonight was amazing, unexpected. Innocent and *wonderful.*

And I don't want it to end.

Because I'm afraid of what he may want next.

CHAPTER 15

Dax
Present

I WAKE UP TO A WARM BREEZE and the smell of sea salt filling the air. I'm sprawled across the most comfortable bed I've ever slept in and make a note to find out who makes it, and order one for each bedroom in my house.

I'm in Mexico at a resort called the Presidential Hideaway. And it's literally hidden. So hidden that I'm one of about two dozen guests in the entire resort. After my little white lie to Alex, I realized I needed to get this trip booked as soon as possible. Stuart, our manager, handled everything, including making a financial transaction for me to put the bike incident behind me. I did something special for Giselle and paid off her car loan. I don't know how he did it, but Stuart was able to find the name of her car financing company from the license plate number I gave him. I don't want to know how many privacy laws he violated, but the remaining balance on her twelve-thousand-dollar loan was paid off this week. She should receive the title to her car sometime in the month or so, at which time I expect her to hunt me down and demand an explanation for the generosity I promised her.

Part of me is actually looking forward to seeing her sassy side. *Again.*

I can't get her out of my head. Everything about her captivates me. When I showed up at her house a few weeks ago, after our gig at The Lounge, I knew I was committing myself to something that I wasn't ready for. Seeing her in nothing but a t-shirt, holding a baseball bat did something crazy to me. She was so fucking hot. *Is* so fucking hot. I feel bad showing up the way I did, unannounced, but I was worried about her. When they told me someone was carried out, practically comatose, I needed to make sure she was okay. I should have known it was her friend and not her. Giselle seems so much more responsible than that. Or maybe not. I mean she did let a complete stranger into her car.

The vision of her bare legs and the tee that barely covered her is back in my head, her perky nipples poking through her practically see-through shirt. *God.*

I need to get in the shower and calm myself down before I spend the entire day in my room, her image at the top of my spank bank. I'm in paradise, after all. I need to get out and enjoy the few days that I have here.

MY SHOWER WAS REFRESHING, in more ways than one. I pull on my swim trunks and t-shirt and slide my feet into a pair of flip-flops I picked up in the airport when I arrived. The walk to the restaurant is quiet, exotic birds flying around and hanging out in the lush trees and bushes. This place is truly relaxing; we should consider doing a retreat with the rest of the band. Garrett could certainly use it and so could Tristan. Whatever he's been going through lately seems to be taking a toll on his nerves, as well. Our tour doesn't start for a few months–I think I'll mention it when I get back. Hell, Garrett can bring Sam and Kai, and if Alex wants to come, he can bring Tabby and the kids. Alex won't be on tour with us, but he's been helping us with the arrangement of some of our songs, as he always does. It's so great still having him involved with us, but I know he's thoroughly enjoying his full-time husband and father status. He and Tabby fought through a lot to be together, and I can't blame him for wanting to focus on his family and their happiness.

The smell of breakfast floods my nose, and I walk into the empty restaurant. The hostess sees me and quickly ushers me to a table on the patio, the Caribbean just a few yards from where I'm seated. *Paradise.*

An extensive menu is placed in front of me, but I already know what I want. A waiter appears with a carafe of freshly squeezed orange juice and fills up my empty glass. "Have you decided what you'd like?" he asks.

"Yes. I'll have the tomato omelet with toast and some bacon." He nods quickly and places the carafe on my table.

The orange juice is amazing, and I refill my glass right away. My phone rings from where I placed it on the table, and I quickly answer it. "Hey, Tristan," I say.

"How's Mexico?" he asks.

"It's incredible. You totally need to come here, it's completely relaxing."

"Since when did you need a getaway? You're the least stressed out of us all."

"Long story," I say. I'm sure he's already heard about my conversation with Alex, and he's just trying to get to me.

"When do you come back?" he asks.

"I'm here for five days." *Five glorious days.*

"Good for you."

"So, what's up? You okay?" I ask.

"Yeah, I'm good. It's just–I may need to ask to postpone our tour for six to eight weeks, and I'm not sure how to approach it with the guys."

"Dude, be straight with me. Are you okay?" I know Tristan has been going through something lately, and he's been very vague about it. I don't want to pry, but postponing our tour could be serious. Especially with this late notice. I think we've already sold out the first dozen or so shows. This would be a PR nightmare.

"I'm fine. I told you that already. I just have some medical things I need to address, and I'll need to be close to home for a few weeks."

"Tristan, when you say medical things, I think the worst. What the fuck is going on?" I take another sip of orange juice and swallow hard. I'm really worried now.

"Trust me, everything's going to be okay. I just wanted to get your thoughts on this."

"I think we can do whatever you need. Talk to Stuart. Talk to the rest of the guys. We can delay the start of our tour, refund tickets if we need to. You tell us."

"Okay, thanks. I'm glad you aren't freaking out about possibly postponing."

"Of course not. Whatever you need," I say. "You would tell me if there was something wrong, right?" *Like if you were dying?*

"Yeah. Yeah, I totally would. I'm fine. I swear. I'm gonna be fine. Thanks for talking. I'll let the guys know that you're on the same page with me, and we can work out the details when you get back. Later." He disconnects, leaving me hanging. *What the hell is going on?*

He's been super secretive, and I can't help but think the worst. He looks good, he doesn't seem sick in any way. In fact, he looks amazingly healthy. I've been watching him for signs of fatigue and other things that I saw back when I was a teenager and Lara was sick. Well, I didn't know she was actually sick because she eluded all of my questions. She was hiding cancer from me, and I'm pretty sure I know what that looks like. I don't think Tristan is going through anything like that, but what the fuck is he dealing with?

The waiter is back with several plates, and my breakfast is placed on the table in front of me.

"Can I bring you anything else?" he asks.

"No. Everything looks great," I say and pick up my knife and fork.

A small group of people are ushered in and seated at the other end of the small patio. The waiter brings them menus and two carafes of orange juice. After he takes their orders, he asks them, "What brought you all to Playa del Carmen?"

One of the guys answers for the group. "We're here for a retreat with our company. The rest of our group will be coming in later this morning."

The waiter smiles and asks, "Oh? How many more?"

"About twenty."

Shit.

I've had this resort practically to myself for the past day and a half, now I'll be sharing it with at least twenty more people, and I'm not pleased. Maybe I can stay hidden back at my room. I'm thankful that I have a private dipping pool beyond my patio, so I won't need to share the resort pool with a bunch of drunken, corporate types.

I finish my breakfast and drop a hundred-dollar bill on the table. I'm over-tipping because I forgot to bring any money to dinner last night. The manager explained to me that this is an all-inclusive resort and their staff doesn't expect anything from the patrons, but I know better. I've been to Mexico before, and the people working in these resorts are thankful for every single dollar they receive from the guests.

The beach is calling me, and I find a private lounge bed, and toss my tank top onto it, and kick my flip-flops underneath. After a swim, I plan to pull the privacy curtains around me and sleep all day on this outdoor piece of heaven. Maybe I'll even get a massage.

But first, I jog toward the water and dive in, taking in all of my surroundings. The turquoise water is beautiful and clear. I can see colorful fish all over the place, and I can even see my feet. Where I go swimming at the Jersey shore is beautiful, but I've never been in water this crystal clear. I float out a little bit more and swim parallel to the coast.

I HAVEN'T LEFT my private little hut on the beach since I came back from my swim a few hours ago. Since then, I've napped, eaten an incredible lunch, napped again, and spoke to Alex twice and Heath once. Epic Fail business aside, I'm thoroughly enjoying this completely impromptu R&R trip. Stuart picked the perfect place for me to escape, even if I really didn't need to escape from anything at all.

My phone alarm buzzes. It's four o'clock. Time for a run. If I don't want to go home twenty pounds heavier, I'm going to have to hit the sand for the next few days. I tuck my phone into the pocket inside my swim trunks and put my earbuds in. There's nothing like jogging barefoot on the beach. My running companions, AWOLNATION, blast through my ears and help me through the next forty-five minutes. The heat is becoming unbearable, and I realize I don't have any sunscreen on. Since

I was in the covered lounge all day today, I didn't think I needed any. Now, I can feel the skin on the back of my neck and shoulders burning up. I see my destination about a quarter of a mile away, and I widen my stride, pumping my arms harder to help get me there faster. As soon as I'm back, I'm going to grab my stuff and head back to my room. The quiet pool is perfectly shaded and will relieve my sunburn.

As I approach my private hideaway, I notice that it's been taken over by someone else, her feet hanging out the end, and the rest of her covered by the privacy curtains that surround the lounge. *What the hell?*

I'm completely out of breath, and I know my bottle of water and several towels are on that lounge, next to the stranger that totally snagged my perch for the day. I don't know what gets into me, but I rip open the curtains, angry that my privacy was breached.

"Excuse me, but…"

I choke on my words. The most beautiful woman I've ever seen is asleep on my lounge. Her hair splayed out behind her, her arms spread wide. She's laying awkwardly as if she literally passed out falling backward. She begins to stir, and as she opens her eyes, recognition sets in.

"Giselle?"

CHAPTER 16

Giselle
Present

"GISELLE?"

I squint to see who just let the massive amount of sunshine through the shades that I drew about a half hour ago. After traveling practically all day, I needed a nap and to be away from all of the commotion at the bar. I found this glorious private lounge, pulled the curtains around me, and was asleep within minutes. I raise my hands to shield my eyes, trying to block out the sun. "Can I help you?" I say, a tall figure standing in front of me starts to come into focus. *Holy crap.*

"Dax?" *It can't be him.*

"What are you doing here?" he asks and folds his arms over his chest. His incredibly toned, tattooed, bare, sexy chest. "And this is my lounge."

I sit up on my elbows, my hair falling around my face. I can feel the remnants of drool on the side of my cheek, and I hope he can't see it. *I'm a freaking mess.*

"Your name wasn't on it," I say and huff. "And I could ask you the same question. Are you following me?"

"What?" he asks.

"Did you follow me down here?" I ask, and I realize by the look on his face that he has no idea why I'm accusing him of stalking me. If anything, he probably thinks I stalked him here because he is a rock star, after all.

"You're kidding, right?" he says and reaches past me to grab a towel from next to my head. His hand brushes my hair, and for a second, I think he's going to climb on top of me. Instead, he stands back up and wipes his sweaty brow and face. He's bright red like he was just working out. Sweat covering his chest and most of his body, and he looks sunburned.

"You're really burned," I state the obvious, and he winces as he wipes the back of his neck.

"Yeah," he says and drops the sweaty towel next to my feet.

"You didn't answer my question, Dax, why are you here?"

"I needed some time away, so I came here. I don't feel like I need to provide an explanation to you, do I?" His attitude is throwing me off. *Is he annoyed that I'm here?*

I'm still trying to figure out this amazing coincidence.

"What about you?" he asks, accusatory.

"I didn't follow you down here, if that's what you think." I grab my cover-up and pull it over my head. "If you must know, I'm here with my company. A group of us received this trip as part of our bonus at the end of last year. While we're here, we have some team-building activities. But most of this trip is R&R for our marketing team."

So there.

"Oh," he says, and his stern look begins to soften. "Sorry, I shouldn't have assumed."

"Yeah, you shouldn't have," I say and slide off the lounge. "Excuse me, but I have to get back to the restaurant. We have a team dinner in a little while." I push past him and walk away. "It's good to see you again," I say over my shoulder, and I can see him standing in place, his jaw dropped in disbelief.

EPIC LIES

"You too," I hear his voice trail off, and I smile.

I can't believe Dax Anderson is here, in Mexico.

AFTER A QUICK SHOWER to wash off the long day of travel and drool I accumulated from the plane ride and the impromptu nap on the lounge, I feel refreshed. I slip into a tank dress and a pair of flip-flops, pulling my wet hair into a quick bun. Thank goodness it's ultra-casual here, and we're not expected to wear any business attire. My boss was very specific that we should consider this a vacation, first and foremost. Any work activities we do over the next few days will be in a casual setting and more focused on team building than anything else. I can handle that as I would prefer not to think about work while I'm in paradise.

"Giselle, over here!" one of my co-workers, Dawn, calls. I wave and walk into the open-air patio bar. Darren and Cody are sitting with her, and the table is already filled with drinks. "We didn't know what you wanted, so we ordered a bunch from the drink specials." She begins pointing to and naming every one of the fruity cocktails on the table. Darren and Cody both have beers. I point to the one with the pineapple draped over the side of a hurricane glass. "That's a rum runner," Dawn exclaims. "You're going to love it."

I take a sip, and it's refreshing. And strong.

"Geez," I cough.

"They put a floater in it," Cody says and laughs.

"You look nice and rested," Dawn says.

"I took a quick nap, and I feel so much better." I really don't like to fly, so I took some Benadryl and Melatonin to help me sleep on the plane. Once we landed, I was in a complete fog. A quick nap certainly did the trick until Dax woke me up, completely surprising me.

"This place is gorgeous," Dawn says as she lifts her own rum runner to her mouth.

"I can't believe they splurged for us to come here," Cody states.

"We won that pharmaceutical account at the end of last year," I remind him. "It's going to bring in marketing and advertising revenue of at least fifty million a year for the next five years. We worked our asses off on that pitch, so I say we deserve this." I raise my glass, and my colleagues do the same. We clink all around.

"Where's everyone else?" Darren asks.

"A group of them went to the restaurant on the other side of the resort. They're with Marilyn," Dawn says, and I nod in understanding. Marilyn is our boss and I can picture the group that followed her to that restaurant, the majority of them being complete ass-kissers. I like our sea-side view and smaller group here.

Dinner is amazing, and I switch to red wine after a few sips of that rum runner, otherwise, it will be a long night fighting heartburn. Rum and I aren't the best of friends, and I have a healthy respect for its power over me. Darren left about ten minutes ago to go back to his room to FaceTime with his kids. He promised to tuck them in remotely for the duration of this trip. He's such a great dad.

Cody stands up and stretches. "I'm exhausted. Do you girls mind if I go to bed?" Dawn and I shake our heads.

"I'll follow you," Dawn says, yawning. The long day of travel has certainly taken its toll on my friends, but I'm still wide-awake. I guess that nap gave me more energy than I expected. Dawn gives me a quick hug and a peck on the cheek. "See you on the beach tomorrow morning?"

I nod. "Sure, I'm going to need to get a run in at some point.

Why don't we plan to meet after breakfast over there?" I point to the private lounge beds on the far side of the beach.

"That's perfect!" she exclaims and follows Cody down the path leading to the rooms at the back of the resort. Thankfully, I don't have too far to walk. My room is just across the way, and I have a wonderful view of the water.

The waiter clears our plates, and I ask him, "Can I take my glass of wine with me?"

"Of course, Miss."

I stand up and slide my flip-flops off of my feet, grabbing them in one hand, my wine glass in the other. I plan to enjoy the glorious sunset that's about to happen.

I walk along the beach, the sand cooling as the sun goes down. It feels amazing between my toes. The sand here is so much softer than the beaches back home. The wind blows the wisps of hair that have fallen out of my bun and into my face. I take a sip of wine and focus on the horizon. That's when I realize the sun is behind me, and I won't see a sunset over the water. I'll have to get up early tomorrow to see it rise. I bet that's spectacular.

I walk a little further around a slight bend on the beach, past the lounge that I was asleep on earlier today. That's when I see him, stretched out on the sand, leaning back on his hands. He's wearing a t-shirt and a pair of swim trunks, and he has no idea I'm behind him. I should just walk away, the coincidence of both of us being here together is too overwhelming for me to address again. I don't want to accuse him of stalking me or vice-versa.

But I can't seem to back away. He's sitting so quietly and contently, and I wonder what he's thinking about. I slowly walk up so I'm next to him, and I drop my flip-flops onto the ground, startling him.

"I'm sorry," I say and laugh nervously. He looks up at me, and his face softens. I like soft. I don't like the scowl.

"Hey," he says. "I was just thinking about you." *Well, that answers my question.*

"Really?" I plop down clumsily on the beach next to him, kicking up a ton of sand in the process. But I saved my wine from spilling. *Score.*

"I owe you an explanation," he says.

"Are you going to admit that you followed me here?" I jest, brushing up against his shoulder. *What am I doing?*

"Is that what you think?" he asks, and I know he's not taking me seriously. His smile gives it away.

"Not really. But it is a crazy coincidence, right?"

"It's an *amazing* coincidence," he answers and brushes against my shoulder. He feels so warm.

"How's your sunburn?" I ask, knowing that I just felt the heat from it through his t-shirt.

"It hurts like hell," he says. "But I found some Aloe Vera at the shop in the hotel, so it should help alleviate the discomfort by morning."

"Oh, thank goodness," I say, taking a sip from my wine. Something crunches against my teeth, and I realize I've splashed some sand into my drink. I swallow it anyway, but look for a place to put down my glass.

"You okay?"

"Yeah, sand in my wine," I raise the glass and laugh. He takes it from my hand, stands up, and walks a few feet away, dumping the contents into the water. He's back next to me before I know it and twists the stem of the wine glass into the sand next to him.

"Thank you." We both look out over the water and watch the horizon get darker as the sun sets behind us. "It's beautiful," I say. "So calm and peaceful."

He remains quiet, but I can see him nod in my peripheral vision.

"Giselle…"

I turn to see him staring at me. Staring *into* me.

My cheeks flush, and I'm not sure if it's from the wine or his proximity to me. His presence does something to me that I haven't felt in a very long time. My pulse quickens, and I remember how I felt the night he came to my house, when I thought he was going to kiss me. How much I wanted him to. Now I want it more than ever.

I lick my lips and taste remnants of wine and strawberry Chapstick. "Dax?"

His gaze falls to my lips, and I lick them again, nervously.

"Fuck," he mutters and exhales harshly.

"What?" I ask. *My God, what is he waiting for?*

"You–you're beautiful. And I don't know why, but I can't get you out of my head. I haven't been able to since that day. And I want to say so much, do so much. And I'm restraining myself. But you're here. Why the fuck are you here?" His rambling is confusing me. He just said so much but nothing at all.

"Why are you mad at me?" The vibe that's coming off of him is–intense. He's frustrated and seems angry. "I swear to God I didn't follow you here." Tears threaten to spill out of my eyes. *Get a grip, Giselle.*

"What?" He looks at me and his eyes soften. "No. No, I'm not mad at you at all. And I believe you, I don't think you followed me. You couldn't have possibly known I was coming here. I'm not even checked into the hotel under my real name," he mutters.

"Oh." I'm still confused. His demeanor is constantly contradicting his mood swings. I can't tell if he wants to kiss me or strangle me. "Then why are you acting this way?"

"I'm not good at this," he answers.

"Good at what? Talking to someone?" I press.

"Restraining myself," he says, and I tense up, my pulse racing.

"Jesus, Dax. Then don't." *What did I just–*

I don't have time to complete the thought. His hands scoop the sides of my face, gently pulling my mouth toward his. His warm breath is the first thing I feel before he crashes his lips into mine. He inhales deeply and exhales into my mouth, his tongue diving in and entwining with mine. His grip on either side of my face becomes tighter as he slides his fingers into the sides of my hair. My bun unravels, causing my hair to fall around my shoulders, covering our faces. I turn to face him, rolling onto my knees. I wrap my arms around his neck and pull him toward me. His breath hitches, and I feel the Aloe Vera on the back of his neck. "Sorry," I say against his mouth, causing our teeth to scrape. He doesn't say anything, but continues his assault on my mouth, slowing down his kisses, savoring my lips. His breathing evens out, and his grasp on my head loosens. He kisses the corners of my mouth and back in the center again, drawing my lips into his. Pulling my tongue into his mouth again. We're breathing each other in, devouring each other. The scent of Aloe Vera and salt swirls in my senses, and I press my chest against his as I settle on his lap. I brush lightly against *there,* and he quickly pulls away, his hand wrapped around the back of my neck.

"We can't do this," he says, releasing me.

"But–"

He slides out from underneath me as if he wants to get as far away from me as possible.

"What did I do?" I ask. My lips ache yet want more.

"This just isn't a good idea."

"Says who?"

"Giselle—"

"You're confusing me. One minute, you're telling me you can't stop thinking about me. Then, you're kissing me like you *mean it*. Now you're all, 'No?'"

"Trust me, this won't work. We won't work. You're better off."

"Oh, so Mr. Brooding Rock Star is suddenly making an appearance," I say sarcastically.

He raises his eyebrows and shakes his head. "What?"

"You can't just tell me all of those things, kiss me like that and not feel anything. Don't you feel it? There's something here, between us. I know I felt *it* the second you came into my car." I'm challenging him, and it feels good. And I want him to kiss me again, despite all of his contradictions.

He stands up and looks down at me. "I don't want this. It was a mistake," he snaps and backs away.

"I don't believe you," I say as I stand up.

"You don't have a choice." His arms are folded against his chest, and the scowl is back.

"I still don't believe you. But I'm certainly not going to stay here and beg, looking like a fool." I bend down and grab my flip-flops.

Our shoulders brush together as I walk past him. My heart drops when I realize he's not following me. *Why would I even expect him to?*

By the time I reach my room, my head is pounding, and my chest is tight. I haven't been in a relationship in years, and something tells me that Dax Anderson isn't the type of guy who'll jump heart first into anything. And neither should I.

From this moment forward, I will not be honest with my feelings, and I most certainly will not be throwing myself at him or *anyone* again.

I've made that mistake too many times, and look where it's gotten me.

Absolutely nowhere.

CHAPTER 17

Dax
Past
Age 21

"WE'RE FINISHED? You're over me?" a female voice yells outside the door, and I roll my eyes. I'm reclined on the couch in the back room of the venue we just performed in. Tristan is sitting at the make-shift bar in the corner. We look at each other and shrug.

"Sounds like Garrett just broke the news to Natalia," Tristan says. "And she's not taking it well."

I shake my head. I'll never understand what draws these women to him. He's constantly on to the next before he's even done with the current one. He and Natalia didn't stand a chance. They've been together for about three months, since our last music video was shot. She was the star of the video, and he fell in lust with her from the moment she hit the sound stage. She is a model, after all.

Alex comes into the room, and he shuts the door quickly. "She just fucking punched him!" he laughs and winces at the same time. "Cold cocked him in the jaw."

Tristan laughs hysterically, and I chuckle along. "He deserved it," Tristan says.

The door flies open, and Garrett comes in, locking it behind him. He's rubbing his jaw and shaking his head. He opens the refrigerator and grabs an ice pack, placing it on his jaw. "Keep your fucking mouths shut," he mumbles, and we all laugh.

"Why would you string her along like that?" Tristan asks.

"I didn't string her along at all. I told her from the beginning it was only for fun. No commitments. Nothing. She was fine with our arrangement."

"That welt on your jaw says otherwise," Alex chimes in.

"Everyone just shut the fuck up." Garrett's personality shines through as usual.

"Next time, don't get involved with the help," Tristan blurts out and laughs hysterically. Garrett throws the ice pack at his head and misses.

"Believe me, I have no intention of ever doing it again." He grabs the bottle of whiskey from the small bar in the corner and swigs from it.

"Great show tonight," I say, changing the subject.

"Yeah, the energy in the audience was amazing," Tristan says and high-fives Alex as he walks over to take a swig of the bottle that Garrett is hoarding.

"This tour is going to be epic," I say, and they all nod in agreement.

"It better be," Alex says and slouches into the couch. He's been a mess lately, and I need to figure out what's going on with him. He told me last night that he can't get out of town soon enough.

Garrett reclines on the couch. "I am swearing off all chicks for the next few months."

All of us erupt in laughter. "Seriously, G. There's not a chance you'll be able to do that," Tristan says.

"Whatever," Garrett says. "Just remind me that models should no longer be on my menu."

EPIC LIES

Chuckles fill the room. "No more models," I toast, and everyone raises their drinks in the air.

STUART LEAVES THE ROOM, and we all sit and stare at each other, slightly overwhelmed. Our manager just outlined the next eighteen months of touring and promotion commitments. Never in a million years did we ever imagine that our high school garage band was going to turn into something more. Practically overnight, we have a seven-digit record deal and a domestic and international tour that will bring in even more money for us. It's completely insane.

Alex is already gone, and even though he says he's ready for a major road trip, I don't believe him.

Tristan stands and places his empty beer on the table. "I'm catching a cab. Anyone want to share?" Garrett jumps up and says, "Yes."

I have my car with me, and since I didn't drink too much tonight, I can drive myself home safely. It's almost two o'clock in the morning, and the only thing I'm worried about is falling asleep at the wheel.

"See you guys tomorrow," I say. I know our tour bus leaves between ten and eleven tomorrow morning, and most of our things are already packed and ready to go.

Garrett and Tristan are gone, and I swipe my car keys from the counter. I'm the last one to leave the backstage area, and security locks the door behind me. I'm alone in a dark parking lot as I walk toward my car.

I unlock my car and open the door when a faint sound startles me. I flash my cell phone flashlight behind me and see someone huddled on the ground, knees pulled to his or her chest.

The figure covers his or her face when my light shines on it. "Hey, are you okay?" I ask, and I see her face.

"Natalia?" I ask as I drop my phone onto the driver's side seat and rush to her side.

"Dax," she says, and I notice she's been crying. Her face is streaked with makeup, and her voice is hoarse.

"What's going on?" I ask, remembering the argument that she and Garrett had earlier tonight.

"Nothing," she says, and I pull her up to her feet. She wobbles and sways in my arms as I walk her toward my car.

"What the hell are you doing out here all by yourself? I thought you left hours ago?"

"Where the hell was I supposed to go?" she says as if I know her personal living situation.

"What do you mean?"

"I was supposed to move into Garrett's place this weekend, and then he—" her sobs continue, and I don't know what to do. The parking lot is pitch black, and I know the best thing right now is to get her into my car and take her—somewhere.

I walk her around to the passenger side and open the door. "Get in, we'll figure something out," I say, silently cursing Garrett in my head.

"Thanks," she says weakly, and I close the door. As I walk around to my side, I realize I'm getting myself into a situation that I don't want to be involved in. I've never had to escort one of Garrett's exes, and Natalia is one of the most beautiful women that I've ever seen him with.

I slide into my seat and turn up the heat. "Are you cold?" I ask. It's chilly tonight, and I know I am.

"Yes, thanks," she says, rubbing her hands together.

"Where can I take you?" I ask.

Her sobs begin again. She shakes her head. "I have nowhere to go."

"Seriously? Do you have a friend in the area? A hotel?" *Fuck, I've definitely gotten in over my head here.*

"No, everyone I know lives out in L.A."

"Oh," I say. Maybe I can put her in a hotel for the night, and she can figure her own shit out tomorrow.

"I'll be fine. Just take me to the closest hotel at the airport. I need to get the fuck out of here," she says.

I punch a destination in my GPS and pull out of the parking lot.

We drive in silence, and her sniffles start again.

"What happened?" I ask, although I don't really want to know the answer.

"You tell me," she says. "Because I have no fucking idea. Yesterday, we were making plans to move in together, and tonight he tells me he's over me."

I shake my head. *Typical Garrett.*

"I don't know what to say," I lie. *She needs to forget about him.*

"Of course you don't," she snaps.

"I'm sorry."

"You know, I've never been one to throw my heart out there and give it to anyone, but Garrett swept me off my feet. He made promises to me! I just can't comprehend this," she says, burying her face in her hands.

I swipe a Dunkin' Donuts napkin from my console and hand it to her. "I don't have any tissues, but I hope this helps."

She grabs it and blows her nose loudly into the napkin. "Do you have any more?" she asks.

"Yeah, sure." I reach into the console, grab a pile of napkins, and place them on her thigh.

"Thanks," she says.

"I'm taking you to the Airport Marriott, is that okay?" I ask.

"Yes, I'm a Gold Club Elite member, I'm sure they'll be able to get me a room this time of night," she says and blows her nose again.

I merge onto the interstate, and her sobs finally subside.

"I'm such an idiot," she says.

"No you're not."

"How many girls like me have you driven away for Garrett? Five, ten? Seriously, if I knew what I was getting myself into, I never would have stayed in town. He led me on. Lied to me. He never really loved me."

"I don't know what to say, Natalia. I don't get involved in his love life, ever. But I can tell you that you've been around the longest, so you must have meant something to him," I say.

"Thanks. But you're no help," she laughs.

Rain starts to bounce off of my windshield, and I flip my wipers on. "I'm really sorry."

She sighs. "It's okay. You shouldn't have to pick up the pieces for your friend. I'm sorry I put you in this position. I should have just gotten a cab."

"I'm glad I can help," I say, uncomfortable even having this conversation.

"I'm stronger than this," she blurts out. "I'm so angry with myself for being so fucking weak. He doesn't control my emotions. He doesn't own me."

Wow.

"See, there you go," I say and have no idea what the hell I even mean. *Girl Power?*

"I should have known this was going to happen. I should have been prepared."

"How could you?" I ask, wondering how any of Garrett's conquests prepare themselves for the inevitable.

"What do you do?" she asks me.

"What do you mean?"

"What do you do when you dump a girl? Is it sudden? Does she see it coming? Is she prepared?"

"I–I don't know. I don't really hook up as much as Gar–I mean, I don't have the same issues." *Fuck, what am I even saying.*

"Oh. I thought you all were the same. Womanizing assholes." Her attitude has completely turned, and now I feel like I may catch the brunt of Garrett's behavior.

"No. I don't use women or take them for granted. It's been a while since I've even hooked up or been in any kind of relationship," I admit, and I see her turn towards me.

"Really? Somehow I don't believe that," she quips.

"I'm serious. Don't lump me into any category that has Garrett's name in it. Don't get me wrong, he's like a brother, but I'm nothing like him."

"Good," she says and places her hand over mine. "Some girl will be very lucky one day if you are exactly who you say you are."

"What does that mean?" I ask, mildly offended. *Does she think I'm lying to her?*

"It means I'm happy you aren't like Garrett. I hope I never meet anyone like him again. It's refreshing that you don't have the same tendencies to consume someone entirely and then throw their heart into the trash."

"Like I said, I'm nothing like Garrett."

We pull up in front of the hotel, and she opens her door.

"Good," she says and walks through the doors like nothing happened tonight. Strong. Confident. Beautiful.

And dangerous.

FLOWERS AND A BOX OF CHOCOLATE peek through the opening in my door attached to a familiar hand. "Happy Anniversary," Derek says as he slides the rest of the way into the room.

Today is the one-year anniversary of our official first date. And it's also the day that we're moving into the dorms to start the first semester of our sophomore year. I wipe my hands on my sweat pants and step over several boxes in the middle of the floor. Mia's stuff was delivered this morning, but her flight hasn't arrived yet, so I'm starting the unpacking process for two.

"When did you get here?" I ask him as he lifts me into a hug, kissing me.

"Rob and I got here yesterday." Mia won't be happy to hear that. She and Rob didn't exactly work out. A few days after the bonfire last year, he saw her kissing 'Thursday' Frank, and he dropped her like a hot potato. Derek told me Rob found the 'love of his life' this summer while he and his family were vacationing in Maine, so we'll see if she's able to make him forget about my best friend.

"Mia's not here yet?" he asks.

I shake my head. "Her plane lands at around nine or ten tonight, and she's taking a cab from the airport."

He drops the flowers and candy onto a pile of books on my desk and pushes me back toward my bed. "Good, we have lots of time to catch up." My sweaty t-shirt is lifted over my head before my body hits the mattress. "God, I've missed you so much." He buries his head in my neck while his hands explore every inch of my torso and chest.

I wrap my arms around him and pull him against me. His touches feel so good. His lips feel incredible. He brushes the side of my breast with his hand and pulls my bra cup down, exposing my nipple. He places his mouth over it, teasing until I'm squirming beneath him. "Derek!" I moan, and he moves over and does the same to my other breast. He slides my sweats off of me and spreads apart my legs, pressing his firmness directly to my *spot*.

"I want you, right now," he mumbles into my neck as his assault on my breasts continues. His mouth covers one of my nipples as I arch my back, pressing harder against his erection. I want him too–but I can't.

"Slow down, before this goes too far," I say, panting into his neck.

"You're killing me, Giselle. We need this," he says and breaks free of me.

"I'm not ready," I say, apologetically.

"When will you be ready? We've been together for a year." He's frustrated, and I know it's hard on him. We've been with each other in many ways, but we just haven't done *that*.

"I don't know," I say.

He lies down next to me and drapes his leg over mine, slowly tracing circles on my stomach. "I love you so much. And I can't think of anything I'd rather do than show you just how much."

Guilt swirls in my gut. I want to give him everything he wants. And I want this for myself. I know he loves me and that he'd never lie to me like Troy did back in high school. But, I just can't shake the feeling that I can't give away the one thing that was stolen from me. Even though it's already gone. *God, I'm a mess.*

"Please, Derek. I'm just not ready." I say, and his hand stops its movement and lies flat on my belly.

"I'm not going anywhere," he says, kissing my ear. "I'll wait as long as you need me to. I'm sorry I tried to rush it today. It's just–you look so hot and sexy in your sweats and your hair pulled up." He nips at my cheek and kisses down my neck. "But, I can wait. And when it does happen, it's going to be perfect. I promise to make your first time the most wonderful thing you've ever experienced." I hate that I've lied to him and told him I'm a virgin, but I can't tell him, or anyone, about Troy. I don't ever want to expose that secret.

"Thank you," I say, and he rolls back on top of me.

"Now relax while I show you how much I love you," he says, and his lips travel from my mouth, down my neck, over my breasts and lower...

"THAT BOY HAS FALLEN hard for you," Mia says as she shoves the last piece of chocolate into her mouth from the box that Derek gave me yesterday. "He's in love."

I smile. "I think I like him a lot, too," I joke.

"Stop! You're in love," she says, and I nod. "This is amazing chocolate, by the way. I would do *so many things* for this amazingness!"

"Mia, you don't need chocolate from anyone to do *things*."

She doesn't seem fazed by my zing and asks like we haven't been talking to each other at least three times a day, "So tell me, how was your summer?"

"Seriously, you're a nut." I swing my feet over the side of my bed and survey our room. All of the boxes are neatly broken down and shoved behind our dressers in the corner. Our clothes are all put away, and for the first, and only time this semester, our room is spotless.

"How many times did Derek come to see you at the beach?" she asks. We spent the summer in Belmar again, and it was amazing. I got a job at a local book store while my father commuted back home a few days a week for work. There were some weeks that I was at the house all by myself, and I smile, remembering the peace and tranquility of our summer house.

She already knows the answer, but I say, "You know that he came to see me twice." My parents have no idea, and I feel guilty.

"Of course I know, but you never told me all of the gritty details. Did you guys finally do it?"

I blush. "No."

"God, girl. What are you waiting for?" she asks. "I mean, get it over with already so you can enjoy having sex with him every single day. He's madly in love with you, and I'm sure will do incredible things to you."

Mia has no idea that I'm not a virgin. I've never felt the need to tell her, and I feel bad lying to my best friend.

She goes on and on. "You'll enjoy it so much better once you get past your first time."

I hold my breath and look at her.

"What?" she says.

"There's something I never told you," I say and instantly regret it.

She sits up on her bed and folds her legs underneath her like a pretzel. "What haven't you told me?" she asks, concerned. I wring my hands in front of me, and I second-guess telling her anything.

"What's going on?" she asks, nervously.

Tears fill my eyes, and I shake my head. "Forget it," I say wishing I never broached the subject. I just want to push the memory of Troy raping me deep inside and forget about it forever.

"No. Something's wrong, and you need to tell me," Mia says as she walks over and sinks onto the bed next to me. "What's going on? You're scaring me."

I inhale deeply and make eye contact with her. Her eyes are wide, concerned. She's my best friend. I have to tell her.

"I'm not exactly a virgin," I blurt out, and she gasps.

"What the hell are you talking about? What do you mean?"

I close my eyes and take a deep breath. "And it wasn't by choice."

"Oh my God. Giselle!" she says, sweeping me into a huge hug. "I'm so sorry, honey. When did this happen? What the hell?"

Surprisingly, I'm able to keep my emotions in check as I calmly tell her what happened back in high school. What Troy did to me. She just sits and stares, tears filling her eyes. She hangs on to every word that comes out of my mouth. Her hands grasp mine, and when I'm finished she pulls me into an embrace. "I can't believe someone did that to you. Stole your trust from you. Lied to you. I'm so very sorry."

I smile into her hair and say, "Thank you. I'm seriously okay, now."

"I'm such an asshole, constantly trying to get you to do it with Derek. I had no idea you were protecting yourself."

"It's really fine," I say. "When I'm ready, Derek will be the first to know." *And I want to be ready. I want to make love to him. But, there's something that's holding me back.*

"If you need any pointers, just ask me," she says, and I laugh out loud.

"I think you could teach me a few things," I say, and she smacks my leg.

"I love you, Giselle. I'm so sorry someone hurt you like that. I wish I could take it all away," she says and hugs me again. "I bet Derek is really bummed about what happened to you."

"He doesn't know," I say, embarrassed. "I haven't told anyone, until today."

"Oh? He doesn't question why you have waited so long to be with him? You love him, don't you?"

"Of course I love him. And, I know he wants to have sex with me, but he doesn't press too hard for it." *Until yesterday.*

"You need to tell him, Giselle. He needs to know what you've been through."

"Why? I don't think he needs to know what happened." *I don't want him to know.*

"If you love him as much as you say you do, tell him. He'll understand why you've waited so long. And maybe he won't pressure you to have sex until you're ready."

"He's been great," I say and smile. "I don't know what I'd do without him."

"He's a keeper. Don't let him go," she smiles. "So, where are we going tonight?" She hops off the bed, changing the subject.

"I'm not connected with the party scene," I say. "I'm sure we'll find something to do."

"I'm getting in the shower. Let's plan to head over to Fraternity Row in about an hour," she says. Derek moved into the Epsilon Phi house, and I'm sure they're having a party tonight. I'm not really big into frat parties, but it's the first weekend back at school, so I'll make an exception just this once. At least I'll get to see where Derek lives now.

But first, I need a nap.

MIA IS DANCING down the sidewalk, singing some song that constantly played over the radio this summer. I finally got it out of my head yesterday, and now she's belting it at the top of her lungs. "Here we are!" she says as we walk up the stairs to Epsilon Phi. Music booms from inside, but it doesn't look too crowded yet. *Good.*

I plan to find Derek and suggest we leave and go back to my room. Mia will be bouncing around all night, and after our talk today, I think I may want to take the next step with Derek. I think I'm ready.

We walk through the doors, and the standard stench of beer fills the air. "Ew," I gag, and Mia laughs. We've been to plenty of parties on campus that smell the same, but stale beer soaked into carpets is not an attractive smell.

The first person we see is Rob. "Hey, girls. Good to see you." He smiles at us both, but he's stiff. Mia isn't his favorite person since she broke his heart last year.

"Hi," I say. "Is Derek here?"

"Oh, yeah. Our room is upstairs. Last door on the left. Can I get you anything to drink?" he asks.

"Nothing for me," I say.

"Show me to the bar," Mia says and loops her arm through his.

"I'll find you in a little while. I'm going to go up to see Derek."

"Toodles," she says, waving.

I walk up the stairs and down the long corridor toward Derek's room. Several fraternity brothers are playing Nerf basketball in the hallway, and the ball flies over my head. "Sorry!" They call out after me.

"No problem," I mutter.

I stop in front of his door and bring my hand up to knock when I hear a strange noise from inside. *What the hell was that?* I grab the doorknob and twist.

Soft music fills the room, and the curtains are drawn. Heavy breathing travels through the air, and that's when I see *them*.

Derek is naked, leaning over a girl whose legs are spread wide in the air.

And he's fucking her.

I hold my breath as I watch the two of them together, and a scream lodges in my throat.

The girl gasps when she sees me, and Derek's face turns pale. I hold onto the doorknob as if it's the only thing keeping me up. I begin to wobble on my feet as the girl tries to cover herself. He attempts to do the same.

"Giselle," he says as I'm frozen in place. Tears fill my eyes, and I shake my head slowly.

A stabbing pain in my gut almost topples me over, but I rush down the hallway before I puke. Another Nerf basketball bounces off the top of my head just before I run down the stairs and out the door.

And I keep running.

Anger boils inside of me. Rage consumes me. That motherfucker has been telling me for almost a year how much he loves me. That he'll wait for me. Blah-fucking-blah. The image of him pounding into that girl makes me run faster. My fists are tight, and my arms are pumping, propelling me through campus. People and buildings blur in my peripheral vision, and I do everything in my power to keep from screaming. I gave him a year of my life. He proclaimed his loyalty and love to me for a FUCKING YEAR!

I reach my dorm and take the stairs two at a time. My adrenaline is a force, and it's driving me beyond my limits. This year, Mia and I are on the eighth floor of our dorm. Eight flights of stairs zoom by as I barrel up them all. I'm breathing heavily when I reach my floor. When I enter my room, I scan it for signs of Derek. They're everywhere.

The vase that holds the flowers sits on the desk next to my bed. I swipe it and tear the flowers from it, shoving them in the garbage. I contemplate throwing the vase against the concrete walls, but I think twice and shove that in the garbage, too. Pictures, notes scribbled on napkins, candy boxes, stuffed animals. They all get shoved into the garbage in our room. I rip out his t-shirts that I have tucked away in my drawers and get rid of them, too. Everything I can find that reminds me of him, smells like him, is gone.

Once the garbage is full, I tie up the bag and drag it down to the garbage chute. I stuff it in and listen to it topple down the shaft and hit the compactor on the first floor. I want to hear it get crushed and then incinerated.

I want his lies compacted and flattened.

And then burned.

CHAPTER 19

Dax
Present

FROM MY PATIO THIS MORNING, I watched Giselle leave with a group of people, who I assumed were her co-workers. There were at least five or six of them in all, and she lagged behind the group, looking as if she were disconnected and not having fun. Everyone else was laughing and speaking cordially with each other, but not Giselle. She hugged a notebook against her chest, a pen stuck in her hair, holding her bun together. Her eyes drawn, staring down at the ground as she walked.

She looked miserable. *And it's all my fault.*

Why did I say those things to her? Why did I kiss her? *Why did she let me?*

I'm not in a frame of mind to start any kind of relationship, and I certainly don't want to just hook up with a girl like Giselle. She's perfect and innocent, and I would destroy that with a one-night stand. She's a normal girl, someone who would have normal relationship goals. *I don't do normal.*

But–I'm so drawn to her, mesmerized by her innocence and beauty. Everything about her relaxes me, despite how I acted last night. Her eyes have an amazing, calming effect that seem to see deep into my soul. Almost like she already knows everything about me, the good and the bad. She has forgiving eyes.

My phone rings at the exact same time it has since the first day I arrived. "Hey, G," I answer. I've been expecting this call, especially since Tristan called me yesterday to tell me that he may need us to postpone the start of our tour.

"Enjoying yourself?" he asks, sarcasm strong.

"Yeah," I say.

"I'll cut to the chase," he says, and I know what's coming. "Tristan spoke to us yesterday and told us he needs us to consider postponing our tour kick-off." I inhale deeply, waiting for the biting words to come out of Garrett's mouth. Fully expecting him to say we can replace Tristan for the first part of the tour and wait for him to catch up to us.

"I'm aware," I say and hold my breath.

"What are your thoughts?" Garrett asks.

I can't fault Tristan for taking some time to figure out whatever is going on with him. He needs to do what he needs to do. We've been flexible in the past with other members of the band, Garrett included. It would be hypocritical to tell Tristan that he can't take some time off when others have had that luxury.

"I don't see the problem with it. Let Stuart and the tour company figure out the logistics, and we can worry about making up those dates later," I say.

"I see," Garrett says.

"Anything else?" I ask.

"No," he says. "You know, I have to agree with you."

What?

"Excuse me?" I ask, fully expecting him to say 'kidding!'

"When one of us needs time, any of us, we should be allowed to take it. You all were amazing when I was going through a rough time with Kai. Nobody asked any questions. Not a single one of you judged me or my son. You just let us be. You let us figure out our lives together. I'll never forget that." His voice trails off. I don't know what to think right now, and I can't believe I'm hearing these words from his mouth.

"Wow, G. I'm glad to hear you're on the same page. Tristan's really got me worried, and if you have any idea what's going on with him, I trust you're doing the right thing entirely."

"I know we are. All he needs is five or six weeks, then he'll be good to go. So it's settled," he says, and I can hear pride in his voice. He's not angry. He's not upset. He's rolling with the punches, and this is a huge step for Garrett.

"Stuart will take care of everything," I say.

"Yes, he will."

"See you soon."

"Oh, you should stay in Mexico for a few more days now that you have some more time to kill."

That's a great idea, but I'm not sure I should be here with Giselle. *Or should I?*

"We'll see. I'll see you when I get back. Take care."

I disconnect and toss my phone onto the lounge next to me. I've taken over the one at the far end of the beach, hoping to remain incognito. This trip so far has been paparazzi-free, and I'm thankful. Even the staff seems indifferent to who I am, and I'm hoping my generous tipping strategy is helping.

My body is exhausted. My mind is exhausted. *Everything* is exhausted. I realize I should take full advantage of the mini-reprieve I've been given, so I text Stuart.

Me: Add five days to my trip. Email me the return details.

He replies almost immediately.

Stuart: Consider it done. Enjoy the rest of your time away.

I turn off my phone and flip onto my side. Having my

schedule cleared up for me for the better part of the next week relaxes me. I need a nap.

A SOFT VOICE PULLS me out of my slumber. The warm breeze wafts under the drawn curtains, and I happily realize I'm still on vacation. As I stretch out, I hear a familiar voice.

"Mia, this whole thing is fucked up, and I don't know what to do." *Giselle.*

She must be in the next lounge over, and she has no idea I'm hidden away in this one.

"You know I can't do that. I was flirting hard last night, and he rejected me completely. I won't put myself in that position again. Not ever."

It's obvious she's talking about what happened between us last night, and my heart sinks. She wanted me to kiss her, I could see it in her eyes, her lips. So I did. *Fuck.* I wanted to kiss her, and as soon as I pulled her lips to mine, I didn't want it to end. She has no idea what she's doing to me. My pulse quickens, and I begin to panic. I have to get out of here. I have no right eavesdropping on her conversation. And it's making me feel like an even bigger asshole. I wanted to tell her last night that I'm no good for her, no good for anyone. I feel terrible that I got her upset.

I hear her flopping around on the lounge, and I assume she's trying to get comfortable. I peek out through the privacy curtains, and I see her stretched out, wearing a white cover-up, her legs bare and bronzed. She's propped several pillows behind her head, so she's looking out at the water while she talks into the microphone dangling in front of her mouth. Her lips glisten, and I remember what they tasted like last night. *Berries.*

She holds the wire steady so the microphone stays put. "I shouldn't have even tried. We come from completely different worlds, and chasing him around Mexico isn't the best idea, is it? I'm sorry, Mia, but I'm not like you. No offense." A smile dances on her lips, and I get comfortable. I can't stop watching her. *I'm a total creep.*

"I'm not listening to this anymore. I'm not going to throw myself at him just because of who he is. We had a connection that day in my car, and it had nothing to do with the fact that he's a rock star. I know he felt it too. I just…" her voice trails off, and she looks toward the resort. There's a group of people sitting at the edge of the pool, laughing and drinking. One of them waves, and Giselle raises her hand in acknowledgment. "Shit, they found me," she says. "My co-workers. I spent all morning with them doing team building and trust exercises, and I've honestly had enough at this point. I'm ready to come home." I can tell she's contemplating closing the curtains around her, but she realizes it too late. She's already been seen.

"I wish you were here with me," she says to her friend on the phone. "Then I wouldn't have to hide away by myself. You'd keep me company." A smile spreads across her face as she stretches her legs in front of her. "I'm going to fry out here." She pats around for her sunscreen and pops it open, squirting some into the palm of her hand. She smoothes the lotion up her legs, rubbing it in thoroughly. Her toes curl as she works it into her skin. "Shit," she says, and she lifts her leg up into the air. "I missed a spot shaving. Lovely," she tells her friend, and I have to turn my face to laugh into the pillow. *She's so fucking hot.*

"It's none of your business what parts of me are shaved and what aren't," she scolds her friend. *Yes it is, tell her, dammit.*

"You're a perv," she says, and I hold my breath. I can't get the image of her out of my head, imagining exactly what is and isn't bare. The throbbing in my bathing suit confirms that fact. I'm rock hard.

She glances toward her co-workers again as one of them walks toward her with two fruity cocktails in his hands. "Crap, I gotta go. I'll call you later. Love you. Bye." She taps her phone and shields her eyes.

"Hey, Liam," she says to the dude approaching her.

"What are you doing over here all by yourself?" he asks and hands her the large drink, umbrellas spilling from the top.

"I'm exhausted," she replies. "What is this?" she asks, amused.

"It's a surprise. But it has rum in it." *What a tool.*

She places the drink next to her on the ledge. "Thanks, but I don't drink rum." Her smile is kind, and I can tell she's trying not to insult him.

He sits down, uninvited, and places his hand on her leg. She tenses up and scoots away from him. "Where did you go last night?" he asks. "When I came back from our dinner with Marilyn, you and the others weren't at the bar anymore. I thought we were going to meet up." She now has her legs curled underneath her, and she's trying to remain polite. I can tell this guy bothers her, her body is stiff, and her smile seems fake.

"I went to bed early," she lies. *She was here with me, and I fucked things up.*

"Don't disappear on me tonight. Promise?" he says and leans closer to her, his arms on either side of her knees, caging her in. Her eyes widen, and her smile is now gone. She almost looks–scared?

Fuck it.

I push the curtain aside and say, "Babe?" *What the hell am I doing?*

A different kind of startled look takes over her face, and she and The Tool both turn to me.

"Now that you're finished with your conference call, why don't you come take a nap with me like you promised?" I scoot over on the lounge, patting the empty spot next to me.

"Who is that?" Tool asks her.

"I'm her boyfriend," I say, and he immediately pulls his hands away from Giselle.

"I'm sorry, I had no idea she even had one," he says, throwing a subtle insult her way. "My bad." He stands up and grabs the drink he brought for Giselle and walks away toward her group of co-workers.

When he's out of earshot, she turns to me, her eyes blazing.

"How long have you been there?" she barks.

"Long enough to know that you missed a spot shaving," I smile, and her eyes widen. And then I'm clocked in the head with her sunscreen.

She immediately regrets her action and rushes from her lounge to mine. "Oh my God. I'm so sorry," she says, softly touching the knot already forming in the middle of my forehead. I wince under her gentle fingers and lay back on the pillow.

"I deserved it," I say.

"Yes, you did."

She gingerly touches the bump and says, "I should get some ice."

I grab her wrist as she's about to stand up. "Don't go." She tenses in my grip, and I quickly let go. "Sorry."

"It's okay." She tentatively sits on the lounge next to me.

"We need to talk," I say, and she sighs.

"You heard everything I said, didn't you?" she asks, and I nod.

"Yes, but I didn't mean to," I lie. I hung on every single word she told her friend. I felt every stab in my heart as I realized how I made her feel last night.

"Oh God." She covers her mouth. "I must seem like a complete loser, fangirl, groupie to you. Chasing you around. Trying to get you to kiss me." She turns seven shades of pink, and she looks like she's about to puke. Her hair is blowing wildly as the wind has picked up on the beach, the privacy curtains flapping around.

"I owe you a sincere apology," I say, trying to calm her mini freak-out. I want to tell her that I was an asshole last night. That I fucked up.

"I practically threw myself at you. I'm such an idiot." Her hands start to shake, and I sit up, our faces so close. The scent of berries surrounds us.

"Giselle, I was an asshole. I *am* an asshole."

"Yes, you are," she blurts out. "But, it doesn't excuse the fact that I put you in an uncomfortable position last night. I guess I misunderstood your intentions."

"No, you didn't misunderstand a single thing," I admit, and she looks confused.

"Oh?" She purses her lips, and I fight back the urge to claim them once again.

"I wasn't lying when I told you I can't get you out of my head. For weeks, you're all I can think about. You're consuming me, and I'm losing the battle." My admission makes her blush.

"Why does it have to be a battle?" she asks, innocently. If she only knew how hard it is for me to trust anyone. To *love* anyone. I've given my heart to only a few people in my life, and every single time it gets destroyed, pieces of it torn out and devoured.

"It's a defense mechanism, I guess."

"I know all about those," she admits and bows her head. "Dax, we've all been there. Trust me."

There's pain in her eyes, and I can tell that she's also struggling with her own inner demons. I hate that anyone has ever hurt her.

"So, now what?" she asks.

"I'm not sure. But I don't want you to walk away from me again."

"You pushed me away," she breathes.

"I know. And I shouldn't have," I admit and brush her wild hair away from her face. I need to see her. All of her.

"Good," she says, and a soft smile plays on her lips.

A strange feeling has taken over, one that I haven't felt in a long time. My heart pounds in my chest as I cradle her cheek in my hand. *What is she doing to me?*

She closes her eyes as I kiss her gently, savoring her softness, her scent, her taste. She remains still, but relaxes into my lips, parting hers slightly, allowing me in. I tease her with my tongue as hers meets mine. She moans gently against my lips, and I wrap my free arm around her waist, pulling her toward me. She wraps her arms around my neck, her fingers teasing the back of my hair. Our kiss becomes more desperate as she slides onto my lap, her legs wrapping around my back and her center exactly where I want it. Our foreheads brush against each other, and I wince.

"God, I'm so sorry," she says as her lips leave mine. She kisses a path from my mouth to my forehead where her lips drift over the aching bump. Her move exposes her neck, and I don't waste any time. I nip and kiss along her jaw and over to her ear, causing her to tense in my lap and moan again. She's now firmly pressed against the bulge in my swim trunks, and *she doesn't stop pressing.*

I pull her face back down to mine and hold her firmly in front of me, placing my lips over hers, inhaling her breaths. Her hips roll into me, and I realize we're going to reach a point of no return. "Wait," I say, and her breathing hitches.

"Hmm?" she says against my mouth, kissing me again. I feel her nipples against my bare chest as she presses into me. *Teasing me.*

I place my hands under her ass and flip her off of my lap and onto her back. I lean over her, taking control back and press down on her arms, holding them in place. She immediately stiffens underneath me and sucks in her breath. Her reaction causes me to quickly release her.

"Are you okay?" I ask, and her eyes widen. "Shit," I say and climb off of her.

"I'm fine," she whispers.

Something clearly got to her, and I'm angry with myself for taking control the way I did. I obviously startled her.

I lie next to her and watch her take deep, even breaths. Whatever got her nervous, I want to take back, make it go away.

"Have dinner with me tonight," I blurt out, and she turns to look at me.

"Okay." She surprises me with her quick answer, and her smile is back again. Her nervousness seems to have disappeared.

"I can't cook," I joke.

"I wouldn't worry about that," she says. "There are plenty of restaurants to choose from right here."

"I don't want to eat in a restaurant, surrounded by all of those corporate people, some of them trying to get into your pants."

She laughs out loud. "I doubt that very much."

I get serious for a second. "You don't think so? I watched that tool try to pick you up just a little while ago. Don't try to tell me there aren't a dozen of them from your office that don't try the same thing."

Her eyes turn dark. "You were totally spying on me. That wasn't right."

"Hey, I saved you from some really bad pick-up lines, didn't I?" I smile.

"I can handle Liam. He's harmless," she says, unconvincingly.

"Have you had to fend him off in the past?"

"Not really. And don't worry, I can handle myself."

"I believe you, I've seen you with a baseball bat." I brush her cheek with the back of my fingers.

She laughs and flashes her bright, perfect teeth.

"So, what's your suggestion for dinner if you don't want to go to one of the restaurants here?" she asks as the warm breeze picks up and blows air underneath her cover up, exposing her bikini bottoms and bare stomach. She quickly presses it down, hiding her body from me.

"Come to my suite. We'll have them deliver food to us," I suggest.

"Like room service?" she asks, teasing.

"Yes, like room service."

"Okay," she says, and I feel completely relieved. Whatever caused her to flinch a few minutes ago has nothing to do with me, otherwise she wouldn't have accepted my invitation to dine alone.

I reach for her hand to pull her off of the lounge. "Let's go now. We can order as soon as we get back to my room."

A look of surprise flushes across her face. "I need to freshen up," she says and blushes.

I pull her against me and kiss her nose. "Be careful shaving," I joke, and she smacks my arm.

"If only I could reach my sunscreen," she replies.

"Yeah, about that. How huge is the lump on my head?" I ask.

She leans back and raises her eyebrows. "Yikes," she says, shaking her head.

"Crap," I say and reach to feel what I imagine to look like a giant goose egg.

When I feel nothing, I exhale. "Exaggerate much?"

"It was huge before, you should have seen it," she blinks and smiles.

"I bet." I pull her in for another kiss, and she giggles against my lips. "Let's go, I'll walk you back to your room and then you can come meet me at mine when you're ready."

We walk hand-in-hand across the hot sand toward the resort. Her co-workers are rowdy and laughing near the pool bar, and as soon as we walk past them, loud whispering commences. Several of the girls cover their mouths, and the guys watch Giselle closely. I can only imagine the gossip that began once The Tool got rejected by her. Now they're all wondering why they didn't know Giselle had a boyfriend and where I've been the past few days. I smile at the group and pull Giselle closer to my side as their jaws hang open. I can only hope I'm not recognized for who I really am, because it's been wonderful being completely incognito these past few days, and I'd like that to continue.

Giselle waves tentatively at the group as they watch us walk down the path to the rooms.

"That was awkward," I say.

"Yeah, especially since you told Liam you were my boyfriend. I'm going to have a lot of explaining to do when I get back."

"Which room are you?" I ask as we walk past the exotic birds that have nested along the trees on the walkway.

"Twelve-twenty."

"Really?" She's literally right next door to me. My suite is the last at the end of the building where it bends to provide privacy for the small dipping pool in the back.

"I'm twelve-eighteen."

"You really are stalking me," she jokes, and we walk down the path to our rooms.

"After you freshen up, put your suit back on. I have a pool, if you'd like to go for a dip."

"You just don't want me to put pants on, do you?" She jokes, and I laugh out loud. I remember the night I showed up at her house, and she answered the door in just panties and a long t-shirt. Giselle without pants is heaven.

"You're on vacation. Pants should be optional," I say as we stop in front of her door.

She swipes her key over the lock, and it disengages. I open the door to let her in, and she immediately looks embarrassed. "Don't come in, the room is a mess."

I crane my neck to see towels and clothes strewn all over the place, and I chuckle. I notice the PRIVACY tag hanging from her door and realize she didn't let housekeeping in. "You know, they can clean up after you."

"No!" She scolds. "I would never make someone clean up *that*." She points to the mess, embarrassed.

"You're too sweet," I say and kiss her cheek. "Come by in a half hour?" I suggest, and she nods.

She enters her room, and I hold my breath as she closes the door between us. I can't believe everything that's happened today. Listening to her tell her friend about how she felt, how I made her feel last night, sparked something in me that I can't quite grasp. I feel terrible that she thought I rejected her, and now I desperately need to prove her wrong. When that asshole hit on her, I had to put an end to it. She doesn't deserve someone like that in her life. She should be cherished, not treated like some hook-up at a corporate retreat.

But, am I doing the same thing? Treating her like a hook-up?

As I walk into my room, I hope I haven't made a colossal mistake inviting her here. She's walking into this eyes wide open, heart exposed. I'm afraid of destroying her beautiful soul. What if she wants more from me?

Can I give her more?

CHAPTER 20

Giselle
Present

HOLY SHIT. HOLY SHIT. HOLY SHIT.

What the hell am I doing?

My heart is pounding, and I feel dizzy. I sit on the bed and try to calm myself. Dax is waiting next door, and I'm over here freaking out like a teenager.

I realize he isn't making any promises to me, but his actions tonight speak volumes. He saved me from Liam, and even though I don't think he's as big of a tool as Dax does, it was amazing to know that our interaction sparked *something* in Dax. *Was it jealousy?*

I strip down and kick my cover-up and bathing suit into the pile of clothes in the corner of the room. I need to clean this place tonight when I get back. I haven't let housekeeping in to clean up because I'm completely embarrassed by how much of a mess I've made. It's now officially become a problem since I've run out of towels and wash cloths, and I'm dangerously low on toilet paper.

Lukewarm water washes the sand and sun from my skin, and I lather up. I swipe the razor from the ledge and make sure

I've removed all stray hairs from everywhere. My cheeks flush as my embarrassment from earlier is fresh in my mind. I can't believe Dax heard everything I talked to Mia about, including my shaving issues. *Holy hell.*

Once I'm out of the shower, I smooth my favorite pink baby lotion all over and look at myself in the mirror. My tan is completely lopsided. My legs are the only part of me that I've exposed to the sun. I have a clear stripe in the middle of my thighs, indicating the line of demarcation from where my cover-up reached. My hair is sun-kissed and wild. It's so dry from the salt air and sand that I've done nothing to tame it over the past few days. I don't bother trying to fix that and wrap it into a bun on top of my head. I'll fight that battle another time.

My face is dry, and I realize how little water I've had over the past few days. I'm terrified of getting sick, and I've been conserving the bottled water to brush my teeth with and add to my drinks when needed. I rub some coconut oil into my face, soothing the slight sunburn and let it absorb into my parched skin. It feels incredible.

Does he really want me to wear a bathing suit to dinner?

I stress out looking at the heaping pile of dirty clothes on my floor. I'm not sure what I have clean, and I don't know if wearing another bikini is a good idea. I open the dresser drawer and find my favorite bathing suit, and it's still clean. I hold it up and know it's the most revealing of all of the ones that I brought. I slip into it anyway, comforted that I have another cover-up that's clean.

He's expecting me any minute, and my nerves set in. I look at my reflection in the mirror again and smile. I have to go over there tonight with no expectations and walk away with no regrets. *No matter what happens.*

I swipe my hand along the spot on my leg that earlier today was covered in stubble. *Smooth.*

EPIC LIES

I'm ready. *I think.*

I KNOCK SOFTLY on his door, and it immediately swings open.

He's freshly showered and in a new t-shirt and swim trunks. The scent of Aloe Vera fills my nose, and I can't help but wonder if his sunburn is still bad.

"I'm glad you decided not to wear pants," he says as his eyes move from my feet up my body.

"You had me at 'I have a pool,'" I say and smile. He grabs my hand and pulls me into his room, letting the door shut behind me. He places a chaste kiss on my lips and pulls away.

"You look beautiful," he says.

I blush as I do every single time he compliments me on my looks. No one has ever said as many nice things about me as he has.

"This old thing?" I joke nervously, and he kisses me again. This time his lips linger, and his arms wrap around my waist. I suddenly want to slow down time and make every second that I have with him tonight count. I don't care what tomorrow brings.

I run my fingers along his forehead. "How's the lump?" I ask.

"Mostly gone, but it still hurts like a bitch," he says as I plant a kiss on the spot where I chucked my sunscreen bottle. He tightens his grip around me, and I realize I'm forgiven.

"Sorry about that," I say, and he laughs.

"You know I deserved it. I'm over it," he says and looks into my eyes. "Or, am I?"

"Maybe I should leave," I joke, pretending to head toward the door. "I certainly don't want any retribution."

His eyes become serious, and he stares into mine. "You have nothing to worry about." His mouth covers mine as his hands move from my hips to my face. I inhale as he kisses me softly, fingers tangled in my wet hair.

"You smell good," he says as he reluctantly pulls away from me, but keeps hold of my hand. He pulls me into his suite, and I'm in awe.

"Your room is ten times the size of mine. And we're right next door to each other," I say in disbelief. This room is totally amazing. The patio has four huge glass doors that open up to a private pool. He called it a 'dipping pool' earlier today, but it's much bigger than that. You could legitimately swim laps in this thing and get a workout. His bedroom is to the right and has two wide doors that are open, leading to it. Another set of glass doors takes up one entire wall in there. "Amazing," I say, and he smiles.

"I had no idea I'd get put in the Presidential Suite," he says modestly. "My manager must know someone to pull strings for me."

"Right," I say as he releases me. I walk through the room and see the dining area to my left. The table is set with beautiful china. "I thought you said this was going to be casual?"

"They've been good to me so far. When I asked to be set for a private and romantic dinner tonight, they took me very seriously."

"I see…" *Romantic.* "You do romantic?" I joke.

"You have no idea," he says, and for the first time I can see how serious he is. His eyes pierce mine, and I feel his energy. If he asked me right now to do *anything*, I would.

"Is there a menu for tonight?"

"It's already taken care of," he responds and walks over to the wet bar by the patio. "Wine?"

"Yes. Red please."

He points to several bottles lined up, and he raises his eyebrow. "Cabernet, Shiraz, or Pinot Noir?"

"Pinot."

He grabs two stemless glasses and fills them both half-way. He walks back over to me and places one of the glasses into my hand; his fingers linger on mine.

"To new beginnings," he says and softly clinks his glass into mine. I nod and sip from my glass quickly. I don't want to jinx his toast.

He leads me out onto the patio, and I see exactly what he told me earlier today. It's totally and completely private. A thick hedge runs around the perimeter of the pool with bamboo trees stacked inside of that, taller than most of the surrounding trees. Candles float in the pool, their flames reflecting off of the small ripples caused by the warm breeze. This is literally the most romantic setting I've ever been in.

"It's beautiful," I say, and take another sip of my wine.

He pulls me over to the lounge next to the pool. It looks exactly the same as the ones we've been spending our time on out at the beach, except there aren't privacy curtains hanging on the sides. We sit, and he doesn't let go of my hand.

"So, I didn't exactly start off on the right foot with you," he says, and I want to stop him. I feel like he has an apology coming, and I don't need it. I'm over it all. I just want to move forward.

"But–" I say, and he raises his hand to stop me from interjecting.

"Just listen," he says gently.

I nod.

"I don't have the best track record when it comes to relationships. I've been lied to, cheated on, and left heartbroken far too many times. I don't trust easily, and I haven't loved anyone for years. My heart is jaded and damaged." His tone is serious, and my own heart sinks for him. I have so many of these feelings myself, but I hold them close.

"Something happened that day you saved my life," he continues. "I don't know what it was, but when I saw you wave to me from your car, I knew something was about to change. I still can't put my finger on it, but when my bike got demolished by the fire truck, I knew you changed my history. My existence. I've been fighting my feelings for a few weeks. I'm struggling with what you mean to me. I know we've only known each other for a short time, but I feel like I've known you my whole life." He pauses and searches my face for a response.

I'm in awe. I never expected to hear any of this from him, or anyone for that matter. "I don't know what to say."

"Say that you feel the same way," he requests. Demands.

"Yes," I say breathlessly. I can't deny the connection that I've felt to him since the second he fell into my car, when he was anonymous to me. He wasn't *the* Dax Anderson. He was just a stranded cyclist in trouble. A stranger, *but something more.*

"I'm sorry for the way I've behaved, and I apologize in advance for how I'm going to behave. I don't trust easily, and my first instinct is to think I'm being lied to."

Me too.

"I can understand that," I say. "I've been lied to enough times in my life to recognize when it's happening again."

"You don't think I'm lying now, do you?" he asks, worried.

"No."

There's a soft knock on his door, and he stands up, grabbing my hand and pulling me through the doors into the dining room. "Dinner's here."

Several staff members roll in trays of food. They place everything on the table quickly and efficiently and then leave.

So many different scents and flavors fill the room. "Wow, it all smells so delicious," I say and walk toward the table.

We sit, and he uncovers plate after plate. "I ordered two of everything," he says, and my mouth waters.

There's even a plate filled with French toast, potatoes, bacon, and eggs. "The all-day breakfast," he says, and I immediately reach for that plate.

"I can't resist bacon." I bite into a crispy piece. "So good." It's literally the best piece of bacon I've ever eaten, perfectly crispy and salty.

He grabs the same dish and sprinkles some pepper over the eggs. "I have to admit, this is exactly what I wanted for dinner."

We both smile as we dig into our all-day-breakfast platters.

"I want to know everything about you," he says with a mouth full of French toast, syrup glistening on his lips.

"Two truths and a lie," I say, and he raises his eyebrow.

"What?"

"I tell you two truths about me and one lie. You need to figure out which is which, and then it's your turn." It's a hokey game we played during one of our ice-breaker sessions this morning, and I found out things about my co-workers that I never expected.

"Okay, you go first," he says and takes another huge bite of his food.

Shit. Now I'm on the spot.

"I'm waiting." He smirks and takes a sip of his wine.

I wrinkle my nose. "Wine and bacon?"

"Yup."

"Okay. Two truths and a lie," I repeat. Now I'm nervous.

He raises his eyebrow.

I take a deep breath. "I'm terrified of sharks. I have a fake tooth. I'm double-jointed."

"This is easy," he says, smirking.

"You're terrified of sharks, TRUTH." I nod.

"You're double-jointed, TRUTH." I smile and shake my head from side to side.

"What?" he says in disbelief. "You definitely *don't* have a false tooth."

"Yes, I most certainly do," I say and open my mouth, turning my head to the side. I pull back my cheek and show him. "Lower right, first bicuspid. It got knocked out when I was thirteen while playing football with the boys from my neighborhood. I got pushed into someone's elbow."

He laughs and shakes his head. "You mean you're not double-jointed?" he asks, disappointed.

"Nope."

He finishes his wine and refills my glass, then his.

"Was it two hand-touch, or tackle football?" he asks.

"Tackle. Is there any other way?" I gulp down a mouthful of wine and say, "Your turn." *Wine and bacon isn't bad.*

He scratches his chin and says, "Two truths and a lie. Hmmm."

His eyes suddenly flash, and I'm excited for what I'm finally about to learn about him.

"I snore. I've run six half-marathons. I'm addicted to ABC Family movies."

I laugh out loud. "This is going to be easy," I tease.

"Then go ahead and guess," he says, folding his arms over his chest.

"You've definitely run six half-marathons. TRUTH." He nods. I know a runner's body when I see one.

"And you totally snore, so TRUTH," I say proudly.

He shakes his head and says, "Wrong."

"What? Don't all guys snore?" I ask, and he shakes his head again.

EPIC LIES

"I've never been told that I do." *Easy way out.*

"You haven't run six half-marathons?" I ask, confused.

"Yes, I told you that I have."

"Shut up. There is no way that you love ABC Family movies. Nope. Not true." I shake my head, refusing to believe he has a soft and mushy side to him.

"Especially the ones that come out during ABC's Twenty-Five Days of Christmas. I mean, have you seen *Holiday in Handcuffs*?" he says.

He's freaking serious.

"Umm, yes," I admit. "It's one of those movies that I'll watch again and again and again. Every single time it's on. In fact, it's still on my DVR from last Christmas," I admit. "Mario Lopez and Melissa Joan Hart's chemistry is…"

"Hilariously painful," he finishes my sentence, and I nearly choke.

"Yes!" I laugh.

"Your turn again," he says and wipes his mouth. His plate has been cleaned, and I can tell he's contemplating digging into what looks to be chicken francaise.

"Hmmm," I muse. *What can I trick him with?*

"I'm training to run a half marathon. My feet are a size twelve. I was in an anti-gas and diarrhea commercial two years ago."

"Really?" he asks. "These are the choices you give me now?" He raises his eyebrow and stands up, walking toward me.

"You're definitely training for a half marathon. I saw you running the other day on the beach, so I believe that one. TRUTH," he says.

I nod and smirk, "You have to stop stalking me."

He's closer now, and I tense up in my chair a little bit. *What is he up to?*

176

"Before I take another guess, I need to do some research." Suddenly, my chair is pushed out, and my bare leg is in the air. He slides my flip-flop off, and I squirm in my seat, curling my toes as he runs his finger from my heel to my big toe.

"That tickles!" I screech, and his face remains serious.

"There is no way this foot is a size twelve. Not a chance. LIE." He positions himself between my legs, still holding my foot in the air. "And I see you got that spot you missed," he says, kissing the stubble free spot on the inside of my ankle.

"You're right," I say as he kisses a trail up the inside of my calf to my knee.

"I want to hear about the gas commercial," he says, pausing to look up.

I don't want him to stop. His lips are so soft on my skin. He kisses my knee again, and he kneels down in front of me, his hands wrapped around my thighs.

"What do you want to know?" I ask, and I realize I'm panting. His lips travel to the inside of my knee, and he looks up at me again.

"Tell me about the commercial? What did you do in it?" His warm breath fills the space between my thighs, and I squirm again.

"Ah, I umm…" He drapes his arms over my thighs and places his chin on his hands, grinning.

"I'm waiting," he says.

"I was involved in this ad campaign, and the actress didn't make it to the shoot. She got sick, or something like that. The director pulled me aside and begged me to step in. So, I did," I say, embarrassed. It was the most awkward thing I've ever done. I felt like a robot in front of the camera. They shot the commercial, and it aired only five times before it was pulled—it was that bad. I'm lucky I didn't get fired from my job.

"Oh yeah?"

I nod.

"What were your lines?"

I blush and shift from side to side. He holds my legs gently, but firmly in place.

"I'm not telling you," I state.

"Then how will I know this is a truth?" He smirks and raises his eyebrows.

"Fine," I say as his fingertips softly tickle the insides of my thighs. I inhale deeply and say, "Gas-Be-Gone: It plugs up the source of your gas leaks." I shake my head and realize I never should have revealed this to him or anyone for that matter.

He laughs so hard that he falls backward onto his ass. "Holy shit, that's hysterical."

I close my legs and cross them, folding my arms over my chest.

"I'm glad you think so. It's not so funny when my dad has it recorded on his DVR and plays it over and over and over again."

"I bet it's fantastic!" he says and runs his hand up my calf. "I think I like your dad."

He stands up, grabs my hands, and pulls me to my feet.

"I don't want to think about gas anymore," I say.

"Me neither," he says, his grin turning serious.

His fingers prop my chin up, and he kisses me. "You have syrup here," he says his lips over mine. "And here." His tongue darts out and licks the corner of my mouth. "And here."

His assault on my lips continues, and I pull him against me, his hands grab my hips and he makes sure I'm firmly held in place.

"I want you to spend the night," he says, his mouth against my ear. I tense up a little, realizing this is the beginning of a one-night stand, something that I told myself earlier that I'd be okay with, but now I'm unsure.

"I don't think that's a good idea," I say, nervously.

He pulls away and looks into my eyes. "Whatever you want. No pressure." He doesn't look angry or disappointed, and I see genuine concern on his face. He's not in this for the conquest, and I'm relieved.

"It's been a while," I say, embarrassed. "I don't normally jump into someone's bed that I just met."

He kisses my nose, then my chin. "Neither do I," he says, and I believe him.

"It's your turn," I say against his lips.

"What?"

"Two truths and a lie," I remind him that we're still playing our game.

He smiles and pulls me against him.

"I love clown feet. Flip-flops turn me on. Honesty turns me on even more."

I laugh against his lips and push my fingers through his hair.

"This is easy," I say as I kiss him.

"Then go for it," he says.

"There's no way you love clown feet, so LIE," I say, and he pushes me against the wall in the dining room.

"Nope. I totally would have sent you packing if your feet were really a size twelve," he says grinning, his arousal pressing between my legs.

"Some women can't help that they have enormous feet," I say as I press against him, letting him know I can feel him.

His lips leave mine and travel past my jawline to my neck. "God, Giselle, are you sure?"

"Sure about what?" I pant.

"About not staying the night?"

"No–I mean. I'm not sure." His lips find mine again, and his tongue plunges inside my mouth. He lifts my legs up around his hips and presses my back into the wall. The pressure he's applying against me causes me to moan loudly into his mouth.

"Are you sure now?" he asks, and I moan again. His hips swirl into mine as his hard length puts the perfect amount of pressure on my–

"Ohhhh," I gasp as a tingling sensation travels from my center to my belly button. *"God."*

"Yes," I say. "I'll stay. Please. I'll stay." All other coherent thoughts leave my head. He carries me out of the dining room and through the main part of his suite until we're in front of his bed.

"Really?" he asks, pulling away from my mouth for a moment.

"Yes."

He places me on the bed and removes his t-shirt and swim trunks before I can breathe. My cover-up is pulled over my head and tossed over his shoulder. He's hovering above me, his eyes fixated on mine. I untie my bathing suit top and let it fall away from my breasts, the ceiling fan above immediately causing me to shiver, my nipples hardening. His fingers loop into the sides of my bikini bottoms, and he pulls them down as he takes in the vision of my naked body. I immediately try to cover my body, blushing.

He pushes my hands aside and kisses by belly, working his way up to my breasts. "You're so beautiful," he mumbles as his lips trace my nipple. I gasp again as he teases it with his tongue. His fingers find their way between my legs, and he slowly massages me, causing a sensation to travel from his fingers to my chest and back again. A ripple of pleasure quakes through my body, and I inhale deeply and loudly. "Dax."

"What do you want?" he asks as one, then two fingers slide into me.

I can't respond.

"Giselle?" he says as he covers my nipple with his mouth, teasing it once again with his tongue.

"Please," I pant.

He reaches for the drawer in the nightstand and pulls out a condom. "Are you sure?" he asks. I hear the package tear open, and I press my hips into him. I want this so much.

"Yes."

He rolls the condom over his length, and his lips meet mine again. "I want you," he says against my lips. I move my hands to his hips and pull him toward me so he's at my entrance. I open my eyes and look into his as he slowly pushes into me. I gasp as his initial thrust spreads me open and he fills me.

"Are you okay?" he asks, slowing down his motion.

"Yes, it's been a while," I admit, embarrassed.

His eyes are now filled with lust, as he realizes that he's in recently uncharted territory. He speeds up his movement and swirls his hips against mine. Our lips collide and tongues entwine. He plunges in and out of me with purpose, each time he pulls out, he slides against my bundle of nerves and back in again. I'm shaking under him, devouring his mouth, pulling him against me tighter but releasing him each time he pulls out and sweeps over my most sensitive areas. My legs quiver, and I gasp for air. I'm burning between my legs, a good burn. A *great* burn. My release is building, and he sweeps and plunges one last time as I completely fall apart underneath him. Quakes of pleasure rippling through my body, and I can't breathe. "Oh. My. God," I pant, almost incoherently. He buries himself as deep as he can go as his body stiffens with his own release, his forehead resting against mine.

"Holy shit," he says, completely out of breath.

As our breathing begins to slow, so do our coordinated movements into each other. His hips briefly rest on mine until he pulls out of me completely. He kisses me passionately before he gets up to go to the bathroom. *What just happened?*

I honestly don't remember the last time I had sex and it felt this good. All of this feels so good.

Maybe too good.

As he's in the bathroom, I reach around for my bathing suit and cover-up. I'm patting the bed, looking for them, when he walks out of the bathroom. "What are you doing?" he asks, concerned.

"Trying to find my clothes," I say. "I should go…"

He slides into bed next to me and pushes my clothes onto the floor. "I asked you to spend the night," he reminds me as he wraps his arms around my waist.

"You were serious?" I ask, surprised. My heart pounds in my chest.

"Yes, I was serious," he says. "All truths. No lies."

He pulls me against him and drapes his leg over mine. "I've extended my vacation until Friday, will you stay with me?" he says into my neck, kissing the tip of my collarbone.

"Yes," I say, without thinking. I have no idea what I'm getting myself into, but his words ring in my head.

All truths. No lies.

CHAPTER 21

Dax
Past
Age 24

"MMM, YOU SMELL GOOD," Natalia purrs against my chest, and I wrap my arms around her tighter. "I smell like you," I say as I kiss the top of her head. "And sex."

"I like that smell on you," she says and slides out of bed. "What was so urgent that you had to leave this afternoon?" She turns the shower on and walks back to the doorway. She's naked. And perfect. And mine.

"Alex needed a ride to the airport," I answer. From what I just found out from him, it's going to be a very interesting trip. Potentially dangerous. When he finds her, *if* he finds her, she's got a lot of explaining to do. I'm on the fence about whether I want to see things work out for them. They both deserve so much. But do they deserve each other?

And, for the first time in months, I finally came clean to someone today about my relationship with Natalia, and it felt great. I admitted to Alex that she and I were together, and he didn't seem bothered by it in the least. Now that it's out in the open, I can finally tell her how I really feel. *I'm in love with her.*

She places her hand on her hip and tilts her head, her long hair falling over her breasts. "Is he okay?"

I shake my head, "I don't know. Something's going on with Tabitha, and he went after her." I am worried about him, which is a constant thing these days. Growing up together, I always looked out for Alex. Not that he always needed protection, but he needed to know that I had his back. I'll always have his back.

"Where did she go?"

"Oregon."

"Wow," Natalia looks confused. "I don't know why he's remained so loyal to her after all of these years. After all she's put him through." Natalia only knows the few things I've told her about Alex and Tabby, which admittedly weren't all good things. They've been through a lot, and neither of their lives has been easy. In fact, they've both been through things that would drive the average person into a tailspin. I respect them both and love Alex like a brother. I hope he knows what he's getting into when he finds her.

"They're—complicated," I say and toss the sheet to the side.

She turns and walks back into the bathroom. "Show me any relationship and I'll find ways to complicate it," she laughs. Natalia is one of a kind. Beautiful. Confident. Cunning. Yeah, she could give someone a run for his money.

"What do you mean by that?" I ask as I follow her into the bathroom. She's already in the shower, and I can only see her sexy silhouette through the steamed door.

"I can find the one thing in any relationship that can tear it apart. Piece by piece."

"Can you?" I lean against the wall and fold my arms over my chest.

"Of course, Dax. Everyone has flaws. I'm good at finding them, and exposing them, if I need to." She's the opposite of me, and I don't like her tone.

"So, you're telling me that you would *purposely* try to destroy someone's relationship if you knew something private or secret?"

Her laugh echoes in the shower stall. "Of course not. What kind of person do you think I am? I'm just good at knowing where to look to uncover secrets. And lies."

I slip my boxer briefs off and open the shower door. "Really?" I say from behind her as I step in, and I wrap my arms around her perfect body.

"You and me. We're lying every single day," she says and presses her back into my chest. She's right. We've been hiding our relationship from everyone, especially Garrett.

"We'll tell him, eventually." I say. I cup her breasts and flick her nipples. She gasps and reaches behind her and between my legs, stroking me roughly. I spin her around and lift her so I can enter her quickly. I plunge into her as I press her back into the shower wall, our bodies move together perfectly.

"I like it the way it is," she pants and bites her lip. "I like hiding and sneaking around with you. It's hot." She grabs onto my shoulders and pulls me toward her, as if she's trying to control my pace. I drive deeper into her and squeeze her ass. She wants it hard, and she wants it quick. I follow her cues and thrust faster. She bites my neck and moans. "God, Dax." One of her hands leaves my shoulder, and I feel it move down my abs near where our bodies are joined. She helps guide my length into her deeper, and then moves her hand between her legs, speeding up her own climax. She quivers around me, and I explode inside of her.

I gently ease her off of me and hold her close until her feet are firmly planted on the shower floor. Her eyes are heavy and seductive. "You always know what I want, baby." She kisses me deeply, but I feel disconnected. I can't get her words out of my head.

"You want to keep us a secret?" I ask in disbelief. She finishes rinsing and turns the water off.

"I think it's best for everyone, don't you think?" she says and brushes past me. She wraps a towel around herself and leaves the bathroom.

"I'm sick of hiding out, Natalia. That's all we do."

"Hiding out is fun. What we just did was fantastic. Last night was amazing!" she yells from the bedroom.

I grab a towel and dry myself quickly, tucking it around my hips and follow her voice.

"I'm in love with you, and I want everyone to know." Her face freezes, and she looks sad. I've never told her this, and I'm surprised by my own admission.

"It just can't be like that, Dax." She dresses quickly and pulls her hair into a bun. I'm tense and worried where this conversation is leading us. She waves her hands between us. "This, right here, will destroy too many relationships. We are a secret that shouldn't be let out. Your band means more to you than life. They're your brothers. I'm just temporary."

"What the hell? *Temporary?* You're talking crazy! Do you not feel what I feel? Is this not real?" I yell and storm toward her. She stands firm and raises her hand.

"Don't do this, Dax. We have a good thing, you and me. This is a good thing. Why mess it up by bringing other people into our private lives?" Her voice softens to her familiar purr. "Don't you want me all to yourself?"

"That's besides the point. You know I love having you here with me as much as possible, but hiding and lying to everyone is something I didn't agree to long term. Garrett will have to deal with this out in the open. He's a big boy. He can handle it."

She looks down at her feet and shakes her head. Her phone rings from behind me, and I swipe it off of the dresser. As I hand it to her, I see the Caller ID. "Who's Edward?" I ask as she snatches the phone from my hands and silences the ring.

She slides the phone into her back pocket and walks past me. She turns and makes eye contact with me before she leaves the room. She looks sad and guilty. My chest tightens as her lips begin to move, and I suddenly realize that she's been lying to me for months.

"He's my husband."

CHAPTER 22

Giselle
Past
Age 21

THE SUN WARMS MY CHEST as Mia snores on the blanket next to me. She's completely hung over, and if I have to admit, so am I. We graduated from college last week, and our summer vacation has begun. I have six weeks off before I start my new job as an entry-level marketing associate.

She rolls over and opens her eyes. "I love it here," she murmurs.

"Me too," I say. I reach for my tank and pull it over my head. The spot between my boobs feels sunburned. "Shit, I didn't put on enough sunscreen." I grab the bottle off of the blanket and rub some onto my chest, shoulders, and arms.

"When are you parents coming down?" she asks.

We're at our summer rental, which we started early this season. My parents knew I'd have some time between school and work, so they signed the lease starting on May 1st.

"They'll be here next weekend."

"So, we have the place to ourselves until then?" She smiles and stretches. "I'm going back to sleep." She rolls over and is out within minutes.

I prop myself up on my elbows so I can look out at the waves. A few surfers waiting for the next big swell and a few people are scattered throughout the beach. I'm going to suggest we start our summer rental before Memorial Day every year from now on. This is awesome. Plus, the bars aren't yet filled with meatheads, and there's no wait at any of the local restaurants. We truly do have this place to ourselves.

"This is heaven," I say to a sleeping Mia, and watch as one of the surfers attempts to catch a wave. He rides a small swell in and abandons it half-way. His friends are shaking their heads, mocking him for jumping the gun. They've been out there for about an hour just floating and waiting. The water is still cold for this time of year, and they're all wearing their wetsuits. Before Mia fell asleep, she was rating them on their looks and presentation. She likes 'Tall Guy' who fills out his wetsuit very nicely, according to her. She plans to talk to him when they finally come in, and I'm on alert to wake her up as soon as that happens.

My phone rings from my beach bag, and I reach in to find it. When I pull it out, I smile. "Hi, Mom," I say.

"Giselle, how are you? Your father and I were beginning to get worried, we haven't heard from you in a few days." She feigns worry, but I can hear the smile in her voice.

"We're good. You don't have to worry about us."

"What have you been doing?" she asks.

"Right now, we're on the beach. It's an absolutely perfect day, you should see it."

"Your father has been keeping up on the weather on his phone," she says, and I hear my father's voice in the background. "It's going to rain between four and five, and then it will be nice the rest of the week. There's a quick clipper coming from the west." He can't help himself. I laugh.

"Did you hear that, honey?" my mother asks.

"Yes, I heard."

"You still have a few more hours on the beach before the rain comes," she says. "Are you two eating okay? Do you have enough food?"

"Yes, we ate at that Italian place on Ocean Avenue last night. It was amazing."

"Oh? They changed owners last year. Your father will be happy. You know how much he loves his chicken parmesan."

Their lives literally revolve around weather, traffic, and food. In that order.

"Are you girls behaving yourselves?" she asks, and I know what she really means: *is Mia behaving herself?*

"Yes, we are." Mia was a little out of control last night, but no more than usual. None of my mother's business, that's for sure.

"Oh good."

"See you and Dad on Saturday," I say, attempting to end the call.

"Wait, I wanted to let you know something came for you today. It was delivered just a few minutes ago."

"Yeah? What is it?" My curiosity spikes. I have no idea what it could be.

"It's a huge bouquet of flowers. The biggest arrangement I've ever seen," she says, excited.

"Really? Who is it from?" Now, I'm really curious.

"Do you want me to open the card?" she asks, and I'm surprised she already hasn't. She's nosy like that.

"Yes!"

"Okay, hold on." I hear an envelope being torn open and paper being unfolded.

"It's from Derek," she says and I hold my breath.

"Really?" I ask. I haven't spoken to him in almost two years, although he's attempted to apologize more than once for what he did to me sophomore year. I saw him at graduation, but avoided him.

"Do you want me to read you the note?" I'm sure she's already skimmed it, but this could be awkward. I never told her why we broke up.

"Yes, please." I hold my breath, my pulse races.

"Giselle, happy graduation. You'll always be the one that got away. I miss you."

I exhale.

"Did you hear me?" my mother asks.

"Yes, thanks."

"Are you okay? You know, your father and I always liked Derek. I wonder what he's doing now?"

Probably cheating on his current girlfriend.

"I have no idea," I say.

"What happened with him? If you don't mind me asking," my mother asks.

"Nothing. It was a long time ago."

"But, these flowers. They are gorgeous Giselle. You should see them. I'll take a picture with my phone and send it to you. Better yet, if they're still alive when we come down this weekend, I'll bring them."

"No. That's okay. I don't need them here."

"Are you sure? They would look great in the front room in that large picture window."

"I'm sure they'll be dead by then," I hope. "Don't bother, okay?"

"I'll just have to keep them on the dining room table then," she says, attempting to make me feel guilty.

"That's fine with me," I say. Then, they'll *definitely* be dead by the time I get home in a few weeks.

"See you Saturday. Tell Mia we said 'Hi,'" she says.

I hang up and toss my phone back into my bag. "Is your mom worried that I'm still a bad influence on you?" Mia groggily jokes.

"She only said that once, and to be fair, you *were* a bad influence on me that summer," I joke. We didn't get arrested after our antics, but my parents had to come pick us up at the police station in Belmar one night. It wasn't fun, and my mother had a long talk with the both of us about drinking responsibly, even if we were underage.

"Oh my God. I'm still so lucky she never told my mother about what happened." Even though Mia lives in Vermont, our families have become extremely close, our parents even going on vacations together. Last winter, they met in New York City and took a cruise to the Caribbean. She's like the sister I never had. *And like the cousin that I lost.*

"Yeah, that was a hell of a night. We're lucky we didn't get arrested."

"So, what did your mom want?" she asks.

"To tell me Derek sent me flowers."

She sits up straight, eyes wide. "What?"

"Yeah. I have no idea what that's about."

"Tell me."

"The card said something like 'I was the one that got away,'" I tell her.

"Oh. My. God. I knew he was still in love with you. I knew it!" She seems proud of herself.

"Stop it. Seriously. That was over years ago."

"He made a really bad decision, but I know how much he loved you."

"So, a chick just accidentally fell on his dick, kind of bad decision?" I laugh. "No, what he did was worse than a bad decision. He betrayed me. Lied to me. Fuck him."

She shakes her head. "What a shame. You would have made beautiful babies together," she laughs, and I slap her arm.

There's a lot of commotion happening behind us on the boardwalk, and we both turn around. There's a group of guys and a camera crew following them.

"Ooh, I wonder who that is?" Mia says, and we both crane our necks to see.

They stop about a hundred yards away, their backs to us. A short woman starts to arrange the group of guys while the camera man directs the shot. A bunch of girls runs past us on the boardwalk, and they're screaming. "Alex! Garrett! Oh My God!"

"Holy shit. That's Epic Fail," Mia says and stands up, shielding her eyes from the sun. A large bodyguard stops the screaming groupies in their tracks as the band poses for more pictures. One climbs the railing behind him and stands tall, his arms outstretched as if he's flying in the air. Laughter emanates from the group.

"How do you know?" I ask her.

"Garrett? Alex? Don't you know their names?" she asks as if I should know everything about them.

"No, not really," I say. I do like their music, though.

"We should go over there," she says.

"No way, I'm not getting caught up in that mess. I'll stay right here and watch your surfer dudes, thank you very much." I place my arms next to my sides and put my head back down onto the blanket. "Maybe I'll even take a nap."

"You're no fun," she says. "There's a group of hot rock stars just over there, and you want to sit here and stare out at those boring surfers."

Suddenly they're boring. I laugh, "You're a nut."

Tall Guy rides a wave in, and she perks up. "I'll be right

back," she says, wrapping her sarong around her hips. She runs toward the water and Tall Guy.

I shake my head and smile. She'll never change, and I love her.

I watch as the band and their crew walk down the boardwalk, toward where I'm sitting. A section of the boardwalk juts out to a gazebo, and the photographer sets up some lights and his camera underneath. They do another group shot and then several individual shots of each of them. One of them sits on the bench, facing the water, facing me. He kicks his legs out in front of him, the sea air blowing through his hair. He watches the waves, and I look at the photographer. *Do I need to move? I think I may be in the shot.*

I stand up and pull my blanket over a few feet to my right, looking back to make sure they know I'm getting out of the picture. The photographer waves his hand as if to thank me and nods his head. The guy on the bench is looking in my direction. He's about fifty yards away, so it's hard to tell exactly what he's looking at. I sink back down onto the sand, so I'm not in his line of vision anymore. They must have him purposely gazing out over the beach, to get a soulful, brooding shot. He seems to still be looking at me when I recline back down onto the blanket. The photographer scales the railing of the boardwalk and leans over as far as he can, getting a shot of him from a different angle.

After about ten minutes, the photographer and his assistant begin to pack up their gear. The guy is still sitting on the bench, and he slowly raises his hand in the air, waving at me. *Me?*

I tentatively wave back.

A dozen more screaming girls rush the group on the boardwalk, and their bodyguard ushers the band away. He turns his head and waves one last time.

That was weird.

Mia's racing back to where I'm sitting. "Dude, was he just waving at you?" she asks, out of breath.

"No, I don't think so."

"It sure looked like it. Oh my God!"

"Whatever," I say, laughing.

"Mark and his friends are having a party tonight. And we're invited!" she says, changing the subject.

"Mark?" I ask.

"Tall Guy. Mark."

"Oh," I chuckle. "Glad he has a name."

I lay back down on the blanket. "I'm not in the mood for a party tonight," I huff.

"Is it because of Derek? Don't let him harsh your vibe," she says as she morphs into her surfer lingo. It happens every summer. By August, she's learned at least a dozen new vocabulary words—surfer style.

"I just don't want to be reminded of that crappy time in my life, Mia."

"Then erase it!" she says.

"You know it's not easy for me. I'm afraid of what will happen the next time I open my heart to someone. I don't think I can handle it anymore."

"I believe in my heart you'll find that person. He's out there for you. He's the perfect guy, and he'll never stray. He'll treat you like his princess; it'll be like a real-life fairytale," she says, pulling me into a hug.

The surfers start to walk our way. The groupies chase after the band.

"You never know what's right in front of you," she says, kissing my cheek.

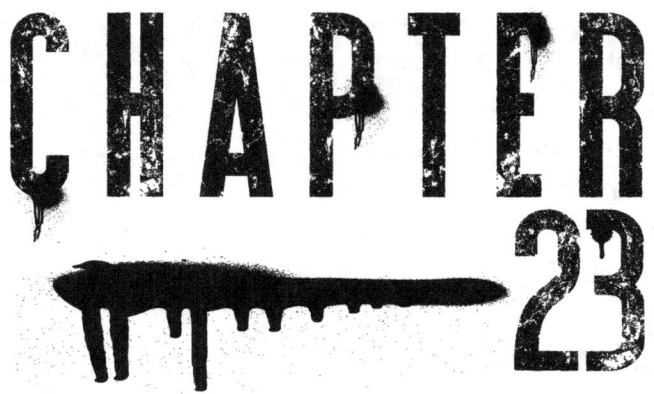

CHAPTER 23

Dax
Present

A WARM, NAKED BODY is pulled firmly against my chest, and I smile. Giselle smells like the perfect mix of baby lotion and coconut oil, and I have no idea how I even know what they smell like. It's hot, sexy, and amazing. I pull her against me tighter, and she begins to stir.

"Hey," I whisper into her hair. "Are you awake?" I press my length against her back, letting her know that I definitely am.

"No," she says, and I hear the smile in her voice. "I'm sound asleep." She fakes a yawn.

I kiss the back of her neck, where my nose has been nuzzled for the past hour. I woke up a while ago and just laid here with her in my arms, listening to her soft breathing. I replayed the events of the last few days, and I realize what a colossal jerk I've been. I was even a jerk when we were back home. She didn't ask anything of me and is genuinely worried about this being nothing. I can tell she's preparing herself for me to leave Mexico and never speak to her again. She's guarding her heart, and I feel bad. I want her to know I'm not like that. I'm not going to use her and toss her to the curb. I need to show her exactly what

I want and keep doing it to her, over and over again. I've been restraining myself from waking her up, but I need to be inside her, *now.*

"I hope you don't mind if I take advantage of you while you sleep," I grin. I slide my hand from her stomach up to her breasts, slowly teasing her nipples. She tenses against me and gasps.

"Who are you again?" she asks, joking.

"You'll remember in a minute," I say, parting her legs with my knee. Her leg is draped over the top of mine. I grab a condom and quickly slide it over me. She inhales deeply, and reaches behind her, helping guide me in to her warmth. I move slowly against her back, going as deep as I can. Her breathing quickens in tune with mine. From this angle, I'm able to easily reach the front of her, so I do and begin massaging her little bundle of nerves as I continue slowly pumping into her. She moans loudly and places her hand on top of mine, slowing my pace. "Too fast," she exhales. "Like this." I let her show me how slow she wants me to touch her, her hand pressing softly on top of mine. This has got to be the hottest thing ever. *Fuck.*

I nip at her ear and kiss the side of her neck while her hand on top of mine slows, then speeds up, then slows again. She's teasing me, and I love it. "Don't stop," she says and groans, "Oooooh."

"God, Giselle," I pump faster into her and almost lose it. It's such a different sensation, entering her from this angle. So much tighter.

She removes her hand from mine, and I rub her pressure point until she explodes around me, her walls convulsing, pulling me deeper inside. My own orgasm rips through me, and I erupt inside of her. She doesn't stop moving against me until she knows I'm finished. I slow down, and my length begins to twitch inside of her.

"Whoa," she says and rolls away from me, onto her stomach. "I think I need a nap after that."

I slide out of bed and quickly dispose of my condom. I grab the mouthwash from the bathroom sink, and quickly swish some in my mouth and bring the bottle out to her. I hand it to her along with an empty cup, so she can swish and spit. She sits up and looks at me funny, but does it anyway. "Ah, I needed that," she says and smiles.

I jump back on the bed and take her face between my hands, kissing her deeply. Mint swirls between our months and she pulls me against her, kissing me back. Our lips remain locked together as our tongues plunge into each other's mouths. This is the hottest post-sex kiss I've ever had.

"I wanted to do that when I was inside you, but I had the worst morning breath ever," I admit, and she smiles against my lips.

"It's so much better with mouthwash," she says. "My lips are tingling," she giggles, and I kiss them again. "I'm tingling everywhere." I'm lying on top of her, with the sheet as the only barrier between us.

"Where else are you tingling?" I ask and raise my eyebrows.

"You'll have to guess."

I pull her lips against mine and devour her all over again. "I know what I want for breakfast," she says against my lips.

"Me?" I joke.

"I want more bacon. And eggs. And French toast." My stomach growls against hers, and she giggles when she feels the rumble.

"I'll order right now. Don't. Move," I say as I roll off of her and dial room service.

I place the order and snuggle into bed next to her.

"No pants today. At all," I decree, and she giggles again.

"You're demanding, aren't you?" She turns on her side to face me.

"This is my room; I make the rules."

She stares into my eyes and looks like she's contemplating something. "What are the rules with us, Dax? Do we have any after we leave here?"

I brush the hair from her face so I can see her entirely. Her brows are furrowed, a line of stress forming on her skin between them. I run my thumb over it then down to her lips. "What do you mean?" I ask.

"When we get home, what are the rules?" The look of concern on her face grows.

"There aren't any rules. I don't make rules," I say, confused.

"No pants. That's a rule. You make rules," she reminds me.

"*Should* we need them when we get home?" I ask.

She closes her eyes, her face drawn. "I suppose we shouldn't." *Wait. She's thinking something she shouldn't be.*

"I know I want to see you again. As much as I can, when we're home. I go on the road in about two months, but I want to spend as much time with you as possible before I leave. And when I get back." Her eyes pop open, and her smile is back.

"Really?"

"What did you think I was going to say?"

"I'm not sure," she says as I kiss her softly on the lips.

"I'm sorry if you were expecting a one-night stand. I'm not that kind of guy," I say, smiling.

She breathes a sigh of relief, "Good."

"And I don't lie," I say, and her eyes glisten.

"I don't like liars," she says, very matter-of-fact. "They're the worst type of people." I know there's more meaning behind this statement, but I don't pry.

"I completely agree." I kiss the tip of her nose. "I think we're on the same page with that."

Her serious tone disappears, and she begins running her fingers up and down my arm. "Last night was amazing. This morning was–ahhh." Her voice trails off, and a smirk forms over her lips.

"Tell me," I say.

"What?" she asks, shyly.

"Tell me how much you liked it when I–" There's a light knock on the door.

"Breakfast," she smiles.

I slip into my bathing suit, pull a t-shirt over my head, and open the door. The delivery person rolls the breakfast tray out onto the back patio so we can dine by the pool.

Once he's gone, Giselle steps out from the bedroom, wearing nothing but her bikini. "Where's my cover-up?" she asks.

I look around, but don't see it. "Maybe on the floor in the bedroom?" I ask, hoping she doesn't find it. "Breakfast is outside." I reach for her hand and lead her out to the patio.

Our platters are on the small table next to the pool, and the food looks amazing.

She sits down, puts the cloth napkin over her legs, and waits for me to sit before she digs in to her food.

"Oh my God. The bacon gets better and better," she moans as she shoves a piece into her mouth. I love watching her eat. It's so fucking sexy. I remember the night in the bar when she ate French fries and a chicken sandwich, and she wasn't shy about it. I love it when a girl isn't afraid to show her love of food. Natalia used to order a salad for most of her meals and never finished it.

Why did I even think about her? Shit.

"I can't wait to take a dip in the pool after breakfast," I say, and she nods.

"I suppose that's just as good as a shower," she smiles.

"A shower can also be arranged." Now she blushes, and I love it. She can be a little brazen, but is reserved as well.

Breakfast is quick as we both devour our food, cleaning our plates. She wipes her mouth and quickly jumps up. "Last one in is a rotten egg," she chides and dives into the pool. She immediately pops up and screeches. "It's so cold. Cold. Cold. COLD!" She bounces up and down in the water, and I can see goose bumps on her arms.

I lean back, put my feet on the chair in front of me, and laugh.

"Get your butt in here, right now!" she demands, and I shake my head. She kicks her leg, and a stream of water covers me, soaking through my shirt. It's so cold, it's hard to believe we're in Mexico. I pull my t-shirt over my head and do a cannonball into the pool, practically on top of her. She screeches again as she tries to swim away from me, laughing.

"Oh, no you don't," I shiver and reach out for her. She tries to wiggle out of my grasp, but I pull her against me. "You didn't think you could soak me like that and get away with it, did you?" I say and quickly dunk her under the water, releasing her almost immediately.

She comes up, gasping for air, "Oh No you did NOT!" she yells and lunges for me, trying to push me under the water by the top of my head. I don't budge, and the frustration grows in her face. It's adorable.

"I can't help it if I'm stronger than you." I smirk. I'm suddenly swept off of my feet as her leg swipes at my knees, and they buckle. She uses that as her opportunity to dive on top of me, pushing me underneath her. My nose fills with water as I'm completely unprepared for her assault. I grab her waist and hold her still as I surface. "You know you're going to pay for that, don't you?" I say as water pours out of my nose, and I cough up some more.

Her laughing turns to cackles, and she's squirming once again in my arms. "Oops," she says and tries to swim away.

"You're not going anywhere," I say and pull her against me. I steal a kiss from her, and she relaxes into my arms. Her arms wrap around the back of my neck at the same time she wraps her legs around my hips. Just like last night when I had her up against the dining room wall, except this time, we're weightless in the water. More free to move against each other with ease.

My lips assault hers, our tongues once again twisted together. She moans into my mouth, and I know I need to get her out of this pool, now. I walk with her in my arms, her body pressing against mine, up and out of the pool, and drop her onto the lounge nestled into the corner of the patio. She's soaking wet, and I pull her bikini bottoms off, tossing them onto the patio with a wet flop. Her top is easier to remove and that, too, hits the ground quickly. Her eyes are wide and nervous. "Out here?" she asks softly.

"Yes," I say and run inside to grab another condom. When I return, I strip out of my swim trunks as she's trying to cover her nakedness with her hands. I shake my head, "I want to see you." She blushes and moves her hands away, exposing her breasts. She parts her legs slightly as I climb on top of her.

"Can anyone see us?" she asks, looking over my shoulder.

"No." The patio is very private. Lush landscape. I'm not worried.

She spreads her legs wider, making space for me to press between them. She gasps as I bury myself deep inside her in one thrust. She's already become accustomed to me, and we fit together perfectly. Amazingly. She throws her head back and pushes her hips up to meet mine, sealing the space between us. "Oooooh," she says, and her mouth opens as a whimper escapes her lips. I have to claim them again as I pull her mouth to me. I'm sucking, biting, and pulling her lips against mine, devouring her cries and moans. Her release comes quickly, feverishly. Her walls convulse around me, once again demanding me to follow suit. I drive deep one last time as I unleash my own powerful orgasm, ripples continue throughout my body, and my arms and legs become weak.

Our breathing begins to slow down, mimicking our bodies as they move against each other. I've never been with anyone like Giselle, she's completely taken all power and control from me. If she asked me to jump off a bridge, I would. I would do anything for her, if I could always see the look she has in her eyes right now. Sated. Seductive. Innocent. All blended together in a look that brings me to my knees.

I reluctantly pull out of her and rush inside to dispose of my condom. I grab a soft blanket from the bed and toss it over her as I slide onto the lounge next to her. Our bodies entwined, her head on my chest. I contemplate never leaving this place, keeping her here with me forever.

"What are you thinking?" she asks as she pulls herself tightly against my side. This is typically a question I dread. A question so many girls have asked in this same position with me. It's a question I've never answered truthfully, until today.

"That I never want to leave here. I want to stay here with you forever." I feel her smile against my chest.

"Oh." She kisses me above my heart.

"All truths and no lies," I say, kissing the top of her head.

She leans up, looking at my chest with a funny look on her face.

"What?" I laugh, suddenly self-conscious.

She's tracing the small tattoo over my heart, and my chest clenches.

"Why is the unlock code for my phone tattooed right here?"

she asks, pressing her finger into those numbers. The numbers that have been etched into my skin since high school.

"What?" I ask, confused.

"Zero-eight-two-four?" she says, her voice shaking.

"It's not your phone code, is it?" I ask, incredulously. That's when I realize why it seemed so familiar to me that day that I punched it into her phone.

"Yes."

"Well, it's been there for years," I tell her.

"Why? What does it mean?" she asks, panic in her voice, and I don't know why.

"It's a date. And it means something to me," I admit.

Her shoulders start to shake and tears threaten to spill from her eyes. *What's going on?*

"It means something to me, too," she says, sighing heavily.

"What?" I ask, needing to know.

She pauses as if she's not going to tell me, but continues. "It's my cousin's birthday. It's also the day she died," she says, tears flowing down her cheeks.

"Who's your cousin?" My chest is tight, and my pulse quickens. Now I know where I've seen her before. Now I know exactly how I know her. It's been bothering me from the moment I stepped into her car and made eye contact. I know her from years ago. *She* was there. At her funeral. *She* was the girl in the rose bushes. I ask her again, "What was your cousin's name?" I'm desperate, and I need to hear her say it.

"Her name was Lara…"

CHAPTER 24

Giselle
Present

"DID YOU SAY LARA?" Dax asks, and I nod, wiping tears from my eyes.

"Yes," I say. "I'm really sorry, I shouldn't have freaked out on you. It's just a date that means so much to me. It's a date that's happy, sad, and scary all in one. Crazy coincidence that you have it tattooed on your chest." I can't believe Lara's birthday, the day she died, and the day that Troy raped me is stained on his skin. My heart races, and I struggle to breathe. Memories of Lara flood my brain as well as Troy's sinister smile. A paradox of emotions rips through me, and I try to remain composed, but it's no use. My shoulders shake as sobs escape. I need to get control of myself. *What the hell is wrong with me?*

He's silent and tense underneath me, and now I feel bad that I cried all over him. He must think I'm an emotional wreck. "I'm not usually like this," I explain to him. "Say something," I beg.

He tightens his grasp around my waist and shakes his head. "I can't believe this," he says, covering his eyes with his free hand.

God. Why is this happening?

He's going to politely ask me to leave, and I'll never see him again. He doesn't need someone with emotional baggage triggered by a freaking date on a calendar.

I move to scoot off the bed and realize we're both naked underneath. "Can I get up so I can get my things?" I ask, embarrassed. I just want to get out of here and hide in my room.

He shakes his head, staring at me. "No," he says, and he almost seems choked up. *What's going on?*

"Dax, this is getting weird. I think I need to leave." Seeing Lara's birthday triggered something in me that I haven't felt in a while. I miss her so much, and I hate that she shares that day with my own inner turmoil. She was a year younger than me and was like my sister. *My cousin-twin.* There will always be a connection between us. Seeing that date on Dax's chest reminds me of all of that and more.

"We need to talk."

"I think I need to get dressed," I respond, and I'm really uncomfortable. I can't believe our little paradise is already crashing and burning. What happened to *all truths, no lies?*

"Giselle, do you remember me?" he asks, and I sit up, holding the blanket over my chest. I look at him, and now I'm completely confused.

"Where would I remember you from?" I ask. He was familiar to me that day, but it's because he's famous, *right*? This is an obvious question.

"Think," he says, and he doesn't let go of me.

"I have no idea," I say to him honestly. "I've seen you before, on TV and stuff, but–"

"When you were a teenager, the day Lara was buried," he says, waiting for my response.

"How would you know when she was buried?" I ask, my heart pounding in my chest.

"I was there."

How can this be? I'm so confused. I begin to sob as I remember that day. She was dead, and our family as we knew it was forever changed. I ran from the church, feeling tremendous guilt as the possible cause of her decision to stop all treatments. I was nauseous and had to get outside before I puked all over the aisle in front of everyone who was there celebrating Lara's life. There were roses, and thorns, and the Virgin Mary. And then I remember *him*, helping me when I was sick. His t-shirt cleaning the blood and puke from my face and body. His kind and concerned voice, speaking softly to me. *Dax?*

"You were there," I repeat his words in disbelief.

He sits up and places his hands on my shoulders, as if he's about to tell me something I don't want to hear.

"You were outside the church, bloody and throwing up in the rose bushes. I helped you." I freeze and hold my breath. *He was there.*

"Oh my God," I say and begin to tremble. "Why didn't you tell me?" I ask him.

"I didn't know who you were. Until now," he says, but doesn't let me go. His grasp on my arms tightens, and I can tell there's more.

"Why is Lara's birthday tattooed above your heart?" I ask, but now I know, and I feel sick.

"I was in love with her," he chokes out. *And she loved you.*

"You're Daxton," I say and realize I know much more about him than he realizes. He's Lara's first love. Her only love. She hid her symptoms. Lied to her parents. Lied to me so she could prolong her time with him, before treatments would begin again. When the doctors realized how far along her cancer had progressed, where it had spread to, she decided to forego treatment altogether. She wanted to spend as much time with him as she could. *With Daxton.*

How could I have not known?

He nods his head and closes his eyes. "I can't believe this," he says, and I pull away from him. He's disgusted now. He's been having sex with his dead girlfriend's cousin.

Fuck.

"I feel sick." I slide, still-naked, out of the covers and run into his room. I find my cover-up on the floor and pull it over my head, hiding my nakedness, hiding my shame and embarrassment. *I need to get out of here.*

He's standing in the doorway of his bedroom, blocking my exit. He's pulled on a pair of shorts, but his chest is still bare, and Lara's birthday screams at me from over his heart.

"Where are you going?" he asks, grasping me by my shoulders.

"This is weird, Dax. I just can't–"

He pulls me against him and kisses the top of my head. "You can't leave," he says, and I stiffen in his arms.

"What?" I ask.

"Hear me out, okay? Just promise me you'll calm down." He grabs my hand and begins to pull me into the outer room.

"I need more clothes." He stops and opens a drawer in his dresser, handing me a pair of boxer briefs. I slip into them and walk over to the door. I need to get out of here so I can attempt to process this insane coincidence.

"I can't," I say. "I need some air." He follows me and places his arms on either side of me, caging me against the door.

"We need to talk about this." Concern fills his voice as he grabs my hands.

"We'll talk. I promise," I say. "But, I–I just can't right now. Okay?" I pull my hands from his.

He shakes his head, "Don't run away, Giselle."

I laugh nervously. "Where would I go?" My chest tightens,

and I feel trapped. His eyes are pleading with me, but I need to leave.

"Promise me we'll talk. *Please*," he begs.

I nod, and he opens the door for me.

"I promise." I back out of his room and turn to walk quickly toward my own. I hear his door shut when I'm safely inside.

"Oh my God," I whimper as I lean into my door. Tears spill down my cheeks, and I grab my sides. *How is any of this possible? How is this even happening?*

"Lara," I cry, looking up at the ceiling, as if she's going to suddenly descend from the heavens. I need her now, more than ever, and I can't imagine telling her what I've been doing with her boyfriend. *Holy shit.*

I find myself once again apologizing to my dead cousin.

"I'm so sorry..."

CHAPTER 25

Dax
Present

I WAKE UP WITH A GASP, my heart racing. It's six-o'clock in the morning, and I realize I've only been asleep for a few hours. After Giselle left, I paced around my room for what seemed like forever. I went out into the walkway between our rooms at least a dozen times, trying to muster the courage to knock on her door and get her to open up to me. But instead, I treaded throughout my suite, crazy thoughts swirling in my head, trying to make sense of this whole predicament.

Yesterday with Giselle started out amazing. Every moment with her felt natural, like we were supposed to be together. Her smile, her lips, her body against mine. Complete perfection. Something I haven't experienced in a very long time.

And then…

Fuck.

After the realization set in, she bolted, and I can hardly blame her. This is so unbelievable. She's Lara's cousin, the one she looked up to all of her life. The one she confided in and trusted more than anyone. *Including me.*

A familiar jealousy rises as I remember how I felt when I

was a teenager, when Lara wouldn't tell me what was going on. She didn't trust me enough to allow me to *feel*.

I clench my fists on either side of me and inhale deeply. Lara died so long ago, and I have to remember, that in the end, she followed the path she wanted. As much as it destroyed me, I can't blame her for the choices she made. Thank God she had someone.

Thank God she had Giselle.

I rest my head on the headboard, a headache ripping through my skull. *Has she had enough time to process this? Have I?*

I want to see her so badly, it's killing me. We need to talk, to sort this whole thing out. We need to make sense of everything and figure out how to move forward. *Together.*

That realization grabs me like a vise. We've only known each other for a short time, yet, I don't think my heart can take the alternative. None of this makes sense to me, but the void in my bed is cold. I'm aching for her to be next to me. We fit together and I need to make sure we can get past this crazy revelation.

I swipe my phone from the bed and call Alex.

"Dax? Everything okay?" he says, his voice groggy. "It's five in the morning."

Shit.

"I'm sorry, I'll call back later," I say, forgetting about the time difference.

"Wait. I'm up. I'm up." He yawns into the phone, and I can hear him fumbling around. "What's going on, dude?" he asks.

"It's a mess," I say and wipe my hand over my face.

"What? Are you okay?" he asks, his voice firm and worried.

"It's Giselle."

"You need to start getting specific. You're scaring me." He laughs nervously. "Do I need to call Sonya?"

"No, nothing like that. Sorry, I didn't mean to be dramatic."

Sonya is the head of PR for the band and is used to getting calls from us when one of us has fucked up.

"Then what the fuck is going on? You're calling me at the ass-crack of dawn and being all ambiguous. Not cool."

I inhale deeply. "Giselle and I have met before," I say.

"Yeah. And? I know this already. You met when she saved your life, and you saw her again a few weeks ago at The Lounge. Old news." He sounds annoyed, and I need to bring him up to speed.

"She's Lara's cousin," I blurt out, and I hear him suck in air. "What?"

"Yeah," I say, bracing myself for what's coming next.

"Whoa."

Alex is silent as he contemplates the situation. His breathing slows, and I wonder if he's still there.

"Hello?" I ask.

"Give me a minute," he says, and I do.

After another long pause, Alex is back. "I don't know what to say. I mean, this is a shocker, right?"

"Yeah, obviously," I say.

"How did you not know they were cousins? Didn't you ever meet her when you were dating Lara? You must have, right?"

I shake my head. "No. Giselle's family didn't live near us. I remember Lara telling me that her cousin lived about an hour away, and the only time they really spent together was when their families rented a house at the beach every summer."

"So, you didn't know who she was?"

"Of course not. What are you getting at?"

"Dude, I know you. You're stressing out over a missed connection. Something that would have prevented you from doing anything with Giselle. A twinge of recognition that would have stopped you from pursuing her. Stop looking for it, it's not there. Take a deep breath and try to think of all of the reasons why Giselle *should* be in your life."

"It's not like I was *really* pursuing her," I say and realize that's exactly what I've been doing since she saved my life.

"Bullshit. You haven't been able to get her out of your head. You know it, and I know it."

"Maybe I couldn't get her out of my head because, deep down, I really did remember who she was. We met once, back then, you know."

"When?" he asks, confused.

"After Lara's funeral. Remember the girl outside?"

"Help me out here, that was so long ago, dude," Alex says.

"She was getting sick outside, in the bushes, remember?"

"Oh, the girl puking."

"Yes. That was Giselle."

"Holy shit."

"See? This is crazy, right?" My heart is racing. I need answers. I need to understand why this is happening.

"That's wild," Alex says.

"So, what do you think?" I ask.

"What do you want me to say? The two of you have somehow found yourselves together in more than one unlikely situation. Stop trying to figure everything out and just embrace it, dude."

He's right.

"Okay," I say and close my eyes.

"Can I go back to bed now?"

"Oh. Yeah, sorry. It's just–"

"Embrace it. Figure it out together. Go find her," he says.

"It's not that easy," I say.

"Nothing ever is." His words ring such a stark truth of reality not only for me, but for him. He had to fight for his relationship with Tabby, and it certainly wasn't easy.

"Thanks, man. Sorry for waking you up."

"Later," he says and disconnects.

No matter what brought Giselle and I together, we need to figure out if we can move forward.

AFTER A QUICK SHOWER, I walk out of my room and knock on her door. I feel bad trying to force the issue, but after my talk with Alex, I'm confident I can convince her to hear me out. She *needs* to hear me out.

She doesn't answer, and I put my ear against the door. I don't hear anything—no movement, no sounds coming from the room. *Where is she?*

Laughter drifts from the pool area, and I jog down the walkway. A group of people are standing, mulling around. Some drinking coffee, others holding notebooks and stacks of paper. They look familiar, and I recognize most of them as Giselle's co-workers.

Then I see her.

Her head is bowed down, her long hair covering most of her face. She's typing feverishly on her cell phone as she shakes her head. She looks miserable.

Fuck.

"Giselle!" one of the girls in the group yells. "Put that damn phone away, and let's go! You've been on it all morning. I can't imagine what's so important to tear you away from paradise." She giggles and grabs Giselle's free hand.

Giselle huffs and tucks her phone into her pocket. She follows the group of people away from the pool, toward the main building. I realize that I've missed my opportunity to steal her away so we can talk.

I walk over to the restaurant and sit at a table on the patio. A waiter immediately pours me a tall glass of orange juice and slides the menu onto the table.

"Coffee or tea?" he asks, and I shake my head.

Without looking at the menu I say, "I'll have scrambled eggs, bacon, and hash browns, please." He nods and quickly walks away.

I look out at the sea and listen to the waves crashing into the beach. The water isn't rough, but there's a constant flow of shallow waves rolling onto the sand. Crystal blue water reflects the early morning sunlight, causing me to squint. It's beautiful. Peaceful. Yet, I'm incredibly tense and preoccupied.

The scent of fresh bacon wafts into my nose, and I realize my breakfast has been placed in front of me, and the waiter has already disappeared. I bite into a warm, crispy piece of bacon, and remember when Giselle unapologetically devoured hers. She savored every single piece, smiling the entire time. It was the sexiest thing I've ever seen.

I swallow, wipe my mouth, and reach for my phone.

Me: We need to talk ASAP.

I hit send and nervously wait for her response. My foot is tapping uncontrollably under the table as I press my free hand against my knee.

After a few minutes, nothing.

Me: We aren't leaving Mexico until we talk.

I finish my breakfast and still nothing.

Me: Don't make me start stalking you—because I will ;)

Still nothing.

I re-read my texts and realize I'm being a pain in the ass. And creepy. I'm sure I'm only making this situation more awkward by spamming her with these messages. I need to back off and just be real.

Me: Sorry. I'll be here—whenever you're ready.

The waiter places the bill next to me, and I scribble my name. I grab my phone and walk back to my room.

My mind is racing with everything I need to say to her to convince her to give this a shot. Give *us* a chance. The pain of what we both went through with Lara somehow connects us, binds us. We were young and didn't know how to process the loss we both experienced. At least I didn't. Giselle seems strong and resilient. Maybe she can help erase my bad memories and help me come to terms with the loss I experienced so many years ago. Would it be fair to even ask her to help me?

The one thing that's clear is we've met again for a reason. We were supposed to meet. We're supposed to be together.

I'm tempted to grab a chair from my patio and sit outside on the walkway between our rooms, but I don't. She'll come find me.

She has to.

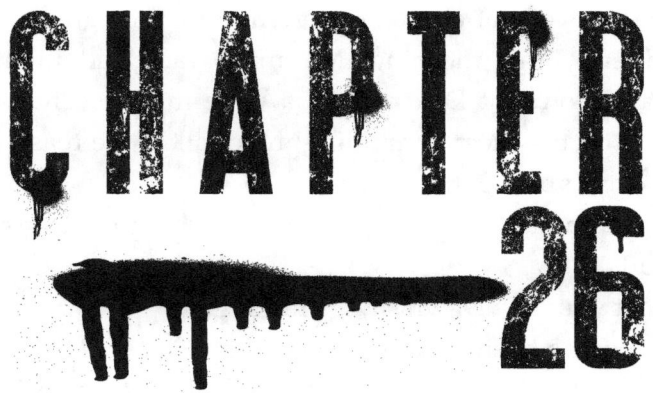

CHAPTER 26

Giselle
Present

"THANK YOU ALL for everything you do for our firm," Marilyn says as I shift in my seat. It's too hot, and I've barely paid attention to her speech that started over forty-five minutes ago. My bare legs are stuck to the chair beneath me, and sweat is pooled between my breasts. "I'm so pleased that you could all join me in paradise!" She raises her glass in the air and says, "Cheers!" The sound of applause and glasses clinking fills the air.

"She's seriously the best manager I've ever had," Dawn says.

I nod. *I need to get out of here.*

"What's with you today?" she asks. "Late night with the boyfriend?"

"Something like that," I say, feigning a smile.

"Why didn't you tell me about him?"

Because there's nothing to tell.

I shrug my shoulders. "I didn't think anyone would care."

"Well, that's one hell of a secret to keep, girl."

The irony of her statement doesn't escape me.

I didn't sleep at all last night, and our final group session started early this morning. My mind raced all night with the realization that Dax and Lara were in love. That date is stamped on his chest, reminding me of all of the reasons why we shouldn't be together. *Right?*

"I need a nap," I say as I stand, stretching my arms above my head.

"I bet you do," Dawn says, smirking.

"I'm going to sneak out of here, okay?"

"Sure, I'll cover for you. We're about done anyway."

"Thanks." I grab my things and peel my legs from the chair. Once I'm outside the conference room, the hot sun hits my face. *What time is it, anyway?*

I pull out my cell phone and turn it on. Marilyn was adamant that we turn off all of our devices when we entered the session this morning. As soon as it powers up, the screen fills with missed messages. Dax and Mia.

First, I scan Mia's messages and immediately call her.

"Hey!" she says after the first ring. "I've been trying to get ahold of you all day. You can't text me like that and leave me hanging. What the hell happened?" She sounds concerned and rightly so. I vague-texted her when I got back to my room yesterday.

"Let me get somewhere private so I can fill you in," I say as I walk across the resort, making a bee-line for the private lounges.

"Seriously, Giselle, you're really worrying me. You better tell me everything."

I reach the furthest lounge and scoot in, closing the curtains around me, and while it's not exactly private, at least I won't be seen. It takes me ten minutes to tell her everything that happened with Dax yesterday. She gasps when I tell her about his connection to Lara.

"Are you fucking kidding me?" she yells into the phone.

"I don't know what to think," I say, hoping she's going to tell me to run far away.

"Giselle, stay with me for a second, okay?" she says. "Hear me out."

Oh boy.

"Okay–"

"You know I don't get all hokey and shit, right?"

"Yes…" *Where is this going?*

"The first thing that came to mind when you told me about your connection to Dax is this is FATE working. Do you hear me? FATE."

"What?" I ask, confused.

"You and Dax. All of this was supposed to happen. You saving his life. Your chance meeting at The Lounge. You being in Mexico, together." She pauses, and I can hear her breathing excitedly. "Now, you suddenly find out about this crazy connection that you have? Seriously, Giselle. FATE."

"It's all a bunch of weird coincidences," I respond. She's grasping at straws, trying to make me feel better about this fucked-up situation.

"Bullshit," she says. "This is more than that, and you know it."

I want to believe her so bad. I want to buy into the whole 'it's meant to be' mentality, but it's so hard.

"Help me, Mia. I desperately want you to be right," I whimper.

"What's holding you back?" she asks.

"Seriously?"

"Tell me."

"Doesn't it bother you that he was in love with *my cousin?*"

"How many years ago was that?" she retorts. "Over a decade?"

"Yeah, so?"

"A lot has happened during that time."

"Right, but–"

"There isn't much you can say right now that's going to convince me that you shouldn't give Dax a chance," Mia says, cutting me off.

I squeeze my eyes shut as I lie on the lounge. "I don't want to convince you," I admit.

"Then what the hell is wrong?" she yells into the phone.

"I don't know," I admit. Everything about Dax just *feels so right*.

"I've seen changes in you since you met him. Since you saved his life," she says.

"What?"

"You've been different. Good–different. *Happier.*"

"Really?"

"Yes!"

"This is all moving way too fast," I say.

"The best things in life usually happen quickly...without warning."

"Literally," I laugh. Finding Dax stranded on the side of the highway was certainly without warning, and my escalating feelings for him has certainly happened quickly. *Too quickly?*

"Giselle, stop overthinking. I'm sorry for saying this, but Lara's dead. She's in Heaven. You're doing absolutely nothing wrong by seeing where things are going to take you with Dax."

"I just–"

"Stop!" she says. "Repeat after me. I'm. Doing. Nothing. Wrong."

"I'm doing nothing wrong," I say softly.

"I didn't hear you," she laughs.

"I'm doing absolutely nothing wrong." I smile, and for the first time in the past twelve hours, I know I'm right.

"Hang up on me right now and go to him."

My heart races, and I smile nervously.

"Okay. Bye." I disconnect.

Before I change my mind, I jump up from the lounge and jog across the beach, toward his room.

I KNOCK ONCE, and his door flies open. His bare chest is heaving as if he sprinted across the room, his hair disheveled. "Hey," he says, panting.

"Hey." I smile.

"I'm sorry," we both say at the same time. He laughs, and I relax a little bit.

"Come in?" he says, stepping aside.

"Okay." I walk past him into his room, and the door closes behind me. I feel him next to me as we walk toward the couch.

"I'm so glad you came," he says, relief in his voice. We sink onto the couch, my knee brushes against his thigh as I get comfortable. He doesn't move, but places his hand on my leg.

"I'm sorry I ran out of here yesterday," I blurt out.

He leans in and places a kiss on my forehead, his lips lingering. *It feels so good.*

"Please convince me that we aren't doing anything wrong," I beg. He pulls away, a confused look on his face.

"What?"

"What would Lara think?" Even though I've convinced myself that this is what I want, I need to be sure he feels the same way.

He shakes his head. "Lara isn't here."

"I know, but–"

He grabs my hand and pulls it to his lips. His eyes lock onto mine. "I've been thinking about our *situation* all day," he admits.

"Me too."

"I've been struggling for years trying to deal with, and understand, Lara's choice. *Her death.* I was a teenager when I found out about her cancer and that it was going to kill her. She lied to me for months. I was so angry that she decided not to continue treatment. I was angry that she wanted to die." He stops and chokes back a sob. His eyes are glistening, and this strong, confident man in front of me is about to buckle and fall apart. I squeeze his hand, and he takes a deep breath.

"Lara–was–extraordinary." He smiles, and I do, too. He pulls me against his side.

"She was." I wish I wasn't talking about her in the past tense. But then Dax and I–this is so fucked up. Guilt takes over my emotions, and I pull away from him.

"I'm not super religious, okay?" he says. "But, I truly believe there was a reason why I found you in front of the church after her funeral. And I know, deep down in my soul, that there was a reason why it was *you* who saved my life on that highway a few weeks ago." His eyes catch mine as tears fall down my cheeks. He reaches up and cradles my face in his hands, thumbs sweeping the tears away.

"Do you get it? Do you see it?" he asks. *Begs.*

"I don't know, Dax. This is all so…overwhelming," I sob. He pulls me against him and runs his fingers through my hair.

"I've been trying to put my finger on it over the past few weeks. But, I've had this overwhelming sense that you were there for a reason. I'd be dead if it wasn't for you. And I know that I wasn't supposed to die that day." His voice grows strong and confident. "Giselle, *you* were meant to save me. I don't know if somehow Lara made sure you were there, stuck in traffic, but the signs, the connections, they've been there hanging before us this entire time." He pushes me away to look into my eyes.

"You have to believe this. We were meant to meet. To know each other. *To be together.*" His voice is unwavering.

"I believe you," I say, choking on my sobs. I nod, and he kisses me softly, his fingers locked behind my head. "I've never been more sure of anything, Giselle. It may be a weird, crazy coincidence, but this is supposed to be. *We're* supposed to be. I feel it in my bones. In my heart," he says and places both of our hands over his tattoo–Lara's birthday.

I run my fingers over the date and close my eyes. *God, Lara, I miss you so much.*

He kisses me again, warmth spreading through my chest. "I'm so glad you found me," he says, kissing away my tears. "I haven't been the same since I lost her, but now I feel whole, and I didn't understand why until now." I gasp as his lips possessively take hold of mine.

"Dax," I cry against his lips. So many emotions are swelling through me right now. I can't get a grasp on them. Sadness. Grief. Guilt. *Love?*

Impossible. We've only known each other for a few weeks. I can't feel love. I won't let myself.

He kisses me softly and pulls away, looking into my eyes.

"Let's not freak out, okay?" he asks, smiling.

"I *am* freaking out." I've been freaking out since I ran out of here yesterday.

"I'm begging you. Please. Stop." His lips cover mine, and I melt into him. My tears stop flowing.

"Okay. Okay," I say. He kisses my eyes, my nose, and my lips again.

"I want to play a game," he says, and I tense up.

"What?"

"Two truths and a lie, with a twist. It has to be about Lara," he says, and his eyes glisten.

I cover my mouth. "I don't know—"

"I'll start," he says. "Ready?"

"Yes," I say, unsure.

He inhales deeply and smiles, his eyes bright.

"Lara was incredibly smart. She put everyone else before her, always. She loved asparagus."

Tears and laughter flow, and my heart warms.

"She was so freaking smart, TRUTH," I say and smile. My pulse begins to normalize, and my heart fills with love.

He nods his head, "Easy so far."

"There wasn't a person that she didn't put before herself, TRUTH." He kisses the inside of my palm and grasps my hand.

"I'll never forget the time she tried asparagus for the first time. Within five minutes, she had to pee, and was literally gagging in the bathroom from the smell!" I start laughing, and so does he. "So, to make it official, that's the LIE."

"You're good at this game," he says. "Have you played before?" He smiles and kisses me.

"Maybe."

"Your turn," he says, hugging me tight. I can feel his heart pounding against my chest, and I know this is just as hard for him as it is for me.

"Okay," I say and pause.

"Lara loved lavender. Everything about it. Her room smelled like it always. She was one of the most passionate and head-strong people that I have ever known." I pause and choke back a sob. *I can't think of a lie. Everything about her was pure and true.*

"And?" he asks, waiting for me to finish the game.

I take a deep breath.

"She was always the center of attention, demanding it even," I say weakly. This is the obvious lie, and I don't hide it.

Dax plays along and begins.

"She loved lavender so much, she thought it would be great to give me one of those diffusers, to keep me calm during final exams. I spilled it all over the place and on myself. I got a horrible rash and never told her about it. I was on steroids for two weeks because I was apparently highly allergic." He laughs and pulls me against him. "So, TRUTH. And don't tell me I'm wrong with that one. I have an epi-pen that proves it to be very true."

"Oh my God! She never told me about that!" I say, laughing against him.

"She didn't know," he tells me, and we both laugh. "I didn't have the heart to tell her."

"Her passion and determination were what I loved most about her," Dax says, and I perk up. "She was so smart. She was a year behind me in school, as you know, yet we were on the debate team together. We did a position paper and prepared a debate about the right to die." He pauses, and his voice changes. He clears his throat. I bury my head in his chest because I know exactly where this is going. She practiced this paper with me, and it's what convinced me that she had every right in the world to decide her own fate, especially with how bad the cancer had spread throughout her entire body. "During this debate, she convinced me, and more than four hundred people in the audience watching our debate, that every human being deserved to die with dignity. The entire auditorium stood on their feet, applause shaking the room."

"I know," I say. "I was moved to tears by it."

"You were there?" he asks.

"Yes, I was her sounding board. I needed to see how it played out. I was so proud," I say, wiping tears from my cheeks.

"She was admitted to the hospital three weeks after that speech," he says.

"Yes, I remember."

"That's when I found out what was wrong with her. She'd been lying to me for months about everything. I was so angry," he admits.

"She loved you, and she understood," I say. I remember the conversations I had with Lara about her boyfriend and how upset he was. But I always assured her that he was just in shock and would come around, eventually. "But, she wasn't exactly lying," I correct him.

"What do you mean?" he asks.

"Well, it's not like she lied to you. She just withheld the truth."

"Isn't that the same thing?" he asks.

"Not at all. One is done with malice. The other with love. She was protecting you."

His breathing changes, and he tenses against me.

"I don't think she ever knew how sorry I was," he says, and I pull him close. "She was in a deep coma by the time I finally told her it was okay to let go." I feel his tears on my forehead, and I lean over him, kissing them away.

"She knew," I say. "I promise you that she knew. You never needed to be sorry, you know that? She was never, ever, angry with you. As soon as you understood exactly what she was going through, that's when she knew you could let her go."

He sobs into my chest.

"You haven't shared your feelings about Lara with anyone, have you?" I ask him, and he shakes his head against me.

"You're the first," he says.

I breathe deeply and feel his strong arms around me. *Did Lara plan this? Is that even possible?*

"So, the last one's the lie, obviously," he says and laughs.

"Obviously," I say and kiss the tip of his nose.

"Wow, that was harder than I thought," he says, wiping the remaining tears from his cheeks. "Thank you for coming back," he says, kissing me again.

"I had no idea about this." I run my finger across his chest. "I'm still in disbelief."

"You said this date was also scary for you. Is that because of Lara's death?" he asks, concerned.

I tense up. The only person who knows about what happened to me that day is Mia.

"No." I turn away from him.

"What happened, Giselle?" he asks as he turns my face toward his. Tears spill down my cheeks one more time.

"I'm not proud of what happened that day," I say.

His eyes turn serious, and he looks scared. "Tell me," he begs.

"I was raped."

His eyes widen. "Who? When? What the fuck?" Rage melts over his face.

"He was my boyfriend at the time. I said no. He didn't listen. I blew off Lara's fifteenth birthday party, and it changed my life," I admit.

"I need to know who it is," he demands.

"No, it's over. I've handled it. Trust me. And it was a very long time ago." I say, but he doesn't waiver.

"Who is he?"

"Nobody." It's true—Troy is literally no one. He means nothing, and he apologized years ago.

"Giselle…"

"I'm serious. I took care of it. He means nothing to me, and he's fully aware of exactly what he did. Trust me, he's very sorry," I say confidently.

"He better be, because I swear to God, I *will* make him pay for what he did to you."

I fall against his chest and hold on tight. *Is this it for us? Can he move on with me?*

"I think I should go." I say and he immediately pushes me away so he can stare into my eyes.

"Are you serious?" he asks, and I flinch.

"Maybe?"

"Giselle, I have never said something so definitive in my life. I never want you to leave. Ever. Do you understand?"

I inhale and nearly cry. We've been through so much over the past few days, our connection so strong, yet oddly coincidental. I don't know what to think about all of this, but his actions tell me that we've got this, together.

"All truths, no lies?" I say, tears threatening to spill again.

"All truths, no lies," he repeats and pulls my lips against his. "No matter what," he adds.

So many familiar thoughts and words swirl in my head, but one thought in particular pops in that I can't shake. I wrap my arms around Dax and bury my head in his chest.

Thank you, Lara.

CHAPTER 27

Dax
Present

MY PHONE BUZZES, and I swipe it from the floor next to my drum kit.

Giselle: What are we doing tonight?

I smile.

Me: It's a surprise.

She hates surprises.

Giselle: You're not nice.

Me: I'm very nice and you know it ;)

Giselle: I'm going to miss you when you're gone.

Me: Then we need to spend as much time together as possible before I go.

Giselle: That can be arranged.

Me: Pack a bag so you can come back to my place tonight.

Giselle: Tempting…

Me: Bring enough so you can stay until Monday.

Giselle: Monday?

We've been home from Mexico for almost a month and have spent as much time together as possible. Our days and nights blend together, time flying by too quickly. I haven't been this happy in a long time, and she's the reason. If I had my way, she'd be moving in to my place. Of course, it's too soon, but I'm hopeful we can figure out a mutually beneficial living arrangement when I get back from the tour. And I certainly don't want to waste any time we have together between now and then. I want her with me for the weekend–or longer.

Me: Or Tuesday.

I hold my breath after I hit send. My heart races with uncertainty. I hope she doesn't think I'm rushing things, but she has to know how I feel.

After a few more minutes, she still hasn't answered my text.

Me: Or Wednesday.

Still nothing. Either she's completely freaking out or her cell phone lost its signal, like it seems to do at the most inopportune moments.

Me: Hello?

Giselle: Who is this?

I laugh out loud and know she's messing with me.

Me: It's C-3P0 reminding you that you haven't responded yet, Master.

Giselle: Hahahahahaha - Stop.

My phone rings, and I answer it immediately. "You had me worried for a second," I say, her soft giggles on the other end of the line.

"Are you seriously asking me to stay with you for five days?"

"Yes," I say, so there's absolutely no doubt in her mind. "It's not like we haven't spent that much time together before." I subtly remind her that she pretty much moved into my room in Mexico for the last five days of our trip.

"Oh," she says. "I'm pretty sure I'm going to have to think about that."

"Take all the time you need. But, I'll be picking you up at around seven, so make sure you have plenty of things packed and you're ready to go."

"Okay," she says tentatively. "Is there anything else I need to consider?"

"Don't pack any pants."

She giggles and says, "I have to go. I have a presentation in two minutes, and I need to pee." She pauses. "I shouldn't have told you that."

I laugh. "Nothing you say could ever faze me, Giselle. Call me later," I demand, and she hangs up, her giggles still ringing in my ears.

"Are you finished?" Garrett asks, and I toss the pencil that I had in my hand across the room at him.

"Yes, I'm off the phone now."

"Sorry to rush you," he says. "What's with this insta-relationship anyway?" he asks, and his tone is more judgmental than I care to hear.

"Seriously? None of your business," I say defensively. My connection with Giselle spans over a decade, and the past two months seem like a blip on that radar.

"I didn't mean to judge. Just looking out for you, man," he says.

I pick up my drumsticks and stand up. "Are we done for today?" I ask. "I think I have the bridge down for *Blue Velvet*. Is there anything else you need to hear before we finish solidifying our set list?" I've been having trouble with the time that he wanted me to keep during that song. I finally nailed it and showed him he has nothing to worry about.

"I'm good, as long as you are," he says.

"Yup. Now lighten up, will you?" I joke, and he slaps my shoulder as we head upstairs from his studio.

"Giselle is good for you," he says. "I really mean it."

"Thanks?" I say, confused. "Five minutes ago, you told me we were moving too fast."

"I'm an idiot," he says, and I immediately nod in agreement. "I don't think I've ever seen you this happy."

"I've never been this happy," I respond.

I thought I was happy a few years ago, but Natalia destroyed that for me. Garrett and I never talk about her. We both know that we each have a history with her, but it's unspoken. And it's in the past. It's better that way because it's too weird any other way you look at it.

As soon as we reach the top of the stairs, I see our publicist talking with Sam. They both turn their heads nervously in our direction.

"Now what?" Garrett asks, and he throws his hands into the air. The press hasn't been too kind to us recently after they unearthed private photos of Garrett, Sam, and Kai, speculating all sorts of things about their family and relationship. Sonya, our publicist, quickly squashed whatever rumors had been flying around, but it still pains them to see anything negative in the papers or on the Internet.

"Nothing to do with you," Sonya says to Garrett, and all of their eyes turn to me.

"Fuck," I mutter and can only imagine what they're about to tell me.

"We have some damage control to do," she says to me, and Garrett chuckles as if to say 'Better you than me.'

"What?" I ask, exhaling.

"Well, first there's this." *There's more than one?* She pushes a tabloid paper across the table and points to a bare ass on the cover. *My bare ass.*

"What the fuck is this?" I ask, looking closer.

"It's you. Naked on top some girl," she says, followed by her standard eye-roll. It's a picture of me, making love to Giselle on my *private* patio in Mexico.

Sonofabitch.

"It isn't just some girl. And you know it." *Giselle is so much more.* "You need to take care of this. Make it disappear," I demand, and Sonya nods her head.

"I'm serious, Sonya. I don't want Giselle's name dragged through the media. She needs to be protected. Promise me you're doing everything in your power to make this go away."

"The tabloids think she's an anonymous hook-up. I think she's going to remain anonymous. But, I promise you that I'll make sure that happens."

Sonya and Giselle hit it off the second they met each other, and I know Sonya is sincere.

"Don't worry, I'm on it," she attempts to reassure me.

"Good," I say. She still looks serious, and I shrug my shoulders.

"Next, we need to figure out what to do about this." She opens the same magazine to the second page.

What I see causes bile to rise in my throat.

Motherfucker.

CHAPTER 28

Giselle
Present

I BARELY MAKE IT to my front door, backpack slung over one shoulder, folders in my hand, mail tucked under my arm. My knee is swollen from tweaking it at the office today as I was rushing in late to my presentation. I'm a hot mess, and all I want to do is open some wine and drink it straight out of the bottle. I drop my cell phone on the counter and plug it in. It died on the way home when I couldn't find the car charger.

I've already kicked off my heels in the foyer, and I limp toward the couch with my mail still tucked under my arm. It's a massive pile of mail today; I can't remember the last time I cleaned out my mailbox. *Maybe last week sometime?*

It drives Mia crazy that I do this. She's completely nuts about taking her mail in every single day. I'll go to the mailbox and just remove one or two things, leaving the rest in there. If I don't pull it out, it means I don't have to react to it. My phone bill can wait an extra few days to get paid.

Today, while I rest my swollen knee and sip a glass of wine, I finally go through the huge pile. Twenty minutes later, there's a mess of torn envelopes and shredded solicitations from various credit card companies. I've weeded out only two or three official pieces of mail that I need to actually do something with. I'm about to scoop up the mess when I see a large manila envelope that I must have missed. I tear it open and pull out a statement from my car financing company. I scan the statement, wondering why it was delivered to me in such a formal looking envelope. I usually receive my statements electronically–another reason why I rarely check my mailbox. I'm surprised when I see that my loan was paid off almost two months ago, and the title is enclosed. *Paid off? There's definitely been a mistake.*

I pull the title out of the envelope and scan it–it's totally legit. I hobble over to the kitchen where my cell phone is charging and pick it up, dialing the financing company. After pushing multiple buttons, a live person is on the end of the line.

"Hi, I think there's a mistake on my statement. It shows that my loan is paid off, and I'm holding the actual title to my car. I still have two years left," I say, rambling to the person who greeted me.

"Can you verify your name, address, and the last four digits of your social security number?" he asks. *Didn't I just punch all of that into the phone?*

I huff and give him what he needs in order to verify I am who I say I am.

"Thank you," he says. "Please hold while I check your account."

I'm expecting him to come back on the line to confirm that they did, indeed, make a mistake when he says, "Our records indicate that your loan was paid in full on June 20th. As you may know, it does take us some time to process the final payoff and to close out the loan. It usually takes us about six to eight weeks to send the title out, and we apologize for any inconvenience this may have caused you."

"No, you don't understand. I didn't pay off my loan." He doesn't get it. I shouldn't be holding this title in my hands right now.

"Your loan was paid in full, ma'am."

"No, it wasn't," I say.

He takes a deep breath and says, "Please hold while I get my supervisor."

Hold music plays as I pace back and forth across my kitchen floor.

"Ms. Andrews?" A new voice is on the line.

"Yes?"

"I see there may be some confusion over your car loan. I'd like to help clear that up, if I can." The supervisor repeats exactly what the other phone representative went through with me before. He confirms that my car loan has indeed been paid off.

"I don't understand. How can this be if I didn't pay it?" I ask.

"Let me check the transaction," he says, and I hear lots of keys clicking on his keyboard.

"Okay, the payment came in from Epic Enterprises. Does that name ring a bell?" he asks, and I almost drop the phone. *There's only one person who could have done this.*

"That clears it up," I say and hang up.

Why would he do this?

Anger bubbles in my chest, and I resist the urge to call him and give him a piece of my mind. *Who does he think he is?* Paying for my car? What's next?

Mia walks through the sliding back door and sees me in the disheveled state I'm in. "Someone's a hot mess today," she says, eyeing the pile of torn paper and envelopes on the floor. "What's up with you?"

"Nothing. I'm just–I'm so mad right now. Look at this!" I shove the title to my car in her face.

She smiles. "Congrats, babe. You own your car. Why would you be angry about this?" She smirks as she shoves something behind her back.

"Dax did this. He paid off my car," I say, throwing myself onto the couch.

"And?"

"And? I'm humiliated. Seriously, why would he do this? Does he think I'm destitute? In need of a handout?"

"Good lord, shut up," she says. "He probably did it to be nice. To surprise you. You did save his life, after all."

Oh. I didn't even think about that. "But still, it's weird. I'm uncomfortable."

She shrugs. "There's worse you could be uncomfortable about." She pulls a magazine out from behind her back and places it on my lap. My stomach churns, and I almost scream.

"He's got a great ass," she says and laughs.

Dax's naked body is on the page in front of me, and I quickly scan the photo. I see all of him. His ass in plain view for the entire world to see. *And he's on top of me.*

"Holy shit, this is from Mexico." I cover my mouth as I fight the projectile vomit that's about to erupt.

"Your face, and everything else, is pretty blurry. The story speculates, but they have no idea who you are, so that's good."

"This is not good. Someone seriously invaded his–our privacy. What the fuck?" I yell, and she flinches.

"At least they don't know who *you* are, right? And I'm sure he's totally used to this kind of thing." She's not making me feel any better.

"There's one more thing…" she says as the doorbell rings.

I walk toward the door, knowing Dax is on the other end. And I'm sure by now, he's seen the same picture I just saw.

Strangely, I think I'm more upset about him paying off my car than a picture of us having sex in Mexico. But, what if my parents see it? Oh my God. My stomach churns as I pull open the door.

"We need to–"

Not Dax.

"Sorry, I thought you were someone else," I say to the woman and child standing in my doorway. She's stunning and nearly six feet tall. A young boy, no more than three is standing next to her, smiling. He looks exactly like her, so I presume it's her child.

"Can I help you?" I ask.

"I'm hoping you can. I'm looking for Dax Anderson, and I was told I may find him here." She peeks around me into my home, and I close the door a little. *Who the hell is this woman?*

My nerves grab hold, and my hand is shaking on the doorknob. My gut tells me to slam the door in her face. I don't think I can take any more surprises today. "I'm sorry, who are you?" I ask, voice shaking.

"Who I am really shouldn't matter to you. Please ask Dax to come to the door."

Mia suddenly steps in front of me, pushing me to the side. "I'm sorry, but you must have received some bad information because there's nobody here by that name," she says and closes the door in her face.

"What the fuck is going on?" I say, trying to catch my breath. Mia ushers me over to the couch, and we sit down.

"Can you get Dax on the phone?" she asks, her own voice shaky.

"Yes–I'm sure I can, but–"

She turns the page in the magazine, and the face of the woman who was at my door is plastered just below a headline that reads: *Dax Anderson Love Child Hidden? Natalia LeFuer Tells All.*

"What the fuck?" I yell. My vision blurs, and my hands are still shaking. *Why is this happening?*

Mia starts reading excerpts from the story. "Was Natalia Dax's hidden secret? What does his son think about his rockstar father?"

"Stop it. Stop reading that shit right now, I can't take it," I say, and the tears begin to flow. Sobs shaking my shoulders and take control of my body. "I'm such an idiot," I cry into my hands, and Mia rubs my back.

"Shhh," she says softly.

"I'm an idiot. I should have known not to get involved with him. He warned me in Mexico. He told me he was trouble. And now this." I slam my finger onto the face of the gorgeous woman, who could still be standing on my front porch for all I know. "And this!" I say, flipping to the first page where we're entangled together, making love. "What's wrong with me, Mia? Why did I get involved with him?" I cry. "Why did I trust him?"

Why did I fall in love with him?

"I'm sure there's a reasonable explanation for all of this," she says confidently.

I huff. "An explanation, yes, I believe there is. Reasonable? I highly doubt that, Mia." She hands me a tissue, and I wipe the tears from my eyes and blow my nose.

"Can I have another one?" I ask.

"Are you okay?"

"What do you think?" My chest tightens.

"I don't like seeing you like this. I'm so sorry," she says, pulling me into an embrace. "You deserve so much better. You deserve to be happy."

Deserve?

"Mia, I *earned* my right to be happy, don't you think? So many fucked up things have happened in almost every single relationship I've ever been in. Troy. Derek. And let's not forget Dale."

"Dale was gay," Mia says.

"Yeah. It would have been nice to know that!" I shout, and she starts laughing.

"What are you laughing at?" I ask her as she cackles even louder.

"What about Jared?" She laugh-snorts.

"He liked his collections more than he liked me. Okay, I think we've hashed out enough of my failed relationships." Jared was really into Star Wars. In fact, he's the one who got me into it. However, he was way into it–more than I could ever have imagined.

"Who buys three of everything? Who does that?" I yell, and she starts laughing again. "Like I said, he was a collector." Embarrassment replaces the anger, and I slap her leg.

"This trip down memory lane is over. I can't do this anymore, as fun as it is for you," I say. "I'm warning you, or I'll start pulling skeletons out of your closet. We could be here all night for that," I quip, and she grabs my hand.

"Listen, the point is, no matter who you've been with since Troy, I haven't ever seen you this happy. There's been something that I completely love about you since you came home from Mexico. Your strength. Your confidence. Your beauty."

I blush. "What are you talking about?" My heart is breaking as she describes what I have–*had* with Dax.

"You've always been the stronger one out of us, Giselle. You always say it like it is–and mean it. Despite the shit that's happened to you, you've never let it bring you down. Yeah, you've dated a lot of assholes and some real losers, but you always find the one redeeming thing in those people and build on it. Even if one of them collected Star Wars figurines well into his twenties."

"Okay, enough." I say.

"Listen to me. Trust what I'm going to say to you. No matter what is going on, find that one thing in Dax to hold on to. Well, make it two. One would be his ass. The other would be something else." She laughs. "I have a feeling he's worth it, and when all of this gets sorted out, you'll see what I mean."

"Mia. I love you, you know that. But, I don't know if I have it in me right now. I'm serious. My head is killing me. My heart is in the process of breaking. Let me deal with this in my own way," I say, and she nods her head.

She squeezes me tight and kisses me on my cheek. "I'll be back in an hour with a couple bottles of pinot and *She's All That*." She slides out my back door, and I stare at the tabloid. *Can a Freddie Prinze, Jr. movie make this all go away?*

Seeing Natalia standing on my front porch, with Dax's child keeps replaying in my head. They're his family and soon I'll be a memory. My heart hurts as I realize a part of my future is suddenly out of reach. I've always dreamed of settling down and having a baby–a family–with the man that I love. Even though Dax and I have been together for only a short time, that reality seemed more real to me than ever. Until now.

Mia's words ring in my head, and I realize she's right. I am strong, and I certainly don't need to sit here and wallow in self-pity and misery. I want answers, and I'm going to get them.

I pick up my phone and call Dax.

He answers on the first ring.

"Giselle! God, I've been trying to get a hold of you," he says.

"I'm sure you were." I crumple the magazine in my free hand and toss it across the room.

"We need to talk," he says. He's right, but I'm going to do the talking. I'm going to ask the questions.

"Two truths and a lie." My voice is shaking, but stern.

"What?"

"Two truths and a fucking lie," I repeat, determined for answers.

"Okay," he says, concern in his voice.

"You paid off my car loan. Your ass is on the cover of a tabloid. You have a child with a gorgeous, seven-foot tall model." I hold my breath, fighting tears. I really don't want to know the answer to the last one. I'm praying it's the *lie*.

He takes a deep breath. "This isn't how you play the game."

Fuck. Are they all true?

"My game. My rules."

"Yes—the first is true."

"Why did you pay off my car? Did you think I needed money? A handout? Did you feel sorry for me?" I'm ashamed and embarrassed that he would feel the need to take care of me like that.

"No—it's not like that," he says.

I don't want to hear his explanation because it's only delaying the inevitable, when he gets to the question about Natalia.

"Tabloid?" I say, skipping to the next truth.

"Yes. And if you saw the picture, you know exactly where it is and who I was with," he says. "And I have absolutely no idea how that picture got leaked or how it was even taken."

"I believe you," I say. "The picture could have been worse." I tense up, and realize again that when this begins to spread, these people will know who I am, and my parents are going to be mortified. "I have some damage control to do with my family," I say.

"I'm sorry about that. I really am. I should have been more careful, more private with you," he says.

Is that regret in his voice?

"Natalia?" I ask and hold my breath. *I don't want to know. I don't want to know. I don't want to know.*

"I don't know," he says. "I don't know if the kid is mine."

I choke on a sob and say, "Well, she was here about fifteen minutes ago. When she finds you, you should ask her, don't you think?" Tears roll down my cheeks, and my hands shake.

"What? She was there?" he yells, anger bubbling through the phone. "What did she say?"

"Nothing, Dax. She said nothing because I didn't give her the chance."

Well, Mia didn't give her the chance, and she slammed the door in her face. But, he doesn't need to know that.

"I have to go," I say, trying to hide the fact that I'm crying.

"Wait. We need to talk," he says again, and I shake my head. I feel like this phrase pops up too frequently in our relationship. There's always something we need to sort out, something to talk about. *It's not supposed to be this difficult.*

"We just did. I have all the answers I need," I respond. "I'll send you the money for my car as soon as I can." *I just need to figure out where I'm going to get twelve thousand dollars.*

I hang up and kick the side of my couch.

Why can't I have a completely uncomplicated relationship with a man?

And why do I trust people so damn much?

I need to get out of here. My mind runs through my parents' calendar as I plan my escape.

I text my mother.

Me: Hey, Mom. Are you and Dad at the shore house this weekend?

Mom: No, we're in Hatteras with Bill and Anne.

Me: Okay, have fun!

Mom: Everything okay?

Me: Totally - bye!

Mom: Love you.

Me: Love you, too.

It's hard lying to her, but I need to get away, without her questioning me.

By the time Mia comes back, my duffle bag is all ready for my escape. It was supposed to be for Dax's place, but now it's been repurposed, and I packed pants.

"Where are you going?" she asks, concern on her face.

"To clear my head–I'm going to the beach," I say, swiping my keys from the counter.

"You're running away is what you're doing," she scolds, her tone judging.

"Running away from what? There's nothing to run away from."

She shakes her head. "Enjoy the weekend. Clear your head. Come back and fix everything," she says, squeezing me tight. "I love you, and I know he does, too."

He loves me?

"I'm good. Practically over it already," I lie.

She follows me out to my car and helps me put my things into the back.

"Be careful. Call me if you want some company tomorrow night," she says.

"I will."

I slide into my car and open the sunroof.

And I laugh.

Because at this point, it's better than crying.

No one deserves to own my tears anymore.

CHAPTER 29

Dax
Present

"FUCK!" I YELL as I slam my fists into my steering wheel. My chest is tight, and I'm gasping for air. Sweat beads on my temples, my scalp tingles.

Seeing Natalia in that tabloid has completely shaken me to the core, especially since she's pictured with a child who looks to be about three years old.

A child who could be mine.

Sonya found out the hotel Natalia is staying at in the city, and I can't get there fast enough.

Why is she back now? Where has she been over the past few years?

I've been trying to get in touch with Giselle since our last conversation, but her phone is going straight to voicemail. I completely understand why she's avoiding me, but I need to apologize. My fucked-up life is destroying hers. This is all my fault, and I need her to hear it from me. I'll do anything to make all of this madness go away.

My phone rings through Bluetooth, and I see Alex's name pop up on my dashboard.

"Hey," I say.

"What's going on?" he says, concern in his voice.

"What *isn't* going on," I respond, clenching my teeth.

"Dude, Natalia? A kid?" He obviously saw the rag magazine. I suck in a breath. "I'm on my way to find out now."

"Good. Get to the bottom of this. I don't trust her," Alex says, echoing my own thoughts since I saw her and the boy in the tabloid.

"Stay calm. Call Doug." Doug's our lawyer, and he was the first person I called when I left Garrett's house.

"Already did."

"What did he say?"

"That I need to immediately demand a paternity test and give her his business card." He also told me that I shouldn't see her in person, a request that I'm clearly violating.

"That's cold," Alex says. "What if the kid's yours?"

"Fuck, man. I don't know. I can't think straight right now." My hands wrap around the steering wheel tighter, and my fingertips start to go numb.

"I'm sorry," he says. "I don't know what else to say."

"Neither do I."

"Have you thought about your options?" he asks, and I practically choke.

"Options? Like what?" I yell. "If the kid's mine, do you think I'm going to ask that crazy bitch to marry me?"

He laughs, "No! Oh my God. Did you think...?"

"I don't know what to think," I respond. The picture in the tabloid wasn't very clear, but from what I saw, the kid resembled Natalia. He has her olive skin tone and dark hair. He was grasping her hand tightly, while looking lovingly at his mother. I tried to pinpoint other features that would make him an Anderson, but I couldn't find any.

"I don't care whose kid he is, Dax. If you ask Natalia to marry you, I'm going to have you committed."

"I can't talk about this anymore." I veer off the highway toward the hotel near the airport. "I'll get to the bottom of it, one way or another."

"Don't do anything stupid," Alex says.

"When have I ever done anything stupid?" I cringe at the thought of him regurgitating my history.

"You should never have gotten involved with her in the first place," he says, and I want to spit.

"You think?" I respond tightly. He's certainly not making this easy; in fact, he's beginning to piss me off. "I don't need a lecture, asshole."

"I'm not trying to be a prick, but she was trouble from the beginning. Look what happened with Garrett." I don't need him to remind me of her history with our friend and fellow brother.

"It's not like I can change the past, Alex. You're right, I should never have fucked her. Okay?" My anger reaches a boiling point.

"You did more than fuck her. You fell in love with her," he says.

"It wasn't love," I retort. I've finally found love again, and what I had with Natalia was nothing like what I have with Giselle.

My anxiety grips me as I realize that I need to see Giselle immediately. But first, I'm going to confront Natalia, once and for all.

"Be careful. Don't let her get the upper hand, okay?" he says, concern filling his voice.

"I can handle her–I just need to see for myself. As soon as I look into her eyes, I'll know."

"Don't let her try to take advantage of you. Stay alert."

"I will," I say, and he hangs up.

I inhale, trying to calm myself, but nothing's working. My sweaty palms slide from the steering wheel as I pull into the driveway leading to the hotel entrance.

I'll fucking stay alert. I already know how manipulating Natalia can be.

The valet raises his hand as I pull up to the hotel. "Keep the car here, I'll only be a few minutes," I say.

He nods as he hands me the claim ticket. "Your car will be right over there." He gestures toward the end of the driveway.

"Thanks." I jog toward the front desk in the lobby.

"Can I help you, Sir?" the girl behind the counter asks.

"Natalia LeFuer is expecting me. Can you call her room and let her know I'm on my way up?"

"Sure, who shall I say is here?" she asks.

"Dax Anderson."

Her eyes widen as she dials the phone. "Ms. LeFuer, Mr. Anderson is here to see you."

She nods and hangs up the phone. "She's on the Concierge Level, Room Fourteen Twenty-Two."

"Thanks," I say and walk toward the elevators.

I press the button for her floor and inhale deeply, running my hand through my hair, trying to keep my nerves at bay.

What is she going to tell me?

Is this kid mine?

My chest clenches as the elevator doors open, and I hesitate. I don't think I want to know the answer. As the doors close, I jump through and see that her room is directly across from the elevator. Before I can change my mind, her door flies open as if she was looking through the peep-hole, waiting for me.

Fuck.

"Dax," she says, and my heart stops.

Her familiar, hypnotic voice floats through the air. Memories flood my brain, and my knees feel weak.

"We need to talk."

CHAPTER 30

Giselle
Present

THE SOUND OF WAVES crashing on the beach is supposed to relax me, but it's doing anything but. My head pounds with each passing wave. The three Advil I've taken haven't alleviated it in any way. My nerves are shot. My heart is a broken mess. I plan to spend the next five days here at the beach, hiding from my life. Hiding from the paparazzi. Hiding from Dax. Despite what I told Mia, I have indeed run away–escaping from my awkward reality.

I'm in love with a rock star.

And to top it off, he has a love child with a fucking supermodel. A child he literally just found out about–that the *world* just found out about.

Pain shoots across my chest, and I massage the tightness in my sternum as I inhale the salty sea air. "Why is this happening?" I say out loud into the ocean breeze. There isn't anyone else within sight, and I'm thankful to have this stretch of beach to myself. The moon is still low in the sky, reflecting brightly off of the ocean. I've been out here since the sun set, and I'm comforted by the darkness surrounding me. I'm anonymous here, nobody knows me. But, I'm sure everyone knows who Dax Anderson is.

I massage my chest harder, trying to work out the knot that has formed. It's been tight since I hung up with my mother. She called me while I was driving here, because she didn't exactly believe my cheerful sounding texts earlier today. I've never been able to successfully lie to her about anything–so I told her everything. Every uncomfortable detail about Dax and me. Even about the tabloid picture of us in Mexico. I was mortified throughout our entire conversation, embarrassed to admit my lack of judgment about many things, including my poor choice of outdoor sex. She was quiet while she listened to me tell her about Dax's connection to me, and to Lara. I cried when I spoke about my cousin, guilt bubbling up again. I've felt her loss so much more over the past few weeks, but Dax and I have worked through so much of it together. We've shared beautiful memories while reliving some of the sadness that we experienced so many years ago.

Now a huge curveball has been thrown our way, and I feel like a complete failure. My mother, once she was over the complete surprise of the situation, offered me some advice: stay true to myself, and everything will work itself out.

What the hell does that even mean?

I know she meant well, but I think I've always been true to myself. I've always been the one to see the forest through the trees, glass half-full. *Until now.*

How can I possibly remain true to myself when there's a naked picture of me, underneath one of the biggest rock stars in the world, on every newsstand between here and London? How can I be true to myself when a woman has come forward, claiming to have a child with him? I can't take it anymore. I just want to scream. My mother means well, but it's not exactly the best advice at the moment.

Before we hung up, she told me she was going to break the news to my father about the tabloid. I'm expecting my phone to ring any moment, with his booming voice on the other end.

As if I just willed it to happen, my phone rings in my hand. *Dammit.*

I look down, expecting to see my father's number, but it's Mia.

A sigh of relief escapes my lips before I answer, "Hey."

"Just checking in. Everything okay?" she asks, concern in her voice.

"I told my mother everything," I blurt out.

"Oh boy. I don't think you need to tell me how that went."

"Actually, not as bad as I expected. But my dad doesn't know yet, so I'm waiting for him to call me yelling and screaming."

"Your mom will take care of him. What did she say?"

I huff. "She told me to stay true to myself, and everything will work itself out."

"Vague," she laughs.

"I guess."

"If there's one thing you can take away from all of this, it is that your mom's pretty freaking amazing. I mean, her daughter is banging a rock star on the cover of a tabloid magazine, and she kept her cool!" I cringe as I imagine my mother reading that article and looking at that picture.

"That's disgusting. Don't put it like that, Mia."

"Seriously. You have no idea how lucky you are to have such supportive parents."

"Like I said, my dad hasn't heard about this yet," I remind her, and my chest tightens again.

"It will all be fine. I promise," she says, and I wonder how she can even make that promise to me.

"Whatever. I just want to forget about everything for a few days."

"Are you going to work on Monday?" she asks.

"Hell. No. I emailed my boss tonight after I got down here and told her that I'm taking a few days off next week. She's totally cool and even told me to take off the whole week, if I need it. I may take her up on that." Marilyn is definitely very understanding. She's very family-oriented and super flexible. She even suggested I work remotely for a few days, if I don't want to take the whole week off. I'm super lucky to work in such a great environment. At least I have *that* going for me.

"Good for you," she says. "You should totally take her up on that offer. Maybe I'll play hooky next week and come join you for a few days."

I love Mia—like love her like a sister, but I need space from everything, including her. I just don't know how to tell her 'no.'

She picks up on my silent cues and says, "Just kidding. I know you need your time alone. I promise I won't surprise you."

"It's okay, Mia. Really. In a few days, I'm sure I'll be looking for something to do to keep my mind off of things." I'm not entirely sincere in my offer, but I say it anyway.

"I'll let you know," she says.

We're quiet for a few seconds before she speaks up again. "Have you spoken to Dax again?"

Another pain grips my chest. "No."

"Are you planning on it?"

"Honestly, Mia, I don't know what else to say to him. He's obviously got some things he needs to work out before he brings me back into the picture." *If there even is a picture.*

"So, you're willing to try?" she asks, surprised.

"I don't know what I'm willing to do. I just can't seem to get the vision of that little boy out of my head. He has a kid, Mia. A. Kid. His life just changed forever, and I'm sure I'm the last person he's thinking about right now."

"Things are going to work out. I'm certain of it."

Her optimism isn't contagious, and I frown. "Listen, I don't blame him for any of this. That woman kept him in the dark for years, but now he has to deal with it."

"Don't you think you should be around to help him?" she says, her voice accusing.

"How can I possibly help?"

"Moral support. Show him you care. Running off and hiding is doing the exact opposite. He needs you, Giselle."

Guilt begins to overwhelm me. She's right, in her own twisted way. I admit that he has no control over what Natalia has done and the revelation she's brought forth, but how can I help without getting in the way? Without confusing the situation even more?

"I think it's best if I lay low. He doesn't need any more of a media circus than he already has. Maybe when things quiet down..."

"Do what you need to do," she says sternly. "But, running away isn't helping either of you."

Suddenly, I feel the urge to apologize to her. To Dax.

"I'm sorry, Mia. You probably think I'm being selfish or childish–"

"Yes!" She cuts me off.

"Let me finish, will you?"

"Fine," she says.

"I need to clear my head and try to make sense of all of this craziness. I also need to decide if I even want to try to fit into his new, complicated life. I need to decide if continuing to pursue a future with him is something I can handle."

"You can handle anything, Giselle. You always have. And you always will."

I smile and recline my beach chair. The moon is higher in

the sky, and the stars are out in full-force. "Thanks for the pep-talk, Mia."

"Also, remember what you both were able to get past while you were in Mexico. He's Lara's high school boyfriend, for God's sake. And you were able to move on and grow closer. Go figure."

Why does she have to make so much sense?

"You have a point."

"Say the word, and I'll be there with a couple bottles of pinot and my charming self."

I giggle and say, "You're amazing, and I love you."

"I love you, too. Call me if you need anything. And call Dax to let him know you're okay." She hangs up before I can respond.

She's right on so many levels. But, I still need to figure out what place I could possibly hold in Dax's heart now that he has a son. And what if Natalia showing up rekindles an old flame that he once held for her. She's incredibly gorgeous, and bringing a child into the picture could make him forget about me altogether.

I inhale deeply and stare at the constellations. So many wishes have been made upon these stars that I'm afraid mine will be ignored.

How can I even wish that a child and his mother disappear so I can finally have my chance at love?

THE HOT SUN BURNS into my skin as I gasp for air, my feet pounding onto the boards below. I glance at my wrist and see I've run ten miles. This is my last long run before the half-marathon next weekend, and for the first time in months, I actually feel ready for the grueling race ahead of me. I stop on the boardwalk and bend over, placing my palms above my knees, sucking in as much air as my lungs will allow. Sweat drips down my face, soaking my chest and my tank top. My legs feel surprisingly strong, when they're usually like jelly after a long run. I see my chair on the beach with the cooler filled with ice-cold water sitting next to it, and I jog toward it. I open one and chug the contents quickly while I hold another to my forehead. It's freezing cold and sends shivers down my spine. Goosebumps quickly appear, and my arms tingle. *It feels so good.*

My father texted me this morning to tell me that the heat index was going to be close to 100 today. He's been tracking my training progress and knows when my long runs are scheduled. He also knows that I'm at the beach, where it's even hotter than at home. He didn't mention a thing about Dax and the tabloids, and I wonder if he knows yet. My mother told me she would tell him soon, but didn't specify when. I have to put my dad out of my mind for now, so I open another bottle of water, chugging it as quickly as I did the first.

After about fifteen minutes of cool-down and stretches, I take off my sneakers and let my bare feet sink into the hot sand. *Should I go up to the house to change?* I cover my eyes and see the house in the distance and quickly decide that I just want to sit and relax for a little while before I make the trek. I remove my sweaty tank top so I'm only wearing my bright pink jog bra and shorts. It's not obscene in any way, and if someone saw me, they would think I was wearing a sporty bikini. A *very sweaty* one, but I'm still decently covered.

As I do after every time I train, I close my eyes and visualize myself running through the streets as people cheer me on. I see myself throwing my arms in the air as I cross the finish line, the shiny medal around my neck. I'm proud, and I know I'm so close to making this vision a reality.

"BAILEY, STOP!" I hear a woman yelling and a slobbering sound in my ear. My eyes shoot open, and a large Golden Retriever is sloppily licking my face, his tongue lapping up every ounce of sticky sweat he can find. I throw my arms up in the air and laugh, petting him on top of his giant head. He doesn't stop and continues licking my face and arms.

"Oh my God, I'm so sorry!" she exclaims as she reaches her overly-friendly dog. I laugh and pet him again, his tail wagging wildly as his legs kick up the sand around us. "I don't know what got into him," she says. "He usually never leaves our side when we're walking on the boardwalk." She points to a man holding a young girl's hand while pushing a boy in a stroller. The man lets go of the stroller and waves back, apologetically.

"It's really okay. I needed to get up anyway," I say and sit up in my seat. *How long have I been asleep?*

The sunburn on my legs tells me it's been a while.

Bailey licks the side of my face again and sits in the sand, sticking his paw out. I grab hold of it and shake. "Nice to meet you, Bailey. You must have known I needed an alarm clock today." He pants loudly and shakes his butt, his tail kicking up sand everywhere.

"Okay, Big Guy, let's go." She tugs on his collar, and he stands up.

"Mama!" the little boy from the stroller yells and giggles.

"I'm coming," she says, attempting to drag the large beast of a dog off of the beach.

"Thanks for saving me from your killer dog," I laugh. "I'm Giselle, by the way. You look familiar. Have we met before?"

"I'm Carly," she says, stopping to wipe her brow. "We live in the next town over, but the kids love the playgrounds here in Belmar. Caleb especially loves the pirate ship jungle gym over there." She points to the play set, and I see at least a dozen other children enjoying it.

"Nice to meet you. I'm here every summer with my family, so I'm sure I've seen you around. That must be it." Her husband definitely looks familiar because I've seen him jogging with Bailey a few times before. He runs the same route I do—down the boardwalk and through Spring Lake.

Bailey takes off running toward the giggling children, and she turns to follow him. "Bye!" she yells as she runs after him.

I laugh and shake my head, grabbing my sweaty tank top to wipe the sticky slobber from my face. I look at my phone and see that it's almost three o'clock. I've been asleep for almost two hours; no wonder I feel burnt to a crisp. Before I stand up, I open the cooler and grab the last bottle of water from the melting ice. As I sip it, I notice someone standing in the gazebo about a hundred yards away. And he's looking straight at me.

Dax.

My heart races in my chest as I raise my hand slowly in the air to wave. He smiles, waving back. He hops over the railing and runs across the sand toward me. "Hey," he says, panting as he stops at my feet. Sweat is already forming on his brow and he looks amazingly hot.

I hand him my half-full bottle of water. "You could use this."

He grabs it from me and chugs it in one gulp. "Thanks." He wipes his forehead with the back of his arm. "It's freaking hot out here. Holy shit."

"Yeah. One of the hottest days so far this year." I'm about to spew random facts about the weather forecast, but I bite my tongue. I'm more interested in why he's here. *And how did he find me?*

"How are you?" he says, softly kicking the sand between us.

Lonely. I miss you.

"Good," I lie. "Got my last run in today before next week's race."

"I figured. You know, it wasn't easy tracking you down. Mia was very tight-lipped about where you went."

"I needed some time alone," I admit and shrug my shoulders, causing him to frown.

"If there's anything I've learned about you over the past few months, it's that you aren't afraid to face things. You don't run away."

"Who said I was running away?" My shoulders tense, and the knot in my chest is back.

He puts his hands out, indicating that he wants to pull me to my feet. I comply and let him.

We're standing toe-to-toe, and I'm suddenly self-conscious about how bad I smell. The sweat has had a few hours to work its way into my skin and running gear.

His eyes travel from mine, down to my chest. He places his hand on the exposed skin on my chest and laughs.

"What?"

"Did you fall asleep with your hand here?" he asks as he removes his.

I look down and see a perfect white imprint of my own hand, surrounded by sunburn. *Oh my God.*

I chuckle at my sunburn stupidity. That handprint is going to take weeks, maybe even months, to blend in with the rest of my skin tone.

"I passed out, apparently with my hand resting right here." I point to the pale spot and blush.

He brushes strands of hair away from my face and leaves his hand against my cheek.

"Why did you run?"

CHAPTER 31

Dax
Present

SHE TENSES AGAINST my hand and looks away.

"I know the past few days have been crazy. Hell, so have the past few months. But, haven't we worked through obstacles together? Why would you take off and not wait for an explanation to all of this madness?"

Her eyes widen. "Does the explanation go something like this? A woman and child show up from your past. You then fall madly in love with your insta-family. The end." She backs away from me, and my hand drops from her cheek.

"You can't possibly believe that," I respond, my heart sinking in my chest.

"What do you want me to believe? Better yet, what do the tabloids want me to believe?"

The beach around us is suddenly more crowded than it was before, and I'm hyper aware that we're out in public. "Can we go somewhere private to talk?"

She nods, folds up her beach chair, and grabs her sneakers from the sand. I pick up the cooler and follow her to the boardwalk, her house just a few more feet away. My SUV is parked in the driveway, and I say, "I hope you don't mind, it was the only spot available."

"It's okay." She unlocks the door, and we walk into the refreshing air-conditioning. She walks through the house, dropping her sneakers and clothes haphazardly. "Do you want a drink?" she calls from the kitchen.

No. I want you to hear me out.

"No, I'm good."

She reappears in the den, peeling a banana. "I'm starving." She takes a bite. "Do you want one?"

I can't help but smile. She looks so cute right now, but I need to focus. I need to make her understand exactly what's going on...and what isn't.

"I'm sorry if it seems like I ran away," she shrugs her shoulders, and sinks into the couch. "And I promise I'm not trying to be an asshole, but when that woman showed up on my doorstep with your son, I just lost it." Tears glisten in her eyes.

I nod. "That's completely understandable, and I don't blame you at all. But, I wish you would have stuck around to hear everything that happened, because it's not at all what you think." I sit across from her on the other couch and lean forward.

"What do you mean?"

"Natalia's son isn't mine," I state, and she exhales loudly, the tension leaving her shoulders.

"Really?"

"It's a long story, but she didn't show up to claim anything. She was trying to find me, to warn me about the tabloid story. Apparently, her husband threw her out two months ago because she'd been having an affair with a professional tennis player, who also happens to be the father of her child. Not me."

A smile plays across her lips, and she shakes her head. "I

feel like a complete idiot." She slumps further into the couch, embarrassed.

"Don't. Seriously. Natalia is, and always will be, a mess. She leaves a path of destruction wherever she goes, and I wouldn't be surprised if this story pops up again. She was hiding the kid from the public eye for almost three years before she surfaced in Spain a few weeks ago. A photographer who used to stalk Epic Fail happened to see her and her son in a cafe, snapped a few pictures, and sold his story to the highest bidder. He clearly embellished the details, getting the entire story wrong. Natalia saw it and freaked out. Her husband was already on the war path, and she didn't need my name dragged into her mess. For the first time in her life, she actually attempted to do something right."

"I see. So, it was a complete misunderstanding."

"But, she shouldn't have involved you, and for that I'm very sorry."

"Me too." She lowers her eyes. "I overreacted a little, didn't I?"

"I wish you wouldn't have taken off. Any anxiety you felt could have been easily avoided."

"But, I'm still mad at you," she smirks.

"How could you possibly still be mad? You know the truth. It's finally over, and we can move on." *Together.* I get up and close the gap between us, standing over her.

"You shouldn't have paid off my car," she blurts out, and I fold my arms across my chest.

"Really? You're still angry about that?" I laugh. "I'm not apologizing. I did something nice for you–so deal with it."

She pulls her knees into her chest and places her cheek on one of them. "I'm working on getting you the money as soon as possible."

"I won't accept it." I grab her hands, pulling her onto her feet and into my chest. She wraps her arms tentatively around my waist, finally settling on my hips. "I'm sorry for not telling you about it, but I won't accept any money from you. You can be mad at me all you want–I'm not budging on this."

"We'll work something out," she says.

"Nope."

She exhales into my shirt and after a few moments, changes the subject again. "I really feel like such an idiot. What was I thinking? When Natalia showed up on my doorstep, looking all gorgeous and intimidating, I snapped. And I ran. I'm really sorry, Dax."

I kiss the top of her head, and she relaxes in my arms. "You don't have to explain any further. I get it. Life in the public eye can be–complicated. Especially when someone like Natalia is thrown into the mix."

"What's your history with her anyway?" she asks, concern in her voice.

I've been dreading this question, but know I have to answer her truthfully. "We were together for a short time a few years ago, after Garrett broke her heart. It was doomed from the beginning, and like I said before–she's a complete and total mess. Not to mention, she's a cheater and always will be."

"I know the type all too well. I'm sorry you had to experience that with her." Sadness and regret fill her voice, and I kiss her head again. "Did you love her?"

"I thought I did," I admit, and she frowns.

"I'm sorry. I also know what that feels like. Loving someone and trusting them, only to have that trust completely shattered by a moment neither of you can ever take back."

I hold her in my arms for a few moments before the silence is broken again.

EPIC LIES

"So, what have you been up to the past few days?" She attempts to lighten the mood in the room.

"Looking for you." I take her face between my hands and kiss her lips. "Are you going to run away from me again?"

"It all depends." She leans her forehead into mine.

"Depends on what?" I smirk, stealing another kiss. *She feels so good in my arms.*

"It depends on whether or not any more of your fictional children show up."

I raise my hand with two fingers raised. "Scout's Honor. I have no other fictional children...that I know about."

"You were a Boy Scout?" she asks, surprised.

"A Cub Scout. And only for two years."

"I bet you were adorable." She runs her fingers through my hair, now completely relaxed in my arms.

"I'm still adorable." I raise my eyebrows, and she giggles.

She wiggles from my arms and backs away from me slowly. "I'm beginning to stink up this entire room. I need to shower. You stay here, make yourself comfortable, and I'll be back in five minutes."

"Sure, but hurry. We have a lot of catching up to do." I say as she slips away, down the hall.

I do everything I can to restrain myself from joining her. I don't like the way things played out over the last few days, and before we jump head-first back into this relationship, I want to make sure she's with me. Like, really with me. She has to be able to weather the storms that come along with my life. Yes, Natalia showing up with a kid immediately sounded the alarms to DEFCON 5, but I need to know Giselle isn't going to freak out over the little things. I need reassurance from her, and maybe some more media training with Sonya is definitely in order–if she agrees.

A door opens at the end of the hallway, and soon she's standing in front of me again. Glistening from the shower. Glowing from the sun. One side of her face is redder than the other, further highlighting her incredibly uneven sunburn. I focus on the white handprint on her chest and can't help but laugh out loud. She immediately covers it up, embarrassed.

"I must have looked graceful sleeping on the beach today," she says sarcastically. I laugh again when I picture her sprawled out on the chair, arms and legs everywhere.

"I bet you looked perfect."

"Yeah, perfect enough for a hundred-pound dog to slobber all over me!"

"Come here," I say, stretching my hand out to her.

She walks slowly over to me and grabs my hand. "Please don't hate me for being scared. And angry. I promise I won't do anything like that again."

"Don't apologize. And of course you're allowed to be scared, angry, and every emotion in between. Just don't hide it from me. Don't *you* hide from me–ever again. We need to work through these types of things together. If your first instinct is to run and not to trust me, then this isn't going to last." I need her to fully understand where I am coming from, and I hope what I said doesn't cause her to bolt.

"You're absolutely right, Dax. Completely and totally right." *Good.*

"Really? You think so?" I pull her against me, and this time I don't plan on letting her go.

"So many emotions took hold of me–it was overwhelming. Things had finally started falling into place for you and me–*for us.* I haven't ever had any luck finding the right guy and actually keeping him. Then, you literally fell into my life. You scared me. Intrigued me. I was drawn to you." She presses herself into my hips and leans her forehead into my chest. "And then one coincidence after another kept throwing us together. I started to feel things for you that I haven't felt in a very long time."

"Yeah?" I ask, wanting to hear her say *it*.

"Yeah." She sighs, and I tilt her chin up.

"What kind of feelings?" I tease.

She blushes and smiles. "What do you want me to say?"

I lead her over to the couch, and we sit. I pull her against my side. "Nothing, for now. But I want you to listen to me."

She stares into my eyes. "Okay."

"We were connected to each other a long time ago–before we even met. We both experienced something as teenagers that we should have never had to endure. Losing Lara to cancer was one of the worst things I've ever gone through, and I imagine you feel the same." She nods and settles against my side. "I didn't know how to process anything I was feeling, so I stayed angry. I lost faith in love and truth, questioning everything and everyone. I went down paths that I knew were no good for me, getting into relationships that were doomed from the start. I tried to trust again, and when I did, was painfully reminded it was a mistake to do so. *Until I met you.*"

"Dax, you don't need to explain anything to me. I know exactly how you feel. My past has also tarnished my ability to trust and to love." Her fingers entwine with mine, and she kisses my shoulder. "Thank you for being patient with me and not hating me."

"I could never hate you."

"Good. Because I think if you did, it would kill me."

"I love you," I say, and for the first time in a long time, I don't regret saying those three words.

She pulls away slightly and takes my face in her hands. "Really?" Her breathing hitches, and she bites her lip.

"Yes, really."

Her eyes light up and glisten. She lets go of my face and throws her arms around my neck. "I love you," she breathes. "I love you so much. I've been afraid to tell you, afraid you would think it was too soon. Everything happened so fast. The day I picked you up–"

I steal a kiss, devouring her words, and pull her tighter against me. I say against her lips, *"That was the day you saved my life."*

CHAPTER 32

Giselle
One Year Later

"DINNER WAS GREAT," my father says as my mother puts the last of the dishes into the dishwasher. He stands up and announces, "We should hit the road before traffic gets too heavy. You know what it's like on Sunday nights when everyone is heading home from their weekend down the shore." Traffic and weather will always be his main concern.

"Bob, we'll be fine," my mother says.

"Mr. and Mrs. Andrews, thank you for a great weekend," Dax says. He stands up and extends his hand to shake my father's.

"The pleasure is all ours, Son," my dad responds, smiling. It's been a long road getting the two of them to feel comfortable around each other, especially after my father found out about the pictures from Mexico. He couldn't look Dax in the eyes for close to three months, and even after that, the awkward meter was through the roof. I can't blame him, honestly. I was in a very compromising position.

"And please call us by our first names," my mother scolds him.

"If you head south on Route 35 and go through Spring Lake and Wall, you might be able to skirt around some of the heaviest traffic where I95 merges with the Parkway," Dax suggests, and my father's eyes light up. They're speaking the same language, and it's making me giddy.

"You're probably right, but I'll let my GPS map out the best route, just to be sure."

"That's a good idea," Dax says. I grab his hand and squeeze to let him know how much this means to me.

"Can I do anything else?" my mother asks, looking around the house. "I think we have everything loaded in the car. If we leave anything behind, you'll take it, won't you?" she asks me, concerned they're going to leave something here. This is the last week of our summer rental, and she's usually the one to take care of moving our seasonal things out and giving the key back to the landlord.

"We've got it under control, Mom." Dax and I will be here for the rest of the week...*alone*.

"Are you sure? I can always drive back out on Friday and help you close up."

"Seriously. Don't worry," I say, kissing her cheek. "Now go, before Dad starts twitching. He's already out in the car."

She kisses me back and pulls Dax into a hug.

"We'll see you both soon. Please, call if you need anything," she says, walking out the door.

We watch through the window as they pull away. Dax falls back onto the couch and I do the same.

"My parents are totally smitten with you."

He lets out a huge sigh, "I was so nervous all weekend. Like I was going to say or do something that would banish me from your family forever."

I snort. "A bit melodramatic, don't you think?"

"It doesn't matter how long we've been together, or how many times we see your folks–it doesn't get any easier. Your father scares me."

"Seriously? Oh my God, you're killing me!" I laugh so hard I get a stitch in my side. "He's a complete teddy bear. What on Earth are you afraid of?"

"I don't know. He may seem nice and sweet to you, but I can't shake the feeling that he will kill me slowly and painfully if I ever hurt you."

"Then don't hurt me, and you won't die a slow death at the hands of my father," I giggle and slap his thigh.

He grabs my hand and pulls me against him, kissing me deeply.

"I feel better now," he says against my lips.

"Good."

"Let's go for a walk." He pulls away from me, just as I was about to attack him.

"Now?"

He's on his feet and reaches out to grab my hand. "Yes, now."

I'm still full from dinner, so maybe a walk on the beach will help me digest. "Okay."

We walk barefoot, and hand-in-hand out to the boardwalk and onto the beach. The sand feels amazing between my toes, and it starts to cool as the sun sets.

"This is my favorite time of the year in Belmar," I say.

"Yeah?"

"Yes. It's the last week before people begin to close up their summer homes. Everyone is hanging on to the last few days on the beach, soaking it all in before their vacations end." It's always been a tradition for us to spend the last two weeks of August here, and I'm glad to keep our family practice alive.

He squeezes my hand, and then kisses my cheek. "I love everything about the beach, especially when I'm with you."

My heart pulls in my chest, and I realize how lucky I am. Dax is perfect. *We are perfect.*

"Can I tell you something?" He stops and faces me.

"Anything."

"It's something I've never told you before, and you're going to think it's weird. Maybe even fate."

I raise my eyebrow, intrigued. "I can't wait to hear."

He points to the gazebo in the distance. "Right there. That's when I first knew."

I remember this time last year when I attempted to escape the craziness that surrounded our relationship. He came to find me, and that's where I saw him, watching me from that gazebo.

"I remember," I chime in. "I was a sweaty, hot mess covered in dog drool. I must have been a sight for sore eyes. You found me during my weak attempt to avoid you and the crazy stories in the tabloids."

He laughs and shakes his head. "Not last year."

Goosebumps suddenly cover my arms as I anticipate his explanation. "When?" I ask.

"About six years ago. Maybe seven. We were doing a photo shoot on the boardwalk, just beyond the gazebo," he points and I gasp. *I remember.*

"I was right here," I say breathlessly. Mia and I were lying on our blanket, almost exactly where we're standing now. She was babbling on and on about the surfers and then about the band on the boardwalk.

"I know. I saw you." His hand brushes the hair that's blown into my face.

"You did," I state. "You waved at me." *How have I not remembered that moment until now?*

"There was something about you that caught my eye. You seemed so pensive, guarded, but strangely free. I was jealous that you had the whole beach to yourself. I wanted to ditch the camera crew and hop over the bannister. I wanted to ask you your name."

"Why didn't you?"

He shakes his head, "It wasn't the right time. Our stars hadn't yet aligned." A warm breeze swirls around us, and he squeezes my hand. "We weren't supposed to meet again until the day you saved my life."

He drops to his knee, still holding onto my hand. "You've kept me alive since that day, Giselle, and I don't ever want it to end."

My heart is beating out of my chest, and tears blur my vision. "Oh my God, Dax?"

"I promise you three things," he continues, unfazed by the whimpers that escape my lips.

"Yes?"

"One—I promise to live as if every single day with you is a gift, always to be cherished."

I cover my mouth with my free hand as my shoulders begin to shake.

"Two—I promise to erase all of the bad memories that we both have on this day and replace them with nothing but love."

I can no longer muffle my sobs as I cry tears of joy. Today is August twenty-fourth, Lara's birthday and the day she died. A date that will now forever connect Dax and me. A day suddenly filled with happy memories and the promise of our future together.

My other memory from this day doesn't deserve a single thought. I've moved on, Troy long forgotten.

"Three—and this one's easy—I promise to always tell you the truth, because lies have no place in our lives or our love."

He reaches into his pocket and pulls something out, his hand still closed around it, but, my heart knows exactly what it is.

"Giselle Andrews, I love you more than I ever thought I could love another person. Please say you'll spend the rest of your life with me?" He opens his hand, and the most spectacular ring appears. I can't believe this is happening.

I love this man so much.

"You want the truth?" I ask, tears streaming down my face.

"No lies," he answers as he has the ring poised, ready to slide onto my finger.

"Yes, Dax!" He moves the ring perfectly into place and scoops me into his arms, kissing my tears away.

"Thank you," he whispers in my ear. "Thank you for trusting me with your heart."

"It's yours–my heart is all yours. *Forever.*"

EPILOGUE

Dax
Sometime in the future...

"ARE YOU READY?" Giselle calls from the foyer. She looks just as beautiful today as she did the day we got married. She's wearing her favorite summer dress, and her feet are bare. We've been at our home at the beach for the past few weeks–the home that I gave to her as a wedding gift. We now spend our summers here in Belmar with her parents' new house down the street.

"I've been ready," I joke.

We just finished dinner, which means it's time for our evening stroll on the boardwalk.

She links her fingers with mine as we step outside into the warm August air. "I love you," I say as I kiss her temple. "Tonight's dinner was amazing."

"You know I didn't cook, right?" She reminds me, and I laugh. Her parents brought dinner to us tonight, and we ate Bob's favorite dish–chicken Parmesan.

"Exactly," I joke, and she bumps her hip into mine.

"I promise, one day, I'll learn how to cook as good as my mother. But, when she's right down the street, it's just too easy to pick up the phone and place an order." She giggles, and then gets serious. "I love you, too."

"What are we going to do with all of our free time?" I ask, knowing we don't have to close up the house for the foreseeable future. Epic Fail is currently on a much-needed hiatus. Garrett and Sam just had a baby girl a few months ago. Heath had to take an unexpected road trip. And Tristan—well, he has his hands full. We agreed to take at least a year off before we make another album, although I know Garrett's been working in his home studio with Chuck and putting together a Greatest Hits album.

"Anything we want," Giselle says and kisses me on my cheek. "We've got all the time in the world."

I walk toward the stairs, leading from the boardwalk to the beach when Giselle pulls me in the other direction. "Let's keep walking down the boardwalk." Her eyes are bright, and her smile is huge. *My gorgeous wife.*

We walk for a few hundred yards, and she pulls me into the gazebo. *Our gazebo.*

"I remember the first time I saw you on the beach—just like it was yesterday," I whisper into her ear.

"I couldn't believe you waved at me," she says.

I turn her to face me and hold her face between my hands. "I would have found you in a sea of a million people." I claim her lips, kissing her deeply. "I love you so much, Giselle."

"A lie and two truths," she mumbles into my mouth, her teeth scraping against mine.

"What?"

"It's a little twist on our game," she teases as she pulls away from me slightly.

"Go for it. You know you can't trick me anymore."

She lets go of me and walks around the gazebo, her hand

brushing along the railing that I leaned on years ago. "You know how much I love you, right?" she asks.

"Of course. Is that one of the TRUTHs?"

She laughs. "No. I just wanted to tell you before I started the game." Her eyes glisten, reflecting the setting sun. *She's never been so incredibly beautiful.* She turns to face me, her back leaning into the railing.

"Ready?" she asks.

"Yes."

She inhales deeply, and her smile widens. "I have size twelve feet."

Good Lord, where is this going? That's definitely the LIE.

"I'm so in love with you, I want to give you more of myself every single day." Tears form in her eyes, and my heart jumps in my chest.

I love you too.

"I'm pregnant."

THE END

COMING SOON

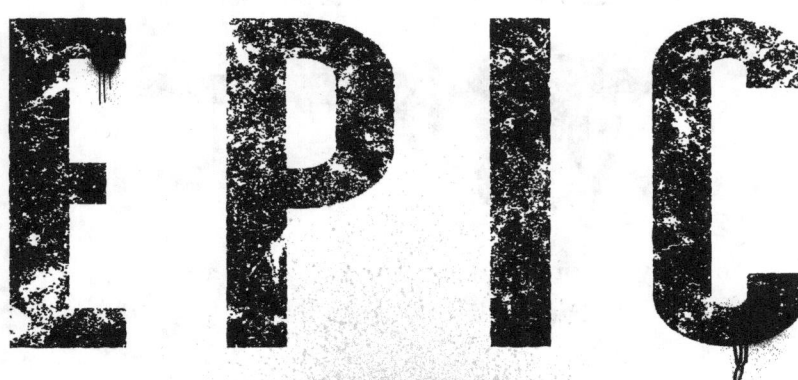

BESTSELLING AUTHOR
TRUDY STILES

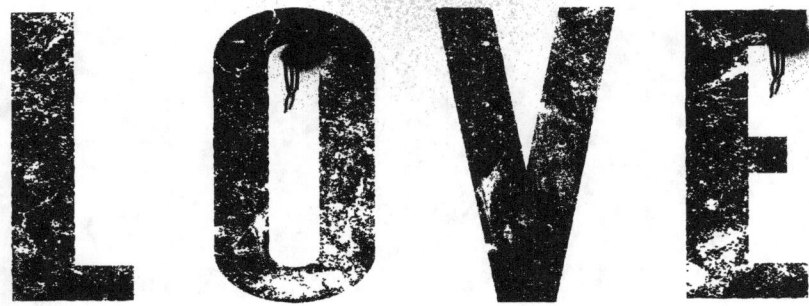

EPIC FAIL SERIES

A Standalone Novel in the
Epic Fail Series

PLAYLIST

The playlist for Epic Lies can be found here: http://trudystiles.com/playlists/.

Featured Bands/Artists Include:
AWOLNATION
Dashboard Confessional
Sia
Young the Giant
The Kills
The Sounds
Arcade Fire
Nico Vega
Swedish House Mafia

NOTE TO MY READERS

Dear Readers,

As you know, I write about connections and how two people eventually find love. Sometimes those connections are obvious, while other times, not so much. I don't start writing a book with the intention to hide the connections or truths from the reader, it's just worked out that way in many of my other books. The reader has found out the 'twist' usually at the same exact moment that my characters do, sometimes eliciting shock and an 'Aha!' moment.

Epic Lies is different — *at least I think it is.*

When I started writing this story, I thought it would flow the same way my others did, just like I mentioned above. However, that wasn't quite working for me. I *wanted* the reader to know early on how these two characters were connected *before* they knew themselves. I *wanted* the reader to be in on the secret. For me, that helped me draw the connections and allowed the characters to live their lives, blissfully (or not so blissfully) unaware, until *that moment*. When I constructed, and deconstructed, this story, that's what worked for me.

And I'm sorry.

Why am I apologizing? Because if you're a loyal reader, and you've come to expect those twists, turns, and shocking moments you've read in my other books, then this book wasn't for you. BUT if you're a loyal reader, who enjoys a story where you can identify with one or more of the characters and are happy with the way their story unfolded, without the crazy twists and turns that I've thrown into my stories in the past—then I hope you enjoyed Giselle and Dax's story.

I think everyone can relate to some aspect of these characters' struggles. I know that I personally have been lied to, cheated on and my own trust has had to be earned. I've given my heart to others blindly, at times. I have more in common with Giselle than I sometimes care to admit. I lived vicariously through her anger, and *it felt so good*.

I've written all types of characters, and my female characters are either loved or highly criticized (it's funny how that works). Why I loved, and connected so deeply with Giselle is because she dealt strongly with the adversity she was faced. She reacted to situations as I would react.

Would I scream? *Yes.*

Would I cry? *Yes.*

Would I be afraid to move forward, for fear of getting hurt again? *ABSOLUTELY.*

So, I hope you didn't mind that this book was a little 'different' than my others. I didn't set out to trick you or make you cry super-ugly tears. I just wanted to tell the story of two people and how they eventually found love.

Thank you for continuing to stay on this journey with me.

All truths, no lies.

Love,
Trudy

PS:
Did you enjoy this book? Please consider leaving an honest review on the site from which you purchased it.

Want to talk to others about your thoughts?

Join The Forever Family Group on Facebook: https://www.facebook.com/groups/808886315794103/

ACKNOWLEDGEMENTS

This is always the hardest part for me. The acknowledgments I normally write usually ramble on and on, but I promise this time, I won't do that.

Thank you to everyone who supports me every single day.

My husband and family: You all inspire me to be a better wife, mother, and person. Writing takes me to places that I both love and hate, some days I'm a disaster, and so is our house. Thank you for never holding my passion against me and for always encouraging me to continue. I love you Kevin, Cara, and Danny. You're my life.

Forever Family: My reader group is my safe place. Thank you all for your words of encouragement and letting me pop in there to tease you about what I'm working on. Thank you for sharing your personal stories and connections to my books. Thank you for laughing and crying with me. Thank you for telling your friends about my work. You're all incredible, and I'm thrilled that you're all still with me.

Amanda Maxlyn: My writing sister. I love you. Every single time we speak, you make me feel better about myself as a writer and as a person. You're my book wife bestie, and I don't know what I'd do without you. Thank you for being a sounding board when I needed it. And thank you for drinking wine with me over the Internet.

Mark Arnold: A quick text exchange, and you were able to give me the perfect slogan! Thank you for all of your support and being one of my 'forever friends.' I love you!

Chelle Lagoski Northcutt: You're a complete lifesaver, in case you weren't already aware. Thank you for putting eyes on this book and giving me feedback that I didn't even realize I needed. You're an incredible woman, and I'm so happy I know you. *Epic Lies* wouldn't be the book it is today, if it weren't for you.

Jade Piccolomini-Grandi: I love you for so many more reasons than the feedback you gave to me. Your heart is huge, and you give it ALL to anyone who needs it. Thank you for your friendship and the care and support you've shown me and my family. Our jar is full of happy and so much of it is because of you.

My BETAS: You all know who you are, and you also know how much I LOVE YOU! Thank you for taking the time to read *Epic Lies*, even when I dropped it in your laps at the very last moment. My schedule has been completely wacky for the past two books, and your flexibility is so much appreciated. Your love for me and my books is astounding. Thank you so much.

Chelsea Kuhel: I bet you didn't know what you were getting yourself into when you took me on as a client. I promise you that I've never been so disorganized with my writing schedule before. And I can't thank you enough for your IMMEASURABLE flexibility. You had your plate completely full, you were in the middle of a move, but yet you still made time for me and *Epic Lies*. Thanks isn't a big enough expression of my undying gratitude for the time that you devoted to my work. Big huge thanks and hugs and kisses.

Julie Deaton: You were my first (that's not dirty, I swear). You're one of the very first people to lay eyes on my first book and you've been with me ever since. Thank you so much for taking the time to read and proof Epic Lies. You're meticulous and one of the best out there. I love you, Julie!

Sarah Hanson: Did I tell you how much I love the covers you created for this entire series? No? Yes? I freaking LOVE THESE

COVERS. You captured the essence of the series, perfectly and dramatically. Your art goes above and beyond, and I'm humbled to call you my cover designer.

Elaine York: Just like the outside cover, the inside of a book needs to look perfect. And for the second time, you've done that for me. Thank you so much for the perfect interior formatting of *Epic Lies.* You're incredibly easy to work with and super talented. I hope you realize you're stuck with me for a long time!

Becca Manuel: I want you to make a trailer about my life. You would make me look super hot and sexy and all to an incredible soundtrack. THANK YOU for what you've done for all of my books, and most recently *Epic Lies.* You consistently capture the essence of the story and take my breath away. I love you so much.

Bloggers: With every new book that I release, there are more and more of you that jump in to support me. I can't thank you enough, for without you, I would have no readers. Thank you so much for sharing and screaming from the rooftops about me.

FTN: You're a bunch of crazy girls, and I love you. No really. You're all nuts and a bunch of lovable lushes. Thank you for your constant support and the only place on Earth where…nah, I'll leave that between us.

Authors: Thank you to my closest author buddies. The support you have given me over the past few years has been amazing. I love all of you so much!

Readers: As I said in my note to you, thank you for constantly trusting me to take you on a journey that is sometimes bumpy, but will always make your heart smile. I thank you all from the bottom of my heart for sticking with me and diving into each story that I write. Please don't go anywhere–I have more stories to tell.

ABOUT THE AUTHOR

Trudy Stiles is a New Adult Romance author, mom to two beautiful children, and married to the love of her life. She's the author of the bestselling **Forever Family** series including **Dear Emily, Dear Tabitha**, and **Dear Juliet**. **Epic Sins** is the first book in the **Epic Fail** series and will continue with at least three more standalone novels. **Epic Lies** is scheduled to release in the Spring of 2016 with **Epic Love** and **Epic Holiday** to follow in the Fall and Winter of 2016. She plans to write many more stories about some of the characters you've already met, and maybe a few new ones. Emily will get her own story, **Sincerely, Emily**, to be released in 2017.

Trudy is a music junkie and you'll know that she's writing when you see her plugged into her laptop with her earbuds in. Her playlist is unique and is a must for her writing sprints.

When she's not writing, she's carting her children to their various activities while avoiding any kind of laundry or housework. She also loves to run along the boardwalk of the beautiful New Jersey shore.

She celebrates Wine Wednesday almost every day.

To learn more about Trudy, visit her website here: http://trudystiles.com.

OTHER BOOKS

The Forever Family Series
Dear Emily
Dear Tabitha
Dear Juliet
Sincerely, Emily (coming soon)

The Epic Fail Series
Epic Sins
Epic Lies
Epic Love (coming soon)
Epic Holiday (coming soon)

Links to all of her books can be found on her website:
http://trudystiles.com/books/

www.ingramcontent.com/pod-product-compliance
Lightning Source LLC
Chambersburg PA
CBHW060858250626
47159CB00008B/2797